Journey of Hope

A Novel of Triumph and Heartbreak
on the Oregon Trail in 1852

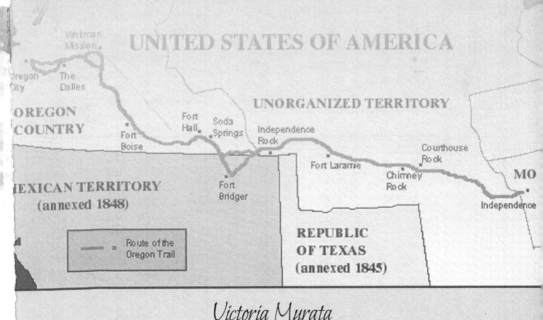

UNITED STATES OF AMERICA

Whitman Mission

Oregon City

The Dalles

OREGON COUNTRY

Fort Boise

Fort Hall

Soda Springs

Fort Bridger

MEXICAN TERRITORY
(annexed 1848)

UNORGANIZED TERRITORY

Independence Rock

Fort Laramie

Courthouse Rock

Chimney Rock

MO

Independence

REPUBLIC OF TEXAS
(annexed 1845)

= Route of the Oregon Trail

Victoria Murata

Dedicated to Daisy, Judy, Mary and
Michele–your enthusiasm is inspiring.
Thank you for the hours spent
reading my pages. Your encouragement
every step of the way kept me going.

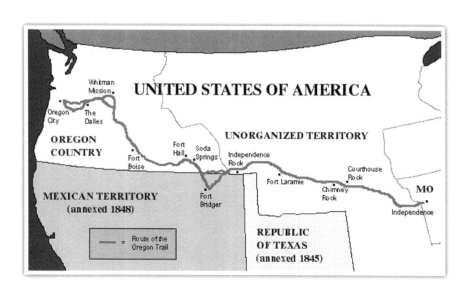

Table of Contents

Prologue

Sunnyvale
Ohio
September, 1851

"Under no circumstances should this be seen by anyone until my death." Henry Lawton sighed deeply as he passed the papers he had just signed to Michael Pound, his long-time friend and lawyer. Henry was a vigorous man. He, his sons, and a dozen hired hands ran all of the operations the large farm required. His dark hair was just turning silver at the temples, but his youthful body belied his middle age.

"Of course, Henry, but you must understand the implications of this decision for your wife Edith," Michael cautioned.

Henry looked at Michael darkly. "She is the only other person who knows the truth about Emily, and even she doesn't know all of it. If anything happened to me, I'm not at all certain she would do the right thing by Emily."

Michael Pound regarded his friend and client quietly. He knew Henry had considered his decision carefully, but he could only imagine the devastating effect these papers would have on his family. "Henry…" he began tentatively.

"No, you won't change my mind, Michael. If I die before Edith, Emily will be at her mercy. This document will protect her."

"Protect her? Or harm her?"

Henry noted the concern on his friend's face and sighed deeply. "That's a risk I'm going to have to take. Emily is strong. She can weather this. You and I have known each other for over eighteen years, Michael, since Emily was a baby. You've served me well all this time. I know I'm asking a lot of you, but I am going to compensate you very well."

"Yes, of course," Michael responded absently. He was thinking of Miss Emily. He had watched her grow up into a confident, beautiful young woman and now she was newly married. She was so young! Perhaps years from now she would have the age and experience to be able to accept what he would be required to divulge. Michael looked up from his thoughts.

"Henry, I hope I will never have to deliver these papers to Miss Emily, but rest assured that I will do my duty by you if that is what you desire."

"I know I can count on you, Michael." The two men stood up and shook hands.

The sound of horses outside drew their attention to the large window.

"Here are Emily and Ernest now. They've come for dinner, and I hope you'll stay, Michael. Emily will be happy to see you."

"I'd love to stay, Henry. Thank you."

"I have to warn you, though, that the conversation may get a little uncomfortable." Henry sat heavily in his chair as Michael stowed the papers in his briefcase.

He looked out the window and watched as Emily and Ernest dismounted and handed their reins to the groom. "I'm still trying to convince that fool Ernest to abandon his plans to take Emily to Oregon."

Michael's face brightened. "Oregon, is it? I've heard lots of conversations from folks about the wagon trains leaving out of Missouri. It sounds like a great adventure." Then Michael's face clouded. "Why would Ernest want to do that? Isn't he set to inherit land from his father?"

"Yes, he would inherit a good portion, but I hear tell that he's been listening to a stranger in town—a man of questionable background—who has been filling his head with stories of the 'wild west' and the opportunities available there."

Michael looked suddenly worried. "Henry, the trip takes six months! It's not an easy thing for a man, much less a young woman!"

"I know that!" Henry said bitterly. "That's why I must convince Ernest to change his mind! I've seen this with young men before—thinking that the grass is greener somewhere else, and I hear he and his father have had a falling out. That won't make matters any easier."

Michael leaned forward in his chair. "Henry, do what you can, but don't alienate Ernest. He's a high-minded young man. Keep him close if you can, for Emily's sake."

Henry regarded Michael's sincere expression. He was a good friend—the kind who could speak freely to him, and he appreciated Michael's candor.

"Yes, I need to tread carefully here." Henry shook his head sadly. "She's not my little girl anymore, Michael. She belongs to another man now, and that's a hard pill to swallow."

"Whatever happens, Henry, Emily is a strong woman. She'll be all right."

Voices from the hallway carried into the room.

"Here they are. Let's have a drink, Michael." Henry poured amber liquid from a crystal decanter into two tumblers. "Perhaps this will give me the steadiness of purpose that I need this afternoon." He handed one glass to Michael.

"To your success, Henry." Michael lifted his glass. "And as far as the other matter," he said, glancing at his briefcase, "may it stay locked safely away forever."

Henry raised his glass and looked soberly at Michael. "Yes. Let's hope for the best."

Earlier that day…

The softly rolling hills stretched for miles across the Ohio landscape. Patches of trees wore bright autumn garments and robust haystacks dotted the fields, waiting for the wagons that would travel down the rows and collect them.

Emily and her husband Ernest Hinton cantered the horses through a copse of yellow trees and scarlet shrubs, the mare and gelding in sync, each making sure the other wouldn't get ahead. Emily skillfully kept her chestnut mare, Calliope, in check, appreciating the youth and friskiness of her favorite mount. She was more comfortable on horseback than on her feet, having been riding since the age of three. Ernest was also a skilled equestrian, but more heavy handed than his petite wife. His bay gelding was enjoying the outing and would have been off at a gallop if not for Ernest's verbal cues and constant adjustments of the reins. Emily laughed gaily as Ernest reined in the large horse and slowed to a trot.

"He's definitely a handful!" Her smile brightened the already brilliant afternoon.

"Nothing that time and miles won't take care of, Emily," he said, admiring her flushed cheeks and sparkling eyes. Her unassuming beauty often took him by surprise.

They walked their horses toward a stream that meandered through the countryside, dividing the land into fields and forest, and dismounted in a clearing next to a pool made by an eddy in the stream. The horses drank thirstily and Emily adjusted her hat, reattaching the long hatpin that secured it firmly to her thick, dark hair. Its brim sheltered her creamy complexion from the sun, but Ernest noticed her smile disappear as she surveyed the vista before her.

"What is it, Emily?" he asked, putting his fingers under her chin and turning her face towards him.

Emily moved her head away. "It's nothing we haven't discussed time and again! I know you have made up your mind to leave, but I'll miss this so much," she exclaimed, gazing out over the soft hillsides.

Ernest sighed. "Emily, where we are going is lush and green like this. You'll come to love it just as you love it here," he said confidently.

"You've said that. But I keep wondering why we're leaving here to go somewhere that's *like* this." She frowned. "I mean, why must we travel across the country through savage Indian territories to a place that's like this when we could just stay here?"

The horses finished drinking and turned to graze on the grass growing next to the stream.

"Emily, we've been over this," Ernest drew his light eyebrows together. "I know what's best for us. We'll have a fresh start in Oregon."

Emily eyed Ernest carefully. She had been schooled in proper decorum and she knew it wasn't her place to question his decisions, but she felt he was concealing something. "You've never told me the entire conversation you had with your father. What exactly transpired between the two of you?"

Ernest looked uncomfortable recalling the hot words that had passed between him and his father. "He and I disagree on a number of things, Emily. Suffice it to say that he isn't happy with my decision to go west."

"You and he haven't spoken since you told him of our plans," Emily reminded Ernest.

"Yes, but he'll come around, I'm sure. Let's mount up," Ernest said shortly, wanting to avoid further discussion. "Your father is expecting us."

"Ernest, you know Daddy is going to try to talk you out of this."

"Like he does every time I see him. At least he's still talking to me," Ernest said wryly, his handsome face barely concealing his discomfiture.

They mounted their horses and proceeded at a brisk trot, traveling the remaining few miles to Sunnyvale, Emily's childhood home.

As Calliope's easy gait carried her closer to home, Emily thought about the turn her life had taken. She was newly married to a handsome man who came from a good neighboring family. Their life had looked so promising. Ernest would be given a large tract of land to farm from his father's ample acreage. They would live close to her family and she would see her daddy often. It had looked like the perfect marriage.

Did she love Ernest? She glanced sideways at him as the horses trotted side by side. His trim physique sat easily in the saddle. His straight nose hooked slightly, but it was softened by full lips and a strong chin that could almost be called obstinate. Dark golden hair was neatly contained beneath his riding hat. He was certainly handsome. He was a good and kind man, if not practical, she was discovering. No, she didn't love him, but love would come in time. At least that's what Nellie, her nanny, had told her, and she was closer to Nellie than she was to her own mother.

Emily sighed. If she had known before the wedding about his wanderlust, she never would have agreed to the marriage. Now it was too late, and she would have to honor her vows and follow him to Oregon. *For better or for worse.* She had lost much sleep over this. *Why does the woman have to make all the concessions?* she wondered. She and Ernest had argued many times, but nothing would change his mind. In spite of his affection for her, this longing to go west was strong, and she didn't know how to fight it. Her tears, although obviously disturbing to Ernest, did not weaken his resolve. He was convinced that a better life was waiting for them out west and that Emily was too young and naïve to realize it.

She sighed deeply, and when the mare's ear flicked back in response, she patted her neck.

"Never mind, Calliope," She murmured, dropping behind Ernest and his gelding. "We are mere females, and we need to remember our place."

Calliope snorted and Emily smiled ruefully.

"I know," she said, scratching the horse's withers. "I don't like it either. Maybe it will be different out west. Maybe women aren't bound by such strict conventions in Oregon."

Emily looked up and saw Sunnyvale in the next valley. Her heart swelled at the sight of her childhood home. On a whim, she turned to Ernest and said, "Race you to the gate!" As she gave Calliope her head and squeezed her calves into the mare, Calliope leaped forward, joyfully stretching her legs into a full gallop. Ernest, at first startled by the horse, quickly followed suit. The pair, forgetting their earlier disagreement, abandoned themselves to the joy of the race like children who never concern themselves with what lies ahead. But like the seasons, life always changes, and the wind in their faces had a promise of the winter to come.

The Beginning

Chapter One

―――――――((☉))――――――――

Independence, Missouri
April 27, 1852

"I refuse to leave even one of these books behind, Mr. Hinton. How am I going to spend all of the long and lonely hours on this journey if I don't have my reading material? I will surely go mad!" Emily Hinton's voice was strident. She had become increasingly difficult the nearer they came to departing Missouri on the overland trail to Oregon.

"Emily, the wagon is too heavy. Some things will have to be left here." Ernest Hinton sounded exasperated. He was looking at a few boxes packed with books.

"All of these books were gifts from my father. They are priceless to me!"

"Emily, are you listening to me? Can you understand what I'm saying?" Ernest was losing patience.

"Oh, I understand very well, Mr. Hinton. My books must be left behind to make more room for your tools."

"We are going to need these tools in Oregon, Emily. The tools are necessities."

Brenna Flannigan leaned against her wagon close by and watched the little drama unfold as Emily Hinton stomped around the boxes and pieces of furniture spread out in the dirt. Ernest followed her with his arms outstretched, imploring her to listen to reason. Brenna eyed the accumulation and couldn't see how they would get it into the already packed wagon's four by ten foot interior.

She had met the Hintons a few days earlier when they pulled their wagon in and camped next to the Flannigans. Emily was a very pretty young woman not much older than Brenna was, but she conveyed a superior attitude, and her deep brown eyes had appraised Brenna's plain and practical dress.

"I'm happy to make your acquaintance," Emily said, squeezing Brenna's hand lightly with her gloved fingers. Her beautiful green dress was the finest Brenna had seen since leaving New York, and her dark brown hair was swept back into a flawless chignon under a matching bonnet.

"Pleased to meet you," Brenna replied.

"This is my husband Ernest and my companion Nellie." Emily's deep-set eyes critically surveyed Ernest, who looked more like he was dressed for church than for wrangling stock and preparing for a two thousand mile journey. She lightly brushed dust from the lapel of his tailored tweed coat. Ernest bowed slightly, tipping his hat.

"Miss." His lips smiled slightly, but the smile never reached his eyes. He was eight years older than Emily and good looking. His features were angular and his expression was serious—almost intense—and Brenna's cheeks flushed under his scrutiny.

Nellie, a small wiry woman about the age of Brenna's mother, glared at Brenna, not bothering to disguise her distaste. Brenna's smile froze on her face and she glanced at Emily and Ernest, wondering what she had said or done to displease Nellie.

Emily spoke shortly to Nellie. "Please get my wrap. The evening air is a bit chilly," and Nellie promptly disappeared into the wagon.

"Pay no mind to Nellie," Emily said cursorily. "She's not in favor of this undertaking, and I'm afraid the whole ordeal has affected her manners." She looked pointedly at Ernest, barely concealing her displeasure. "I'm inclined to agree with Nellie, but my husband insists that we go to Oregon."

Brenna mumbled something about how she thought the journey might be exciting, and Emily sniffed.

"It's time for tea, Ernest," Emily said, and she took his arm and they walked through the dust and back to their wagon.

Brenna remembered the icy looks from Nellie over the next few days. They weren't just for her—the rest of her family had remarked on the obvious unfriendliness of the woman. Everyone else they had met since setting up camp in Independence was cheerful and helpful. The Flannigans had spent many evenings with the Bensons after the day's work was finished. They were a large family from Iowa. The oldest daughter, Rebecca, was Brenna's age, and a couple of the boys became fast friends of Brenna's younger brother Conor. Brenna's father Michael and Thomas Benson were both farmers and liked each other immediately. They had spent hours discussing tools, methods of farming, and farm animals.

Brenna sighed, feeling the warm wood of the wagon against her back. It was a beautiful April morning. For as far as her eyes could see, Independence, Missouri was a sea of people making final preparations to embark on the overland trail to Oregon. She had never seen so many people in one place before. Not even in New York City. She watched the bevy of activity around her. Teams of oxen and mule were harnessed to farm wagons and prairie schooners. Large rounded hardwood bows held up oiled cotton bonnets that covered the interior of the wagons to create more space. Children, animals, and barrels and crates of tools and supplies were everywhere as the next wagon train was preparing to depart. Brenna's slender frame was tight with tension. Although to the casual eye, her posture may have given the impression that she was bored or disinterested, her intense blue eyes and furrowed brow belied this and discouraged any passers-by from striking up a conversation.

Her dark eyebrows drew together when she saw Ben Hansson, the blacksmith's son, walking in her direction. She looked around for somewhere to escape, but she was too late. He had spotted her and his pace quickened. At eighteen, two years older than Brenna, Ben was easily six feet tall and one hundred eighty pounds. His father had started him shoeing horses and mules at twelve years of age, and his build reflected the hard work. His arms looked like the limbs of large trees. Ben and his father Hans Hansson had met most of the people as they made the rounds, making sure the teams were properly shod for the journey. Soon, he was standing next to Brenna, his cheerfulness irritating her on possibly the most important morning of her life.

"Hi, Brenna." His easy grin extended up into his sun-browned face and slanted his pale blue eyes upwards. A floppy hat covered most of his straw-blond hair. "What're you doin' standing out here in the sun?" Ben talked easily and had a quick smile. He had befriended Brenna and enjoyed teasing her. She didn't feel like being teased this morning. Brenna tucked a stray black corkscrew curl behind her ear.

"Waiting on my folks," she replied, trying to hide her annoyance.

"What're they doin'?" Ben asked conversationally.

That's a good question, Brenna thought. They had left an hour ago with Conor, her younger brother, to get some last minute supplies and talk to the captain. Her anxiety was increasing by the minute as the sun rose higher in the sky, and the tension from the crowd seemed to be rising with it. Ben tilted his head to one side, thoughtfully surveying her, waiting for a reply. Brenna realized she hadn't answered Ben, and she felt the blush on her cheeks.

"They're talking to the captain," she said shortly. Redheaded Tommy Benson ran past them laughing, trailing a blue ribbon behind him. Four-year-old Deborah Benson ran after him complaining loudly, her blond curls flying behind her, trying to catch the elusive ribbon. Fifty feet away, burly Thomas Benson cursed as he struggled to harness a young ox.

4

"Captain is bound and determined to leave on time whether folks are ready or not," Ben said affably. "Some are goin' to have to wait for the next train."

"Oh, we're ready," Brenna said firmly, looking at the teams of oxen harnessed to the well-stocked wagon. They didn't have to carry much feed for the oxen because the grass would be abundant. It was almost May, and the prairie was already greening. There were provisions in barrels for six months, and the journey to Oregon could take that long. Two hundred pounds of flour took up a lot of room. There was also chipped beef, rice, tea, vinegar, mustard, saleratus (baking soda), and tallow. That along with the bacon, coffee, lard, beans, salt and sugar, and cooking pots and utensils also took up precious space in the small interior. Her father's Sharps rifle, powder, lead, shot, and some of her mother's furniture were packed also. Ben looked appreciatively at the carefully packed wagon. The tar bucket hung from the side, ready for caulking the wagon bed for river crossings.

"What's your pa bringing in the way of tools?" he asked, surveying the jockey box hanging on the side of the wagon. Brenna lifted the lid and they gazed inside.

"Looks like he has most everything he needs here," Ben murmured. "Bolts, linchpins, skeins, nails, and a jack. He's got some extra leather to repair harnesses and some farm tools. But what about hoop iron? These wooden wheels shrink from the dry air and dust, and then the hoop iron comes off."

"He was going to try to find some this morning."

"We've got extra if you need any along the way."

Brenna imagined what the Hansson wagon must look like. She pictured it full of tools and parts—a conglomeration of metal, wood, and leather. Men seemed to require lots of tools. Her mother left household items behind in order to make room for her father's "necessary and important" tools.

"Are you pretty good at butchering chickens?" Ben asked playfully, checking out the clucking chickens in the coop slung on the side of the wagon next to the water barrel.

"I've butchered a few," Brenna grimaced. It was a chore she cheerfully left to her mother.

Ben noticed her distaste and chuckled. "I'll bet you're a pretty good cook. Do you like to cook?"

Brenna mentally rolled her eyes. She liked Ben, but he was getting on her nerves. She scowled at him and crossed her arms over her chest. "No. I don't like to cook. Do you?" she retorted sharply. Ben guffawed loudly. His generous mouth stretched across his face and his twinkling eyes almost disappeared behind his cheeks. His laughter was deep and highly contagious. Brenna blinked once and then couldn't help but join in. It was hard to stay angry with Ben. After a minute, he wiped his eyes with his shirtsleeve and smiled at Brenna.

"Actually, I do enjoy cooking. I make a mean chicken pot pie," he said, eyeing the chickens. His face became serious. "It's hard to believe we're about to leave Independence. We won't see another town 'till we get to Oregon."

Brenna had waited for this day for so long, and now that it was here, she could barely contain her agitation and anxiety. Mixed emotions flooded through her as she thought of the family and friends she had left behind in New York and the new life her family would make in beautiful Oregon.

It was over four years ago when her family emigrated from Ireland, and she vividly remembered the journey. It had been difficult and heartbreaking. Many of the passengers on the ship from Ireland to America had been sick, and quite a few had perished during the crossing. She hoped this journey would be easier. Her whole life was ahead of her, across that prairie and all those mountains and rivers she had heard so much about. Ben must have sensed her mood because he suddenly touched her shoulder. "Don't you worry now, Brenna. It's a long trip, but I'll look out for you."

She looked at the concern on his face and the tension suddenly left her body. Her eyes welled with tears. She hadn't realized how nervous she had been. "Thanks, Ben. I'll be fine," she replied, smiling at him gratefully. "Here are my folks." Her parents and brother were walking towards them. Her father carried a pick and some extra hoop iron. Her mother had a bolt of dress material and one of homespun. Conor was sucking on a peppermint and playing with a length of rope.

"Good morning, Ben. We just spoke to Captain Wyatt, and it looks like we're leaving on schedule," her father said in his lilting Irish brogue. "Conor, let's check everything over one more time."

"I'd best get back and do the same thing," Ben said. "Let me know if you need anything, Mr. Flannigan." With a quick smile at Brenna, he turned and walked back the way he had come. Brenna watched him go for a few seconds until her mother called to her from inside the wagon. As she walked to the back of the wagon, she looked towards the Hintons' camp and saw Nellie staring at her. Nellie's face was twisted into a look of pure hatred. Brenna quickly looked away, and she shuddered as she felt a chill on the back of her neck. *What is that woman's problem?* she thought.

Two hours later, the forty-two wagons were organized into the order they would travel over the next two thousand miles. Many more wagon trains would leave within the following week. The wagon train would travel roughly fifteen miles a day. Oxen were slow beasts, but they could make the trip easier than horses, and they would eat almost anything.

The captain had met everyone in the previous two weeks, and now he rode down the line making last minute checks.

"Everything looks in order, Mr. Flannigan."

"We're ready, Captain Wyatt."

The signal was given, and the first team strained forward under the weight of the loaded wagon. Brenna watched anxiously from her position next to their wagon. Everyone except the very young and the elderly would walk to Oregon, but that was fine with her. She wanted to walk because she didn't want to miss anything.

Conor was hopping up and down, waiting for their wagon to begin moving. They were the ninth in line, and finally Michael Flannigan coaxed the teams to move forward. Brenna had a huge lump in her throat. *This is it,* she thought. *Here we go.* Her eyes were bright as she looked up into the endless sky towards the far horizon. What would she find in the days and months ahead? She inhaled deeply, smiled, and stepped forward with the wagon, the first of many steps taking her into her future.

Second Night

Chapter Two

Mile 25

The campfires glowed warmly in the early evening outside of the large circle of wagons that kept the stock contained. The animals had been fed, watered, and bedded down for the night. Women were busy heating water and preparing the evening meals. Many of the men were sitting around one of the fires discussing the day's events. "Brenna, dinner is nearly ready. Will you find your brother?" Kate asked.

"Sure, Ma,"

It didn't take Brenna long to find Conor. She simply followed the sound of children's voices and found him in the middle of a lively discussion about "redskins." Brenna tightened the shawl around her shoulders against the chill of the evening. She wandered closer to the fire to listen to what the men were discussing. It seemed that some of them were unhappy about being at the end of the line and having to breathe in the dust from all the wagons traveling over the trail. They were discussing different options and seemed to be coming to a consensus.

"Tomorrow we'll separate into four lines, and the wagons will be rotated back to front every day. Is that acceptable to everyone?" Captain Wyatt asked. There was unanimous agreement and the conversation moved on.

"The Donation Land Act is why I'm going to Oregon," one voice stated. "How can you pass up one hundred sixty acres of rich fertile land?" Other men agreed. Indeed, that was the reason the Flannigans were on this journey. When Brenna's father Michael had heard about the Oregon Donation Land Act two years earlier, it was all he could talk about. Kate would be eligible for one hundred sixty acres also, bringing the family's total to three hundred twenty acres—enough for the farm her father had dreamed of since leaving Ireland.

Brenna scanned the faces around the fire. Some she recognized, having met them in the weeks they spent camped at the jumping off place in Independence. Others were new to her. There was Ben Hansson next to his father. The resemblance was remarkable. Both men were big-boned and fair. Their faces were friendly, although Ben's father Hans wore a more care-worn expression, and his light hair was graying at the temples. Ben's face looked soft in the firelight. His generous mouth stretched into a wide grin over something someone close by said. She watched the way his eyes slanted upwards when his smile broadened. She couldn't help smiling too.

"Hi, Brenna." The voice startled her, and she jumped. A girl about her age giggled. "I'm sorry; I didn't mean to scare you."

"Oh, hi Rebecca," Brenna replied. She had met Rebecca Benson at the camp in Independence, and they had taken an instant liking to each other. Rebecca's large family was from Iowa. They had relatives in Oregon waiting for them.

"My ma sent me to round up the brothers for dinner," Rebecca said. She looked in the direction of the children's voices. "Sam, Tommy, dinner's ready," she called, and turned back and looked at Brenna, her warm eyes glowing in the firelight. "We made fifteen miles today," she said.

"Yes, I heard. Are you tired from walking?" Brenna asked.

"No! Compared to all the chores I'm used to doing, today was easy!"

Brenna looked at Rebecca's face shining with excitement. She felt the excitement too. The walking had been slow and not strenuous, just dusty. She knew Rebecca had a lot of responsibility. She was the oldest of six children, and her pregnant mother, probably in her mid-thirties, seemed older than her years. Rebecca, on the other hand, was robust. Even in the firelight, Brenna could see her ruddy face and eager expression.

"How's your mother?" Brenna asked. She wondered how Rebecca's mother would handle the birth of her seventh child on the trail.

A small shadow crossed Rebecca's face. "She's riding some in the wagon, but she says she's feeling fine," Rebecca replied. "Thanks for asking."

"Listen, if you need any help with the children, I'd be happy to lend a hand," Brenna said.

"Thanks, Brenna. I may take you up on that!" Rebecca grabbed Brenna's hand and gave it a squeeze. Just then, Sam and Tommy ran up to them. Tommy threw his thin arms around Rebecca's waist. His young face looked up at her, eyes wide.

"Is it true that the redskins will cut my scalp off and stick it on a pole and ride around on their horses waving it and hollering their war cries?" his voice wavered.

"Yes, it's true," thirteen-year-old Sam said gleefully, "and they're going to want your hair 'cause it's bright red," he finished confidently.

"Noooooo!" Tommy cried, tightening his hold on Rebecca. She glowered at Sam and cuffed his ear.

"What are you doing scaring your brother like that?" she said angrily.

"Ow! He's such a baby. Why does he have to follow me everywhere?" Sam said, rubbing his red ear. Rebecca grabbed the thick red hair at the top of Tommy's head and gently pulled his head back. She wiped his tear-streaked face with her apron. "And you shouldn't be believing everything you hear! Now the both of you go and wash up for dinner." The boys ran off in the direction of the Benson's wagon. "I'm going to have to talk to Daddy about finding some more chores for Sam. He's thirteen and he has too much time on his hands. He shouldn't be hanging out with the young'uns and scaring them like that."

"Do you think there's any truth to the Indian stories?" Brenna asked.

"From what I hear, most of them are friendly if you leave them be. Captain Wyatt said there would be chances to trade with them for fresh meat along the trail. I don't know about your dad, but mine isn't much of a hunter."

"Da spent some time at target practice when we got to Missouri, but I think we'd starve if we had to depend on his skills with a rifle!"

The girls giggled amicably. "I'd better get back and help Ma. Goodnight, Brenna. I'll talk to you tomorrow!" Rebecca followed her brothers into the darkness. Brenna watched her fade into the night. When she turned to find Conor, she saw him walking toward her.

"When's dinner? I'm starved!" He said.

"Come on, let's go. I'm sure Ma's waiting on us."

As they passed the Hintons' wagon, Brenna saw Nellie bent over the fire cooking the evening meal. Nellie glanced up and immediately looked away, busying herself with the fire.

"Good evening, Miss Nellie," Brenna said.

Silence greeted her, and she thought that perhaps Nellie hadn't heard her. Then Emily emerged from the tent and saw Brenna and Conor.

"Good evening, Brenna, Conor," she said as she walked up to them.

"Hello, Emily."

Emily Hinton looked beautiful in a dark blue dress with an intricately crocheted shawl over her shoulders. She didn't seem to have any of the dust of the trail on her clothing. Her hair was beautifully done up, and her skin showed no evidence of sun exposure like everyone else's.

"I do believe I will perish if I have to walk another step."

Brenna knew she had ridden in the wagon most of the day.

"Well, we only have nineteen hundred and seventy miles to go!' Conor said cheerfully.

Emily gave him a withering look.

"And the captain made me leave some of my most precious belongings on the side of the road!" she exclaimed.

"I'm so sorry, Emily," Brenna said.

"He said our wagon wouldn't be able to keep up because it was too heavy. Humph! I don't believe that's true. Besides, everyone could just travel a little more slowly. What will I do without my organ?" she pouted. Leaving the organ on the side of the trail had broken her heart. Music had always been a comfort to her.

"That must have been difficult, Emily." Brenna commiserated.

"Don't worry! People from the town will be out in the morning to get all the stuff that's left on the trail," Conor said helpfully.

Brenna gave him a cautionary look and discreetly pinched his arm.

"It's true," he piped. "I heard some of the men say that people from Independence furnish their houses with stuff the overlanders have to leave behind." He didn't notice the misery on Emily's face. "Mrs. Taylor had to leave a big old bed and dresser. She was mad!"

"Well, at least someone will get pleasure from playing my organ," Emily sniffed.

"Miss Emily," Nellie called, "Come into the tent now. Dinner is ready."

"I must go. Do come by and visit in the evenings, Brenna. And you, too, Conor," Emily said sweetly, her southern hospitality surfacing. "I want to hear all about New York City. I hear it's very civilized there," she said, and she turned and walked into the tent.

"She's pretty!" Conor said appreciatively. "Let's come back tomorrow night."

Brenna grabbed Conor's arm. "Come on, Conor. Ma's waiting on us." She had no intention of spending any time with Emily Hinton. There were a thousand other things she would rather do.

Indian Encounter

Chapter Three

———————◦((◦))◦———————

Mile 150

In the early morning, the last wagons in the four lines moved up to the front positions. This rotation system would work until the road narrowed when they got to the mountains. Even though the wagons on both sides of theirs were a hundred feet away, Brenna liked having wagons on the right and left. She felt safer. If truth be told, the Indian stories scared her. She'd never seen an Indian up close, and she was pretty sure she didn't want to.

The Benson family was on their left, one wagon back. She could hear Annie, the youngest, crying. Rebecca's mother was in the wagon with Annie. Soon, the crying stopped and Brenna knew Annie was no doubt nursing. It was difficult keeping the eighteen-month-old occupied. She was too little to walk alongside the wagon, and the days were long for an active toddler to be cooped up in the small enclosure. Sometimes Rebecca carried her in a makeshift harness strapped across her back. Soon there would be another baby, and Annie would have to learn to cope with that. Rebecca was shepherding the other two girls, keeping them close by. Thirteen year-old Sam, Brenna noted, had been given the job of herding the oxen and keeping their wagon at a safe distance behind the wagon in front of it.

The Hintons' wagon was behind theirs, much to Conor's delight. He made no attempt to hide his infatuation with Miss Emily. At eleven years old, he was growing up, and he wanted to help his Da. He was taking on more responsibility, and Michael was teaching him to lead the oxen.

"You just have to watch them, Conor. Don't let them stray or they'll try to graze. Keep them moving."

Brenna was relieved, since it meant less babysitting for her. She loved her little brother, but she was glad to see him growing out of some of his immature behavior. His curly black hair was like hers—only short. Still, it corkscrewed in all directions, giving him an unkempt but angelic look. Yesterday he had gotten burned from the sun, and his pink cheeks made his startling blue eyes stand out even more. One of Rebecca's sisters obviously liked Conor, and that annoyed him. Now that their wagon was so close, Mary Benson was always dancing over to Conor to ask him questions and walk beside him. He would scowl and look down, ignoring Mary, but she seemed oblivious. Brenna liked Mary. She was a delightful girl. Her sunny disposition and bright smile warmed the coolest of days. She talked non-stop, but her conversation was light and easy, and sometimes remarkably insightful, as it was today.

"Brenna, why is Conor so quiet?" she asked cheerfully, her soft brown eyes looking up at Brenna as they walked companionably next to the Flannigans' wagon. Brenna looked ahead to where her younger brother walked next to the team.

"Oh, he's concentrating," Brenna replied, smiling down on the eleven-year-old, whose chestnut braids reached almost to her waist. "He's trying to learn how to drive the team, and it's hard work." Brenna watched some of the men struggling to keep the teams moving at a steady pace. The oxen wanted to graze on the rich grass. They were allowed to graze morning and evening, and they were watered once more during the day—usually early afternoon.

Conor was too young to drive the team alone, so her father Michael Flannigan was with him, encouraging his son's efforts.

"Why don't any of the girls get to drive the teams?" Mary queried.

"Because it's men's work," Brenna replied.

"And cooking is women's work?"

"That's right."

"Mr. Cardell cooks for himself," Mary reflected.

"Yes, but Mr. Cardell doesn't have a wife."

"Why doesn't he have a wife?"

"I don't know. I suppose he never found a woman to his liking."

"Do you think he gets lonely?"

Brenna cocked her head to the side, considering the question. James Cardell kept to himself, mostly. She had noticed him tending to his chores in the evening, and cooking over a small fire. "Maybe he gets lonely, or maybe he likes peace and quiet," Brenna replied.

"Yeah, I think you can feel lonely sometimes, even in a big family like mine," Mary said sagely. Brenna looked down at the small girl marching steadfastly next to her.

"You're right, Mary." Brenna reached down and hugged the narrow shoulders. "If you ever feel lonely, you can come and talk to me."

Mary's face brightened. "Thanks, Brenna! Now, I'd better go and make sure Conor isn't getting lonely!" She skipped ahead to catch up to Conor. Brenna smiled fondly. She hoped her brother would warm up to Mary. In the meantime, she knew the girl would be cheerfully persistent.

The wagons were slowing next to a stand of trees and brush following a creek. This would be a good place to stop for the midday meal and water the stock. Brenna helped her mother prepare the lunch, and afterwards, her mother sent her off to the creek with a few pieces of laundry, a washboard, and a bar of lye soap. Brenna was heading downstream, well away from where the stock was drinking thirstily. She heard someone coming up behind her, and when she turned, she saw Mary hurrying to overtake her.

"Where are you headed, Brenna?"

"Just downstream a ways. I have a little laundry to do."

"Can I help?" the girl asked eagerly.

"Sure," Brenna said with a smile; she was glad of the company. After a few minutes, they found a suitable spot—not too deep—with large boulders along the shore to pound the clothing dry. The water rushed over smooth rocks covered with green mossy algae. At this point, the creek was only twenty feet across and two feet deep in the middle. The high brush was thick on the other side. Brenna and Mary busied themselves with the few items, scrubbing the bar of soap over the soiled material. Mary took her shoes off and waded in.

"Brrrr—this water is freezing cold," Mary cried, and she laughed delightedly when Brenna scooped a handful of water and tossed it at her. As she backed up, her foot slipped on a mossy rock and she tumbled backwards into the water. When she tried to stand, her bare feet slipped on another rock and she only succeeded in putting herself deeper in the water and farther from shore.

"Brenna! Help! I can't stand up!" Mary's terrified voice called as she tried unsuccessfully to right herself.

"Mary!" Brenna screamed, as the small girl was carried downstream by the rushing water. Brenna ran along the shore, trying to think of how she could catch the thrashing girl. Suddenly a dark form stepped out of the thick cover on the opposite side of the creek, just downstream of Mary. A strong arm reached out, grabbed the gasping girl, and helped her balance in water that was now up to her chest. The dark man helped Mary to the bank where she crawled on hands and knees, coughing up the water she had swallowed and inhaled in her struggles. Brenna rushed up, gasping for breath.

"Are you alright?" she cried, throwing her arms around the shivering shoulders.

"Yes," Mary choked, drawing in deep breaths. She stood up shakily, and Brenna supported her. They both faced the dark native who had been calmly observing the girls. Brenna had never seen an Indian before, but she knew that this dark young man was one of the savage scalp-taking redskins. He was taller than Brenna was, and scantily clothed. He looked to be about eighteen or twenty years old, and his black hair trailed down his back. *Redskin is not very descriptive,* Brenna thought. His skin glowed like burnished copper. He watched them curiously. The deep-set eyes, Brenna noted, were the darkest she had ever seen, and the high cheekbones and sharp brow shadowed them. Brenna's heart pounded in her chest. What would he do to them? Just as she was considering the worst, Mary piped up.

"Thank you," she said sincerely, taking the Indian's hand and giving it a squeeze. The young man looked startled, and then he slowly smiled. Brenna incredulously watched this interplay. Then he said something incomprehensible, looking at Brenna intently. Brenna shook her head, not understanding. He reached out towards her, and she flinched and stepped backwards. He paused, and then when she stood still, he gently took a lock of her hair, rubbing it between his thumb and fingers, and said the words again.

"Curly!" Mary proclaimed, laughing. "He's never seen curly hair before!"

Brenna was paralyzed with fear. Did he like her hair enough to want her scalp? The Indian looked at Mary curiously.

A shout from upstream carried down to them, and the young man straightened. He placed his hand briefly on Mary's head then turned and crossed the creek, disappearing into the brush. Brenna exhaled loudly. She hadn't realized she had been holding her breath. She knelt down in front of the soaked girl, raking her eyes anxiously over Mary's shivering form. "Let's get you out of these wet clothes," Brenna said. Just then, Ben came running up. His eyes took in Mary's sodden clothing and Brenna's anxious expression.

"What happened? Is she all right? Where'd that Indian go?" he asked, looking around nervously.

"She slipped in the water and couldn't get her footing," Brenna explained. "The Indian saved her."

"H...H...He was n...n...nice," Mary stammered, shivering violently.

"I'm taking her back to her wagon so she can get some dry clothes on," Brenna said.

"Come here, Mary," Ben scooped her up in his arms. Brenna looked at him gratefully.

"Next time, stay closer to the camp," he said, glancing at Brenna and moving off toward the wagons.

Brenna flushed darkly. Her relief turned into irritation as she tried to keep up with Ben's long strides. She was still composing a scathing retort to his insensitive comment when they neared the Benson's wagon. Rebecca hurried towards them, her eyes taking in the girl who looked happy and warm in Ben's arms.

"She fell in the creek," he said, setting Mary down.

"Thanks, Ben. I'll get her dry," Rebecca said, smiling warmly up at him.

"I'm not cold anymore," Mary said, looking adoringly at Ben.

"Good! I'll come back and check on you later," He said, pulling one of her braids playfully.

"Please do," Rebecca said, giving Ben a dazzling smile. Then she turned and helped Mary to the back of the wagon. Brenna took all of this in, realizing that Rebecca was flirting with Ben. Ben, however, seemed oblivious. He turned to Brenna.

"What were you doing down there?" he asked, but his clenched jaw belied the casual tone of his voice. Brenna blinked twice, and then exclaimed, "The laundry! I left it there!" She turned and started back to the creek when Ben grabbed her arm.

"You're not going back there alone," he said matter-of-factly. "I'll go with you." The two of them walked together back to the spot where the laundry lay on the creek bank. Brenna gathered it up with the soap and the washboard. She was glad for Ben's company. The encounter with the Indian had unnerved her.

"Thanks, Ben; I'm glad you came along when you did. The Indian seemed friendly, and I'm grateful he was there to help Mary, but he still scared me," she said solemnly.

"I watched you two heading down here. I wanted to tell you not to go far, but I figured you knew better." Brenna felt her face flushing again.

"I was looking for a shallow place to do the laundry. I wasn't expecting to see any Indians!" she retorted angrily. He stepped in front of her, put his strong hands on her forearms, and shook her gently. His eyes, normally a light blue, were dark.

"You need to be more vigilant," he said tensely. "You're not in your backyard in New York City anymore. We don't know anything about these Indians. Count yourself lucky that this one was friendly."

Brenna looked up into his eyes. She had never been so close to him before. He seemed different—not the easy-going Ben she thought she knew. His gaze was intense and unblinking as his hands squeezed her arms tightly. "Promise me that next time you'll think twice before doing something so foolish."

Brenna angrily wrenched herself away, her heart pounding. Her electric blue eyes seemed to shoot sparks as she gave him a venomous look. "I'm not responsible to you, Ben Hansson," she shot back at him. "Who appointed you as my protector?" Her heart was pounding, and she struggled to control her voice. "Don't you worry about me. I can take care of myself." She stomped off toward camp. Ben watched her rigid back as she walked away from him and he slowly exhaled and relaxed his clenched fists.

The rest of the day was uneventful, but the news of the Indian encounter spread like wildfire through the camp. That night, Mary entertained the travelers with a much-exaggerated version of the story. Brenna watched in amazement as Mary acted out in great detail her near-death experience and the heroic rescue from the dark native. Brenna observed the girl's animated face in the firelight. She was a born actress. Someone else was watching Mary intently. Brenna looked at Conor. He was engrossed in Mary's story. She smiled, thinking that maybe he wouldn't be so aloof towards Mary anymore.

Then she saw Ben sitting behind Conor. He wasn't watching Mary. He was looking at her. Brenna blushed and looked away, but not before Ben saw what he was looking for. A slow smile spread over his face. He folded his arms over his broad chest. *It's a long way to Oregon*, he thought. *A long way.*

The Crossing

Chapter Four

—————— ((•)) ——————

Platte River crossing

"Calm down, Miss Emily. You may as well get used to these river crossings. I'm told this is one of the easier ones." Nellie looked nervously at her young mistress.

Emily Hinton's brows knit together over her deep brown eyes. Her perfectly groomed dark coiffure was neatly tucked into a frilly blue bonnet that shielded her face from the sun. The pretty dress she wore flattered her figure but was impractical for the trail. Emily didn't care. She was going to look presentable, even in this God-forsaken country.

"One of the easier ones?" Emily scoffed. "Why, look at that rushing water, Nellie. I will surely drown if I try to cross!"

Emily Hinton could barely bring herself to watch the wagons crossing the Platte River. She wasn't just nervous about the crossing—she was petrified! She had always been unreasonably afraid of water. She couldn't trace this fear back to any traumatic event from her childhood. When her brothers and friends played in the pond, she hung back, unsure of what lay beneath the surface. She had never been a timid child. She was bold in other areas. She loved riding horses, and she and her mare were often at the front of the hunting parties. Her sometimes-risky behavior was often admired by the other young men and women. She was outspoken in mixed company and often got disapproving looks from her mother. Her father, however, was indulgent and secretly smiled at her self-confidence.

Nellie sighed loudly. "Miss Emily, I know how stubborn you can be. There's only one way to get from here to the other side of this river. Mr. Hinton is going to insist you cross. You're just making it harder on yourself."

Emily's jaw was set firmly and her arms were crossed tightly over her chest. She had refused to attempt the crossing earlier in the day when it was their turn. Her husband had moved their wagon to the side to let the others cross. He looked frustrated and preoccupied, and he wasn't sure how to convince his wife to make the crossing.

"Emily, we have to cross this river," Ernest had implored.

"No, Mr. Hinton, I will not. You never told me this journey would require crossing rivers!"

Emily had been difficult from the beginning of their marriage. They had been wed less than a year, and she was only eighteen. Ernest knew she still resented his taking her away from her family and the Ohio farm where she had grown up, but he was her family now, and she finally and reluctantly had consented to accompany him on the overland trail to Oregon. It was her father who had decided for her.

"He is your husband, Emily. You go where he goes. I don't like it one little bit, but I can't make him see sense."

Ernest Hinton recalled a conversation weeks before with his friend Abel Brown in a saloon in Missouri.

"Her father doted on her—gave her everything she wanted," he confided to Abel. "I don't believe he has ever refused her anything."

They had just finished the last poker hand, and it had been a good night for Ernest. He was feeling superior and savoring a particularly smooth shot of whiskey.

"What attracted you to her, Ernest?" Abel asked.

"You mean aside from the obvious?" Ernest laughed. Abel joined in. Emily was a beautiful woman.

"I believe it was her spirit. She has always been independent, and that has sometimes been a problem for me. I love that in her, but I don't quite know how to control it." He tipped the glass, draining it of the last swallow of the amber liquid.

Abel masterfully hid his contempt as he listened to his young companion. Aside from Emily's physical beauty, he admired her fiery spirit that animated her features. *She's above and beyond anything you could ever hope to control,* Abel thought disdainfully.

Ernest regarded his wife's profile as she watched a wagon crossing the river. Her chin jutted out stubbornly, and her brows met in angry furrows. Nellie stood next to Emily looking uncertain. Ernest felt like wrapping Emily in his arms and shaking her at the same time. His feelings were often conflicted when it came to his wife. She could drive a man to distraction. He decided it was time to be firm.

"Emily, we have to cross now. We can't make these people wait on us again." He was referring to her habit of painstakingly packing everything from the tent each morning while the other travelers waited for them to take their place in line.

A few nights ago he had complained about this to her. "Why do we have to make this tent look like a parlor every night? Most of these people are happy if they're moderately comfortable."

"Moderately comfortable is not acceptable, Mr. Hinton."

Ernest looked exasperated. "All this furniture—your frilly doodads," he was referring to her collection of intricately crocheted doilies.

Emily's face darkened. "These things are my treasures, Mr. Hinton, and you won't bully me into abandoning one more item." She was referring to the end of the first day when she had been pressed to leave the cook stove and a small organ on the side of the trail when their wagon lagged behind the others. The captain had insisted they lighten their load or be left behind. She had unsuccessfully tried to sweet talk Captain Wyatt. Ernest had watched her batting her eyelashes and putting her hand on his sleeve.

"Why, Captain, I'm going to need my stove when we get to Oregon. What am I going to cook on if I don't have my stove? And that organ was my grandmother's. Why, I've played hymns on that organ for twelve years. Surely the wagon train can go a little more slowly so that we can keep up."

The captain had been polite but firm. His shadowed eyes regarded her from under the wide brim of his western hat. His raspy voice was firm. "I'm sorry, Mrs. Hinton. Other families have had to lighten their wagons. We all need to be able to keep on schedule if we are going to make good time and get to Oregon by next October."

No amount of cajoling would change the captain's mind, and in the end, he and Ernest had unloaded the stove and the organ.

"You are both heathens and barbarians!" Emily had cried, while Nellie had stomped around muttering under her breath about having to leave the stove.

Over the next few days, Ernest had endured accusing looks from Emily, and her stony silence had lasted until he had brought her a puppy from one of the wagons where a dog had had a litter before they left Independence. She had tearfully hugged the little dog, exclaiming over his "precious little face," and had promptly named him Buster.

Ernest walked over to talk to some of the men who were helping wagons cross the Platte. Emily could barely hear their muffled conversation, and when they looked over at her, she imagined they were complaining about her obstinacy. Nellie stood next to Emily, intently watching the activity on the water.

"Well, they can just complain all they want, because there is no way I am going into that water. No self-respecting woman would debase herself by floundering around in that filthy river."

It was true. The water was a muddy brown from all the wagons and livestock that had crossed over. There were shallow stagnant pools and mud flats. A three-foot-deep main channel meandered from side to side, and there were numerous sandbars between the shores. Previous travelers had set willow poles out to mark the stable sand bars that would support the weight of the wagons.

Nellie looked at her mistress. She recognized that determined jaw-set.

"I don't want to go into that water either, Miss Emily, but I don't see any way around it."

Abel Brown separated himself from the group of men, walked over to Emily, and tipped his hat.

"Afternoon, Miss Emily. If I could have a word with you?" He was secretly amused by the little drama, but he played along with the men and did his part. He was supposed to distract Emily while the other men unloaded the wagon and transferred everything to boats for the crossing.

Emily liked Abel. He was polite and good-looking, and he always paid her a compliment when he saw her. She smiled at him tightly.

"Don't think for one minute, Mr. Brown, that you're going to talk me into crossing that river."

Abel regarded her studiously. "Ma'am, I will personally guarantee that you will arrive on the other side safe and sound. Don't you worry one little hair on that pretty head of yours." His dark eyes regarded her solemnly, but she detected a glint of humor around the corners. Behind Emily, men had commenced unloading the Hintons' wagon. Abel kept her attention on him and off the activity.

"Why Mr. Brown, you are too kind. I thank you, but I will not be needing your assistance today. Perhaps Mr. Hinton and I will cross over in a few days when the water settles down a bit."

Abel looked up at the gathering clouds in the sky and then back to Emily. His eyes seemed to be calculating the best strategy to convince this obstinate but very pretty woman to cross the river.

"Ma'am, that river isn't going to settle down, and if it rains it will only get worse. Today is the best day to cross. Believe me; most of the wagons have had no trouble, and we haven't lost any stock. I know it looks fearsome, but it's an easy crossing."

Emily's heart pounded in her chest as she watched a wagon maneuver through the muddy water. Many men were helping to keep it stable through the deepest part of the river. She shivered as she thought of herself tipping out of the boat and being swept downstream. Abel watched the play of emotions across her face. He knew Ernest was sometimes beside himself over her stubbornness, but he admired her feminine wiles, and he couldn't help but be drawn to her compelling eyes and the firm set to her chin when she made up her mind.

"Mr. Brown, I do appreciate your offer, but I must decline." A motion caught her eye and she turned and saw some men carrying pieces of her furniture from the wagon to a boat. "No! Wait!" she cried. She ran up to one of the men to detain him, but Ernest stepped in front of her. His expression was stony and his voice was low and controlled.

"Emily, we're crossing today, and I don't want to hear any more objections."

Emily stamped her foot angrily. "We are not going near that river, Mr. Hinton. Have I made myself clear?"

Ernest looked at his wife. Her hands were on her hips and her stormy eyes regarded him fiercely. Behind her Abel tried to hide a smile, and Nellie looked distraught.

"Emily, you have no choice," Ernest said, and then he bent down, grabbed her behind her knees, and threw her over his shoulder. She screamed and kicked and beat his back with her fists.

"Put me down, you brute!" she cried. "I will never forgive you for this! I insist that you put me down this minute!"

The men carrying her possessions snickered under their breath. One guffawed loudly.

Nellie followed Ernest. "Mr. Hinton! Put Miss Emily down! Please!" Buster yipped and jumped up on the back of Ernest's knees trying to lick Emily's face. Emily continued her tirade all the way to the boat where Ernest deposited her. Nellie grabbed Buster and scrambled in beside Emily, and Ernest swiftly pushed off. He and two other men forded the river, guiding the boat through the deepest water as Emily shrieked and clung to the sides. Brenna and Conor Flannigan were standing on the other side of the river with other families and watched the frantic woman rocking the boat in her panic.

"If she would just sit still the boat wouldn't tip like that," Conor observed sagely.

"She's really scared," Brenna said.

"I should go and help them."

"No, you should stay right here," and she put a protective hand on her brother's shoulder.

For a while, it looked like they might see the first capsize of the day, and they could clearly hear the refined aristocratic young woman use language that would make a grown man blush. One woman covered the ears of her young son.

Once they made it to a stable sand bar, Emily and Nellie jumped out of the boat and waded across the rest of the muddy and shallow river. When they finally reached the far shore, Emily angrily trudged past the group of onlookers, dragging the muddy and sodden hem of her cornflower blue dress. Ernest watched her rigid back as she moved toward a stand of trees. He ran after her and they had heated words. Abel Brown watched and a cynical smile spread over his lips.

Soon, Ernest emerged from the trees and helped the men bring their wagon across the final distance of the river.

Emily found a shady and secluded bower and collapsed in a flood of frustrated tears. She had never felt so humiliated, and she was sure all of the other women regarded her as a child. She was shaking from anger at her husband for forcibly making her cross in the manner that he had, but she felt relief at the realization that she hadn't drowned after all. It was a few minutes before she was able to compose herself and breathe more normally.

She looked at her dress. It was very wet and dirty. She searched for a dry part of her sleeve to wipe her face. She would never forgive Ernest for this. She could still hear the men snickering and see the disdainful expressions on the faces of the women as she had stormed past them. She had a mind to take a horse and ride back to Independence. She was a fine horsewoman, and she had been riding almost since she was able to walk. From Independence, she could catch a train to Ohio. She spent a few minutes enjoying this fantasy while her breathing calmed.

She was abruptly brought out of her self-pitying reverie by the sound of her husband calling to her. He had come to the edge of the trees.

"Emily, it's time to load up."

"You load up," she muttered miserably. Then she pictured what the wagon would look like if Ernest loaded it. That thought motivated her to get up and find her way to their wagon.

Buster yipped and leaped up happily into her arms when he saw her. She hugged him and he licked her face. Nellie was complaining about the crossing, the river, her muddy dress, the state of the wagon, and the supplies scattered all around.

"What a mess!" she exclaimed. "I hope no one is in a hurry, because it's going to take a while to repack all of this! How many more rivers are we going to have to cross? I declare, I didn't sign on for any of this!"

Ernest had hitched the teams to the wagon, and the horses were tied to the side. Without a word, Emily began the task of organizing everything. In Independence, she had carefully packed to conserve space. Once the stove and organ had been left on the trail she had more room to spread out. Still, she liked to have everything in its place. She and Nellie busied themselves with the task while Ernest handed them boxes, bags, and crates. Ernest had not brought any hired help along on the trail. He had left not speaking to his father, and he had only his own money to outfit their trip and buy the supplies they would need to build their home in Oregon. Some of that money he had lost gambling. He wasn't very good at poker, but he could never pass up a game. Abel Brown held quite a few of his I.O.U.s, but he was confident he would earn the money to pay him back once they got to Oregon.

In a short while, they were ready.

"Well that wasn't too bad, now was it?" Ernest asked cheerily.

Emily regarded him stonily. Nellie didn't reply, but averted her eyes and crossed her arms. The sun disappeared behind a gray cloud and thunder rolled ominously in the distance. The smile left Ernest's face and he realized that this was going to be a long day.

He was wondering what he could do this time to lighten Emily's mood when Abel Brown sauntered over.

Abel enjoyed watching the way Ernest handled his wife. He lacked finesse and diplomacy. He realized that Ernest had never been a lady's man like himself. Ernest had been smitten with Miss Emily from the first time he met her, and he had pursued her until she consented to be his wife. It hadn't been difficult to convince Emily's father, since Ernest came from an established and wealthy neighboring family.

Abel knew Emily had consented to be Ernest's wife because she thought she would always be close to her daddy. He speculated that Emily would most likely never see her daddy again.

Abel's family wasn't well connected, and their money was newer, mostly earned through risky and often illegal pursuits. They had made their fortune through horse-trading. Abel had a good eye for horseflesh, and by the young age of twenty-six, he had won a small fortune at the racetrack. He was an accomplished poker player and had funded this trip with money he had won at the tables in many towns east of the Mississippi. He usually had no trouble winning, but he wasn't averse to cheating if he had to. There were always plenty of rich farmers who thought they were good at cards, and Abel encouraged their vanity until he had gained their confidence, and then he would play his hand and take their money.

He had met Ernest at a poker table in a saloon in Ohio, and when he won the final hand, a very large pot, Ernest had been good-natured about it.

"You're a good poker player, Mr. Brown. You're going to have to give me a chance to win my money back."

Abel had encouraged Ernest's fondness for poker. He hadn't been averse to taking advantage of his young friend whenever he had the opportunity. Ernest already owed him quite a lot of money, and he planned to get more I.O.U.s from Ernest and some of the other travelers. He was already making plans to get a game up at the fort where they would camp tonight. Abel knew he would be a wealthy man when they reached Oregon. As he walked over to where Ernest was adjusting a harness, he saw that the Hintons' wagon had been re-packed and was ready to roll.

"The captain says we're going to camp at Fort Kearny this evening. It's just a short ways from here." He looked over to where Emily and Nellie were climbing down from the wagon.

"Miss Emily, it looks like you made it across safe and sound and are none the worse for wear!" His eyes couldn't hide his amusement as he noted her scowl.

"Thank you, Mr. Brown. Fortunately, I didn't drown," she replied tersely, and gave her husband a dark look. Abel noticed she looked a little pale, but considering her ordeal, she was remarkably controlled.

"There's a trading post and a post office at the fort if you have any letters you'd like to send home." He tipped his hat at the women and returned to his wagon.

Emily's expression brightened. She resolved then and there to write to her daddy and tell him she was coming home!

The Letter

Chapter Five

Fort Kearney
Mile 319

Nellie walked next to the wagon the short distance to Fort Kearny. Emily was inside pouting. Ernest was stonily silent as he concentrated on driving the team. Nellie sighed. Their behavior was typical in this marriage. Put two spoiled young people together as husband and wife and this is what you get! She regretted her choice to accompany Miss Emily.

Emily's family had come from Virginia and settled in the Military District Lands of Ohio shortly after Emily was born. Ernest himself came from landed gentry, and he and his brother were set to inherit large tracts of rich Ohio farmland. But Ernest had been bitten by the bug and wanted to seek his fortune in the wild and untamed west. Both his father and Emily's had tried to talk sense into him, but when Ernest's mind was made up, no one could dissuade him.

Emily's father, Henry Lawton, had persuaded Nellie, her personal servant, to travel with them and be a companion to Emily.

"Nellie, I know how much you love Miss Emily—like your own flesh and blood. You've raised her from a baby. I would be eternally grateful to you if you would accompany her and Ernest to Oregon."

"Mr. Lawton, I am not young. I know the journey is difficult, and I don't think it's a good idea for any woman."

"I agree with you, Nellie." Mr. Lawton's face looked troubled. "I certainly don't want my only daughter traipsing across this country with who knows what in store for her. I've pleaded with that fool husband of hers, but he won't be persuaded." His eyes misted and he took Nellie's hands in his.

"Please, Nellie. If you go with Emily, I'll rest a little easier."

Nellie's heart softened. She couldn't refuse the man who had always been so kind to her.

"Alright, Mr. Lawton, I'll go. God help me, I'll go with Miss Emily to Oregon."

Henry Lawton had hugged her then. Nellie remembered the embrace. She had always been fond of Mr. Lawton.

"Thank you, Nellie. I will never forget your sacrifice."

Nellie was small and wiry, and twice Emily's age. Her features were sharp, but her warm eyes softened an otherwise fierce expression. She had married young, and two years later her husband had been killed in a brawl in one of the bars he frequented. Columbus, Ohio had been predominantly German, and once the Irish moved in with their Catholic ways, trouble was always brewing. Nellie's husband had joined in when fighting had broken out between the German Protestants and Irish Catholics, and when the brawl was over, he was dead.

Nellie had been a young childless widow with no prospects until she found the ad in the *Ohio State Journal* placed by Emily's family for a domestic servant. When she began working for Emily's family, Emily was nearly three years old, and Nellie was twenty-two. Nellie had lost her only child in childbirth, so she quickly bonded to Emily, and the family made her Emily's nanny. She loved the little girl, and Emily had always returned the affection. Emily's own mother was cool and distant towards her, saving her love and attention for the younger brothers.

Fort Kearny appeared ahead, and Nellie looked forward to the lay-by. A number of long, flat-roofed low buildings made from sun-dried bricks were strung along the mostly flat landscape. Captain Wyatt was instructing the leading wagons to camp to one side.

Later that evening after camp had been made next to the fort, Emily composed a letter to her father. Buster lay at her feet asleep.

Dear Daddy,

> *As I write this letter, I am shaking from cold and exhaustion. We crossed a raging river today and I nearly drowned. Many of my fine dresses are ruined from the dust and mud on this horrible trail. My skin is so brown I look like a darky! The food is unpalatable, and it's the same morning and night. Most of the women are not friendly, and there is no one to talk to besides Nellie.*

> *I cannot go any farther, Daddy. I am not a pioneer, and I cannot go one more step towards an uncertain future with a husband who is determined to see me to an early grave. In the morning, Ernest and I will turn our wagon around and head back.*

> *I will send you a wire as soon as we get to Independence, and from there we will catch a train to Columbus.*

> > *Your loving daughter,*

> > *Emily*

> *P.S. In the event that I cannot convince Ernest to give up his plan, Nellie and I will be coming home without him.*

Nellie found her in the tent holding pen and paper, tears streaming down her cheeks. She looked knowingly at Emily.

"It would be best for all concerned if you would quit your mooning and be the wife and partner you promised to be in your marriage vows."

Dismayed, Emily looked at the woman who had been more mother to her than her own mother had. She saw the sympathy in Nellie's eyes despite her sharp words.

"I can't do this, Nellie. I'm tired and dirty." Her voice broke. "I want to go home!" Nellie felt compassion for this girl who was like a daughter to her, but she knew she had to be firm. She knelt in front of Emily and looked into her eyes.

"Your home is with your husband now. Where he goes, you must go. Whatever you've written in that letter, it had better not be crying over something that can't be helped. Think about your father. He's already worried sick about you. Do you want to cause him more grief?"

Emily sniffed loudly. She hadn't thought of it that way. She found her handkerchief in her sleeve and blew her nose loudly.

"No, I don't want to worry Daddy." Her voice was almost a whisper. She sighed loudly. "You're right, Nellie. It will do no good to complain." Her shoulders slumped dejectedly. She belonged to Ernest—for better or for worse, and she had promised to love, honor, and obey him. Those vows spoken at her wedding held a bitter taste in her mouth. The married life she had pictured looked nothing like this. In a way, she felt betrayed.

"That's my girl. Things may look bleak right now, but remember, every cloud has a silver lining." Nellie patted Emily's shoulder and left the tent to finish the evening chores. Emily looked down at the letter in her lap. She thought of her father reading it at his large oak desk in the study. Slowly she tore the letter into small pieces. Maybe Nellie was right. Maybe things would get better.

That night the travelers had time to gather around one of the campfires and talk about the day. Some of the men from the fort joined them. They were familiar with the trail, and a few had traveled it more than once. Many people wanted to know what to expect in the days ahead.

"Will all the river crossings be as easy as this one?" James Cardell asked. He was transporting fruit trees to Oregon to start an orchard.

"Will there be trouble with the Indians?" Thomas Benson inquired.

"Will we be able to restock supplies at the other forts?" Michael Flannigan asked. Many people had read accounts that had been written about the overland journey. There was a lot of discussion and speculation.

Later there was music and some of the women and girls danced. The mood was light. Emily joined in the singing and her voice was clear and strong until someone started singing "Where Home Is." Then she was reminded of her family and the beautiful farm she had left when she married Ernest. Her melancholy returned, and she left the circle of people and retired to the tent.

As she crawled between the blankets and closed her eyes waiting for sleep, her last thought was that conditions couldn't get any worse. Buster curled up next to her and licked the chin of the sleepy young woman. Emily resolved to look on the bright side. Tomorrow would be a better day.

The next morning it began to rain.

The Dream

Chapter Six

———————⟫⟨⟫⟨———————

Mile 427

Michael Flannigan looked across the campfire at his wife. Kate was bent over the pan of water, cleaning up the dishes they had used for dinner. Her riotous dark hair was tied in a bun at the nape of her neck, but a few strands had worked free and corkscrewed over her forehead. He noted the dark circles under her eyes. This journey was taking its toll on her. The everyday tasks for a woman of packing up in the mornings, unpacking in the evenings, cooking, washing, gathering firewood or buffalo chips, building fires, and carrying water were hard enough in the best of conditions, but it had rained for a week and this evening's was the first fire they had been able to build. The rain had been steady and everything was dripping wet or damp. His fingers deftly worked on the harness that needed repairing, and his thoughts drifted far away, back to Ireland seven years earlier.

* * *

It had been a cool, wet summer in 1845. That fall the potato crop had failed throughout the whole country. Wet rot, they called it, and few farms had been spared. He remembered having to sell his livestock to pay his rent and buy food for the family. A few months earlier, the British prime minister had resigned. Then the new man in charge had ordered the closing of government food depots to prevent the Irish from becoming "habitually dependent." Michael's face contorted as he remembered his county, with every farm and family destitute. His neighbors and friends had sold all they had to buy the Indian corn the British government had been selling for a penny a pound, but soon there was mass starvation when there were no pennies left. He sighed deeply, remembering all the people who had been evicted by their landlords when they had no money to pay their rents.

* * *

He watched Kate methodically doing her evening chores. She looked worn out. All the travelers were bone tired from struggling to keep the wagons moving over muddy and rutted trails. Sometimes the mud was like sucking quicksand, and it had been hard to keep shoes on feet. His thoughts returned to Ireland—to his neighbor Maggie Donahue and her two small children.

* * *

He found them one morning standing in the rutted road wet to the skin from the rain, their feet up to their ankles in mud. Her husband had recently been imprisoned because he couldn't pay the back rent, and the landlord had evicted Maggie and her children. Michael and Kate took them in, even though they had barely enough food for their own family.

* * *

Michael shook his head sadly, remembering how they had been so hopeful the summer of '46 that the fall's harvest would be a good one after the devastation of the year before. He remembered his deep disappointment that September when the new crop succumbed to the blight.

* * *

He held the rotten black potato in his hand that he had pulled from the ground, and for the first time in his life, he could not think of what to do. They had nothing left: no money and no food. He knew it was only a matter of time before they would be evicted. He stared at the rotten potato for a long time, unseeing. Kate had been calling his name, but all he could hear was a roaring in his ears like the sound of a train. Then Kate had come up to him and angrily taken the potato from his hand, throwing it as far as she could. She looked at him fiercely, her eyes flashing.

"We're done here, Michael. We're going to my sister's in Dublin, and then we'll decide what to do." She didn't wait for a reply but turned on her heel and packed up their few belongings. Soon they were on the road to Dublin with hundreds of other displaced families.

* * *

Michael worked oil into the leather harness, carefully covering both sides. The wagon train hadn't been making good time in the persistent rain. One day they traveled over a particularly mucky stretch of the trail and barely made five miles. Everyone was either pushing the wagons from behind or pulling them from the front. Michael could see the discouragement on the faces of many of the travelers. He knew they were concerned about the possibility of early snow if they didn't get to the Blue Mountains in good time. His brow furrowed when he was reminded of the journey his family had made to Dublin six years earlier.

* * *

When they reached Dungarvan in County Waterford, the scene was riotous. People were amassing together in angry mobs, shouting and raising fists against British troops that were protecting stores of grain to be shipped out to England. Michael and Kate watched, horrified, as starving peasants picked up stones and hurled them at the troops. Michael saw the enraged face of the officer, and although he couldn't hear him over the angry crowd, he knew what his shouted orders were.

"Quickly! In here!" he yelled, and Kate and the children ducked into an abandoned building as they heard the first shots and the screams from the crowd. The pandemonium seemed to go on forever, and the shots continued until two peasants were dead and several others were wounded. The crowd fell over each other attempting to get away. Many were trampled, and many others were arrested.

* * *

Michael's hands froze on the harness he was oiling as he remembered narrowly avoiding arrest.

* * *

A raggedy man ran into the building where they were hiding. His eyes widened when he saw Michael, Kate, and the children huddled in a corner.

"You're done for if you stay here," he said, and darted to the rear window where he quickly climbed out. Michael helped his family climb out that same window as the troops descended upon the crowd. The terrified family fled deeper into the village where they were swallowed by the crowds of starving people.

In other villages along the way to Dublin, they saw British naval escorts guarding the grain on riverboats that passed before the eyes of starving peasants who watched from shore.

* * *

Michael bitterly remembered the defeat and hopelessness on his countrymen's faces. He could see this defeat on Kate's face now across the campfire. He had worried about her the last few days. She had been uncharacteristically quiet, and even Conor and Brenna had noticed and had tried to cheer her up, but she had been unresponsive. After dinner, Rebecca Benson had come by to invite them to visit. Brenna and Conor had gone to the Bensons' wagon, but Michael said that he and Kate would visit later. Michael wanted to take this opportunity to find out what was troubling his wife.

"Are you all right, then?" he queried. She didn't answer him, and he thought that maybe she hadn't heard his question. She hadn't looked at him or acknowledged that he had spoken.

"So, are you all right then?" he asked again, a little more loudly.

She raised her eyes and looked at her husband. The firelight did not brighten her dark look. Slowly she straightened her thin frame and her right hand went to her lower back, massaging sore muscles. Her dress was stained with sweat down the front and the back, and a full eight inches of the bottom of the skirt was caked in mud.

"No." Her voice was almost a whisper, but he heard her. "No, Michael Flannigan, I'm not all right at all."

Alarmed, he got up from where he was sitting. Kate had always been a pillar of strength, and to hear her sounding so defeated caused him great consternation.

"Kate, the rain has stopped. Everything will dry out now." He walked over, took her shoulders in his hands, and turned her towards him. He looked carefully at her. Kate was only thirty-five, but she had aged in the months they had been on the trail. Weary eyes looked back at him, not really seeing him.

"I don't care anymore, Michael. I'm sick of this trail. I'm sick of this wagon and this food—the same thing every day. I can't remember why we ever thought this would be a good idea. Why did we ever leave New York? We had good jobs and we were making money enough to put some aside. The children were in school. What is the point of all of this? Tell me, Michael. Tell me why we're killing ourselves going to a place we've never been." Her voice had started out calm, but it had slowly risen to near hysteria.

"I don't want to be here!" she exclaimed, tears streaking the dirt on her cheeks. "Please, let's go back." She had grabbed the front of his shirt, and he realized that she was beside herself.

"Katie, girl, things will get better. Sure and it's been rough, but the rain has stopped." Michael drew her close. His voice was gentle, and he rested his cheek on her head. "You're bone weary. You've worked harder than anyone, Kate. You're the one that's held this family together through it all." He held her tightly, and he felt her rigid body go limp as she sobbed softly against his shirt. "You've been so strong, Katie. I know you can do this. I never would have started if I didn't know you wanted this as much as I do. It's our dream—yours and mine. Remember all those nights in the crowded tenement in New York when we planned this? It's that dream that kept us going, Kate." Michael held her at arm's length and looked in her eyes. "Tell me, Kate. Tell me what our dream looks like. Tell me how we pictured it all those years that we scrimped and saved for this."

She ran the back of her hand across her nose and took a few ragged breaths. For an instant Michael thought she wouldn't answer him, but then in a quavering voice she said, "There's a beautiful green valley at the base of rolling hills. A log cabin sits next to a wandering stream. There's smoke coming from the chimney." Her chin quivered slightly, and she paused and took another deep breath.

"What's behind the cabin?"

"There is a paddock for the horses, and there's a barn. Every morning I go out to the barn to milk the cows." Her voice was getting stronger now, and her eyes began to focus on him.

"Tell me about the fields."

"Well, and they're full of our crops. Everything is growing and thriving. You and Conor have plowed the rich land and planted the seeds and the sun and rain have made everything grow."

"And tell me about our neighbors."

Kate's eyes were clear now. "If you follow the gentle winding road around the hill, you'll find our closest neighbors, a family like ours with children that Conor and Brenna will have as friends. The woman of the house and I share recipes and help each other sew quilts and clothes. You and her husband smoke your pipes on the porch and talk about the weather." She smiled then at her little joke, and Michael took her in his arms and smiled with her.

"There's my girl," he said. "Have faith, Katie. It will all happen just as we've planned. I promise." He dipped the end of her apron into the pan of water sitting by the fire and gently wiped the dirt and tears from her face. "Tomorrow we're going to start late so that you women can do some laundry in the creek, and maybe you can get a bath."

Kate sighed, "A bath! I can hardly wait for morning!"

The sound of Conor and Brenna's voices drifted out of the half-light, and soon they rounded the wagon, talking companionably. Brenna trotted over to her parents standing by the campfire. She sensed that something had transpired between them while she and Conor had been gone. There was a difference in her mother. She was animated again, and her father looked relieved and happy. *Maybe Conor and I should leave them alone more often*, she thought.

"Look, Ma. James Cardell sent some dried apples and apricots. Here, try one." Brenna held an apricot to her mother's mouth, and Kate bit into it gracefully, closing her eyes to savor the sweet taste.

"I've never had anything so delicious."

"Here, Ma, eat some more." Conor put a handful in his mother's hands and then gave some to his Da.

That night Michael Flannigan lay wide awake thinking about his wife and all she had endured. Their lives had looked so promising when they were just married, and the first eleven years had been happy. Their small holding was enough to support the family and pay the rent, and they lived the life their parents and grandparents had lived in their small, close-knit community. But the past seven years had seen heartache and despair. He remembered arriving in Dublin.

* * *

Kate and her sister Chloe hadn't seen each other in a few years and they threw themselves into each other's arms, crying, with Chloe exclaiming over Kate's thinness. Chloe and her husband had little room to spare but readily took them all in.

The situation in Ireland was dire, with no relief in sight. Although there were many cases of death by starvation, most died from typhus or dysentery, and the dead were so numerous there were not graves enough to contain the bodies, or living people with the strength to bury them. Warehouses were full of food, but the masses had no money with which to buy it.

Michael, Kate, Brenna, and Conor lived with Chloe and Donald for over a year while Michael and Kate worked on a public works relief project building stone roads. It was backbreaking work, and they were paid almost nothing, but they were able to save enough for passage to America. In 1848, they boarded a ship and set sail for America and better opportunities.

* * *

Michael tossed and turned in his bedroll while Kate slept like a baby next to him. He had found James Cardell and asked him for herbs to brew a calming tea for Kate. She dutifully drank her tea, and when they finally lay down for the night, she sank into a deep sleep. All of his restlessness failed to rouse her, and he was glad of that. She needed the sleep. So did he, but he couldn't quiet his mind. The emotions of the evening had brought a flood of memories.

* * *

When they left Ireland, it was under semi-martial law. British troops were all over Dublin expecting a rebellion. Anyone could be arrested and imprisoned indefinitely without formal charges or a trial. Michael remembered having mixed feelings when their ship left from the River Liffey: Heart-wrenching sadness over leaving his homeland, anxiety about the long journey to New York, and relief in the promise of a better life.

Conditions on the ship were not good. Hundreds of men, women, and children lived below decks with no ventilation and no sanitary facilities. Many were sick, and burials at sea were frequent, and usually, to the dismay of these devout Catholics, without religious rites. Michael insisted that his family spend as much time above decks as was permitted, and he adamantly refused to allow Kate to minister to the sick. He had watched too many caregivers succumb to the illnesses they were treating. He had brought some food aboard to supplement the pound-a-day they were each allotted, and he kept a close watch on these secret stores. Starvation, sickness, and poverty brought out the worst in people, and he observed otherwise kind and generous people steal and commit other crimes out of desperation.

* * *

"But we made it," he muttered, half asleep. A cousin had taken them in to live in his lodgings in an overcrowded tenement in New York City. The tenement was barely livable but it was a roof over their heads, and they lived there almost four years until they had saved enough money to head west.

"We made it then, and we're going to make it now." With those words on his lips, he finally drifted into sleep. He slept peacefully the few hours before daybreak because it wasn't soldiers and starving people he dreamt of, but a beautiful green valley at the base of rolling hills and a small log cabin with smoke curling from the chimney.

The Long Night

Chapter Seven

━━━━━━━━━⫯⟨◉⟩⫯━━━━━━━━━

Ash Hollow
Mile 504

Brenna Flannigan lifted the bucket of water she had drawn from the cool spring nearby and poured some into the pan. The trip down Windlass Hill that morning had been strenuous. All the travelers had helped each other and used ropes to prevent the wagons from barreling downhill. The glade where they were camped was beautiful and abundant with wild roses and ash trees. Mrs. Mueller watched Brenna carefully, her shoulders stooped, and her gray head bent.

"Just a bit more water, dear," she said in German-accented English.

Brenna dutifully poured another cup into the pan. She was helping Mrs. Mueller with the mid-day meal. She first met Mrs. Mueller when the Mueller wagon had been moved up from the back of the line to a position behind the Flannigans' wagon. Mrs.

Mueller's son John, a pastor from Ohio, was with her. His wife Greta had died a few weeks ago, an early victim of cholera, and the captain had moved them forward when Brenna, with the permission of her parents, had volunteered to help them. Mrs. Mueller was a small elderly woman who, as Brenna noticed, bore a strong resemblance to Brenna's grandmother who had died in Ireland. The resemblance was uncanny, especially her eyes, which were always smiling. Even when her grandmother had been too sick to get out of bed, she would smile at Brenna, and her blue eyes would twinkle as she would take Brenna's hands and say, "Your destiny is in the stars, a gra'."

Brenna had been born Christmas night in 1835—doubly lucky as her grandmother loved to tell her.

"It's good luck to be born at night as you have the gift of seeing spirits and the Good People. And being born on Christmas is also good fortune."

Her grandmother had seen a shooting star shortly before Brenna was born.

"That was a sign that your life will be remarkable."

Any time Brenna was blessed with fortune or happiness, her grandmother told her it was because she was special. Brenna came to believe she was special, and she believed that if she saw the Good People, they would bring her wealth. But she hadn't seen the Good People yet, and she hadn't seen any spirits, even though she was always on the lookout. Sometimes she felt her grandmother's presence watching over her and protecting her.

Her grandmother was always telling her stories of the Good People.

"Some call them the Little People or the fairies, but that's bad luck," her grandmother warned.

It was also bad luck to put shoes on a chair or place a bed facing the door. And one should never bring lilacs into the house or cut one's fingernails on a Sunday. Oh, there were so many admonishments, and Brenna was careful to always keep them in mind. But as lucky as she was supposed to be, she wasn't able to keep her grandmother from dying, even though she had spent hours on her knees praying. No, her grandmother had died, and Brenna blamed herself. She hadn't been good enough or lucky enough to save her, and she had cried bitterly for many weeks after. Her parents and the parish priest had tried to console her, but nothing had helped.

"Don't let that tea steep much longer, dear. John doesn't like it too strong." Mrs. Mueller's heavy German accent was fun to listen to.

"Yes, ma'am." Brenna poured hot tea into tin cups and gave one to Mrs. Mueller, who carefully measured a teaspoon of sugar into it.

"Go and tell John that lunch is ready, dear." Brenna looked about and saw Reverend Mueller leading one of the oxen back from the river. He was short and slight, and had no facial hair. His dark chin-length hair was always tucked behind his ears, giving him an almost feminine look. She walked up to meet him as he guided the large animal back to the wagon.

"Reverend Mueller, Mrs. Mueller sent me to fetch you for lunch." John Mueller smiled gratefully at Brenna.

"Thank you, Brenna, you've been such a great help to us. Since my wife Greta died, my mother has had a hard go of it." His voice was soft and deep—surprising for such a small man.

"'Tis my pleasure to help, Reverend," Brenna replied shyly. This man of God was a bit of a curiosity. Not a priest, but like a priest. He held Saturday evening prayer meetings for any who cared to attend, and his simple and generous nature and quiet piety had attracted many followers. Brenna's parents, sorely missing the community of worshippers from the crowded borough of New York City, were among the attendees. As the days and weeks passed, sickness and tragedy had touched everyone in the wagon train, and the travelers increasingly turned to prayer for strength and guidance.

Two days ago, one of the scouts got sick with cholera. The wagon train, already behind schedule, had left the man on the side of the trail with a "watcher" who would stay with him the short hours he would live and then quickly bury him. Brenna had seen this happen more than once, and she grieved for the poor souls who didn't even have a marker for their graves. They had passed other graves on the trail, and one was so shallow that wild animals had dug up the body and left the bones lying about. Someone from their group had taken the time to bury the remains.

Brenna handed Reverend Mueller his lunch and tea. Lunch consisted of breakfast leftovers of biscuits and bacon.

"Will you share this with me?" John asked.

"No, thank you, Reverend, I've already had my lunch." Brenna always ate with her family. She knew every wagon was carefully rationing their food. She wanted to help the Muellers—not be a burden to them.

"She never eats our food," Mrs. Mueller said, "even though we have plenty now that Greta is gone." Her voice caught as she said this, and John looked at his mother sadly and sighed.

"It's true, Brenna. You know you're always welcome." Brenna smiled at him as she busied herself cleaning up the campsite. It was a hot day, but Mrs. Mueller still wore a heavy shawl over her dirndl. She had lost weight over the past weeks, and Brenna was worried about her. Still, in spite of everything, Mrs. Mueller's blue eyes twinkled merrily each time she saw Brenna, and she usually had a story from the old country to entertain her. As Brenna finished up the dishes, Mrs. Mueller asked, "Have you ever heard the tale called 'Little Red-Cap'?"

"Nay, I have never heard the tale. Will you tell it to me?"

The minutes slipped by as Brenna sat transfixed, listening to the story of a little girl who had walked to her sick grandmother's house in the wood with a basket of food, only to find a wolf there who had eaten her grandmother, dressed in her grandmother's clothes, and was waiting in her grandmother's bed for little Red-Cap to arrive. Then the evil wolf had swallowed her! Luckily, a huntsman happened by and cut the wolf open, and the little girl and her grandmother sprang out! They then filled the wolf's body with heavy stones, killing him. Brenna's eyes were wide as Mrs. Mueller finished the story, dissolving into giggles.

"That's a good story, not?"

"Yes, I'll have to tell it to Conor and the Bensons. They always want to hear the new stories you tell me."

"Well, I have a lot more to tell. You know, I went to school with Jakob and Wilhelm Grimm in Kassel in the old country. They're the ones who wrote all the stories I tell you. They collected stories from everywhere and they wrote them down. I have one of their books. Those boys made a name for themselves!"

Later that night as Brenna lay in her blankets unable to sleep, she thought about Mrs. Mueller as a young girl in school with the Grimm brothers. She imagined them playing by the Fulda River that flowed through the little town of Kassel. Mrs. Mueller had described Kassel in vivid detail, and Brenna loved picturing it. She finally drifted off to sleep, dreaming of meandering rivers, wolves, and little girls in red velvet caps.

The next day, the weather changed. The morning was foggy and cool, and traveling was pleasant, but by mid-morning, what had started as a fine mist had developed into a steady drizzle. Everyone was exhausted after maneuvering down the steep grade of Ash Hollow. They were camped at the bottom next to a cool spring for the mid-day meal. Mrs. Mueller was uncharacteristically quiet during the break. Brenna thought that maybe she hadn't slept well and left her to her thoughts.

By the time the wagons circled to make camp for the night, everyone was wet through to the skin. Brenna spent longer than usual at her chores before going to the Mueller wagon. When she finally did, Reverend Mueller told her that his mother was in the wagon and hadn't been feeling well. Brenna tried not to look alarmed as she went to the Mueller wagon and climbed up. The small space John had made for his mother to rest was empty. Brenna climbed out of the wagon and found the reverend attending to the oxen. The drizzle was steady, and her hair was stuck to her head. Her clothes dripped water and hung from her slender frame.

"She's not in the wagon, Reverend. Where could she have gone?"

John looked instantly alarmed and ran to the wagon in disbelief. "She was here when we made camp," he said. "We've got to find her. She's not well! Go and ask people if they've seen her. I'm going to look by the river. Maybe she went for water." But even as he said it, they both saw the water bucket hanging from the wagon.

Brenna ran from wagon to wagon asking everyone if they had seen Mrs. Mueller, but no one had. Everyone was busy trying to get chores done and dinner made in the steady drizzle. The evening was getting grayer, and so were Brenna's hopes. Where could the little woman have gone?

Brenna's search had taken her away from the camp, and now the voices were barely audible. The drizzle had mostly stopped, but the mist was rolling in from the river, and visibility was poor.

"Mrs. Mueller!" Brenna called over and over as she wandered farther from camp. *Where could she be?* Brenna wondered. *I have to find her!* The sound of a wolf howling a ways off startled her. She stopped, shivering in the cool damp air, remembering the evil wolf from the story of Little Red Cap. Then she shook her head, realizing that the h owl was probably a coyote, not a wolf. Brenna strained her eyes, trying to make out what was ahead of her. A form materialized briefly, insubstantial in the mist. Brenna squinted trying to make it out and softly called, "Mrs. Mueller?" She felt the hair on her arms and on the back of her head rise. Her grandmother had said she was able to see spirits. Was that a spirit she had just seen? Surely Mrs. Mueller would have answered her. Brenna moved forward slowly towards where the vision had been.

"Mrs. Mueller? It's me, Brenna." She could barely get out the words. The mist moved over her, engulfing her in its damp clutches. The coyote called again, mournfully. There! A vague form drifted ahead, tendrils of hair swirling about a gray face. The mist cleared momentarily, and Brenna felt a scream in her throat.

"Grandmother!" Yes, she could see spirits! There was her grandmother, just ahead. In the next instant, she realized it wasn't her grandmother. It was Mrs. Mueller! Brenna ran to the old woman. Mrs. Mueller was chilled to the bone and seemed unaware of Brenna's presence. She shivered violently, but her skin was hot when Brenna put her arm around her shoulders.

"Come on, Mrs. Mueller. Let's get you back to the wagon and into some dry clothes." The mist had lifted enough for Brenna to find their way back, and John Mueller met them when they were almost to the camp.

"Thank God you found her! Mother, where were you going?" he asked. Mrs. Mueller didn't respond, and Brenna looked anxiously at the reverend.

"She's feverish," she said. They hurried to the wagon, and Brenna helped the old woman change into dry clothes while John heated water for hot tea. Brenna kept up a steady stream of conversation, but Mrs. Mueller didn't respond. She didn't even seem to recognize Brenna.

News spread through the camp, and many people stopped by to see how Mrs. Mueller was doing. Everyone was nervous about cholera. Brenna's parents were worried too, but Mrs. Mueller didn't have the symptoms of cholera. Ruth Benson and James Cardell decided that she had caught a chill and the resulting fever was very debilitating to her weakened condition. A quick consultation determined that she should be given a drop of aconite in a bit of water every hour for six hours—no more, no less. Aconite would be effective in reducing the fever, but if taken in larger doses it could be fatal. As they were discussing who would administer the medicine, Reverend Mueller spoke up.

"I'll give her the medicine."

"You can't stay up all night, John. You'll be no use in the morning. You need to get your rest," Thomas Benson said. The wagon train would not stop or slow down for sickness. Captain Wyatt kept everyone on schedule no matter what happened.

Brenna looked around at the concerned faces. "I want to stay with her," she said quietly.

"Brenna, you'll have to stay awake all night. You're already exhausted. We'll all take turns," Kate suggested, glancing around at the others for confirmation.

"No! I want to take care of her. I can do it, Ma." The strong set of her jaw convinced the others that it would be futile to argue. Ruth Benson took the aconite tincture from her medicine bag and showed Brenna how to mix the drug. Then she gave Mrs. Mueller the first dose and watched her swallow the medicine weakly. Her eyes were tightly closed, and her body shuddered with the chills.

"Keep her warm, and in one hour give her the next dose, and then four more doses, one each hour, after that."

Thomas Benson gave Brenna a pocket watch, and Brenna opened it and watched the second hand slowly tick away the seconds.

"It's very important not to give her the next dose too early," Ruth admonished.

"Don't worry, Mrs. Benson. I'll take care of her." As the others returned to their wagons and settled in for the night, Brenna got comfortable in the wagon with Mrs. Mueller, but not too comfortable—she didn't want to risk falling asleep. Reverend Mueller looked at his mother. His face showed worry.

"You're a godsend for doing this, Brenna. I won't forget it."

"My grandmother had a saying. She used to tell me that people live in one another's shelter. I want to take care of her." Brenna took Mrs. Mueller's hand gently. "She's going to be all right, Reverend Mueller. Go to bed. I'll be right here."

A look of relief passed over the reverend's face. He bowed his head and said a quiet prayer for his mother's quick recovery. Brenna bowed her head too, and together they said, "Amen."

"Please call me if there's any change." He slipped into the darkness, and Brenna was alone in the quiet with Mrs. Mueller. A single candle illuminated the dark interior of the wagon. Brenna looked at the old woman's face. It looked pinched and strained, and Brenna dipped a cloth into some cool water and bathed it gently.

"There, now, that should feel a wee bit better." The truth was that Brenna was very worried. Mrs. Mueller was so small and frail. How would she weather this storm? Brenna's thoughts went back to Ireland and to her grandmother. Brenna had been a young girl when her grandmother had passed away, but she remembered that night as if it was yesterday. It was a night much like tonight.

* * *

The day had been dreary, but it had cleared and the night was chilly. Her grandmother had been suffering from a fever for three days. There had been no medicine except for Godfrey's Cordial, a children's medicine, but the laudanum in it, an opium tincture, made her grandmother rest a little easier. Brenna was the only one awake when her grandmother passed. She had gone to bed while her grandmother seemed to be resting, but she couldn't sleep. After a while, she crept over to where her grandmother lay in her narrow bed. Her eyes were open and she was looking out a small window at the stars. She turned her head when she heard Brenna. Her eyes were unusually bright as she looked at her granddaughter.

"Do you know that I saw a shooting star the night you were born?" Brenna nodded, a lump forming in her throat. "That's a sure sign, a gra'. You have always been special to me, and I know you will make a difference in the lives of others." She took Brenna's hand and squeezed it feebly. Then she closed her eyes. Brenna sat with her grandmother until the small hours of the morning and she was holding her hand when her grandmother took her last breath.

* * *

Tears stung her eyes as she remembered her grandmother's words. She looked down at the small form of Mrs. Mueller. If only she could make a difference here, but the tiny woman was pale and unresponsive.

"Have I ever told you the stories of the Good People?" Brenna asked the old woman. Mrs. Mueller's chest rose and fell under the blanket. "Well, let me tell you about them. They can be very tricky, and it's best to always be on your guard." Mrs. Mueller's body shivered, but otherwise made no acknowledgment. "And did you know that they are angels? Well, not the best of the angels, but not as guilty as some." Brenna spent the next half hour telling the tales of the Good People and recounting true stories of people she knew who had had encounters with the wee folk.

"I have it on good authority that I shall meet them some day, and when I do, I can ask them for some of their gold. If I don't let them out of my sight, they will lead me to it. Then I will be rich for the rest of my days!" She imagined she saw a slight smile on Mrs. Mueller's face.

Brenna opened the pocket watch and checked the time. She then dutifully administered the next dose of aconite. Mrs. Mueller swallowed it but didn't open her eyes.

Brenna looked around at the contents of the wagon. Everything was organized and carefully put up. She noticed a leather folder open to a daguerreotype of a handsome young woman with light hair sitting in a stuffed chair. The woman wore a stylish hat and dress. *This must be Greta*, she thought. She saw a well-worn book entitled *Kinder-und Hausmarchen* by the Brothers Grimm and took it from the shelf. She opened it to the table of contents and looked at the list of stories—eighty-six total, but she couldn't read the German text. She entertained herself for the rest of the hour by looking at the illustrations throughout the book. Soon she saw an illustration of a little girl wearing a cap and talking to a very large wolf. *This must be the Little Red Cap story*, she thought. A noise outside the wagon caught her attention, and she looked up to see her father peering in.

"Da! You startled me!"

"How is she doing?"

"No change, except that she might be resting a little easier." Brenna opened the pocket watch. "It's time for her third dose of aconite." Brenna carefully measured a drop of the liquid into the tin cup containing a small amount of water. She lifted Mrs. Mueller's head and held the cup to her parched lips. She slowly poured the contents into her mouth, and Mrs. Mueller swallowed. Brenna poured more water into the cup, and Mrs. Mueller drank again. "I think she's thirsty, Da."

"Give her as much as she will drink. The fever is drawing the fluids out of her."

After another drink, Brenna carefully laid Mrs. Mueller back against the pillow and made sure she was comfortable.

"You're a good nurse." Her father looked askance at Brenna and frowned slightly. "Brenna, we all know that you're doing everything you can for her." He paused, and Brenna knew what he was thinking.

"Why did Grandmother die, Da?" she asked.

Michael Flannigan looked at his daughter, and then he looked at the ground. He sighed deeply. "Everyone who was old or very young died, Brenna. There wasn't enough food in Ireland to nourish people, so only the strongest survived. Your grandmother had been weak, and the last fever was too much for her."

"Did she have cholera?"

"No, no she didn't have cholera, although many people did."

"Do you know what Father O'Brien told me, Da? He said that when death comes, it will not go away empty."

"Yes, I've heard that before."

"I saw Grandmother tonight," Brenna blurted out.

Michael studied his daughter and said gently, "Did you now?"

"Yes, I'm sure of it. I was looking for Mrs. Mueller, and right before I found her, I saw Grandmother. She led me to Mrs. Mueller, Da." She looked beseechingly at her father. "Do you believe me?"

"Aye, I truly do."

"Sometimes I feel like Grandmother is so close to me. I miss her so much!"

"I know you do, Brenna." Michael sighed again. "This trip has been hard on folks. Mrs. Mueller is old, and she may not have the strength to…" Brenna put her finger to her lips.

"Shhhh. Better not to speak the words else the Bean Si' will hear you and come for her. Mrs. Mueller's resting now, and she'll awaken soon."

Michael Flannigan looked at his daughter. *Where does she get her strength*, he wondered. Perhaps his mother was close by, watching over her. She had always had a deep affection for Brenna.

"Right, well I'll go back to my bed, Brenna, unless you want me to sit with her for a while. You could get some rest."

"Thanks, Da, but I'm fine. I want to be here when she wakes up." Michael smiled at his daughter. He bid her goodnight and silently retreated into the darkness.

Before the next dosing, Ben Hansson kept her company for a while. He told Brenna about his mother.

"She was beautiful. She had long yellow hair that she used to brush out at night, and she had the brightest blue eyes—like your eyes, Brenna. She would tell me stories and read to me from the Bible. What I remember most about her was her smell. She smelled like fresh baked bread."

"What happened to her?"

"She died when my little brother was born. He died too."

"I'm so sorry, Ben."

"It was a long time ago. I was young, but I still remember certain things about her. She used to do her sewing in the evening, and I would crawl into her lap for attention. She would always put her needle and thread down and hug me and tickle me. I know my dad misses her. He keeps a picture of her and I catch him looking at it sometimes."

"It would be hard to lose your spouse."

"Yes, when you love someone it's hard to let them go." He looked at Brenna a long moment. Then he smiled and said, "Try to guess what I'm thinking of." They spent the next half hour playing twenty questions and trying to stump each other. She finally told him he wasn't playing fairly when he started thinking of tools she had never heard of before. He laughed.

"I have to win, Brenna. Don't you know that about me yet?"

Brenna gave Mrs. Mueller the next dose, and Kate Flannigan showed up. She watched Ben and Brenna bantering back and forth for a while, and then Ben said goodnight.

"He's a nice boy, isn't he?"

"Ma, he's not a boy."

"Well and I suppose you're right. He's eighteen, isn't he?"

"Yes."

"You two seem to get along well."

"I like Ben. He's funny."

"It's too bad he isn't a Catholic."

"What does that have to do with anything, Ma?"

"I'm just saying you two seem to be getting close, and I think it's a shame he isn't Catholic."

Brenna looked at her mother incredulously. What was she getting at? It was time to change the subject.

"Ma, how do you make your bread pudding? Mr. Benson was raving about it the other night."

Kate was flattered and spent the next minutes instructing her daughter on how to make her famous bread pudding. Then she said goodnight and went back to their tent.

It was nearing three o'clock in the morning, and Brenna was alone again. The stillness was deep, but she was not sleepy. She was filled with a calm and serene peace. She dipped the cloth into the water and wrung it out. As she put it on Mrs. Mueller's forehead, she noticed that the heat from her head was much diminished, and she seemed to be sleeping peacefully. "Now that your fever's broke you can rest and get strong," Brenna said quietly. Mrs. Mueller's eyes opened.

"Hello, dear," she said weakly, looking at Brenna curiously. "Why are you in my wagon?"

"You've been sick, Mrs. Mueller. I've been taking care of you. I'm so happy you're better! We've all been worried about you!"

"Oh, I'm sorry I am such trouble. I remember not feeling well. You look tired, dear. You need to get some rest. Why don't you go to bed? I'll be fine, now."

John came out of the darkness smiling broadly. "Mother, you gave us a scare tonight. Thank goodness for Brenna. She's been your nurse and brought you back to health."

"Yes, she's been very good to me, but now she needs to go to bed. I feel so much better—just tired. I want a drink of water, and then I'm going to sleep myself. It looks like the morning isn't too far off."

Relief flooded over Brenna. It was so good to see Mrs. Mueller's twinkling eyes smiling at her, even if her face was paler than usual.

"Let me give you the last dose of your medicine and some more water. Then I'll let you sleep, and I'll come back in a few hours and make your breakfast if you're hungry."

Brenna gave Mrs. Mueller the last dose of aconite and a good drink of water. She made sure the old woman was comfortable and then said good night. John thanked her warmly again, and she walked the short distance to her wagon. In spite of her fatigue, her feet felt light. She looked up at the night sky. A million stars spread across the heavens. Her heart was overflowing with joy.

"Maybe I made a difference tonight, Grandmother," she said softly.

Just then, a star broke away and trailed its light across the night sky. Brenna's breath stopped. She closed her eyes. A gentle breeze caressed her cheek. "Thank you, Grandmother," she said softly, and she climbed between her blankets and slept peacefully until the dawn.

The Invitation

Chapter Eight

Scott's Bluff
Mile 596

One evening after dinner as Emily Hinton and Nellie were read-ing in their tent, Ernest came in.

"Reverend Mueller is here. He'd like to visit with you ladies."

It hadn't taken Nellie long to make the acquaintance of the reverend and his mother. Mrs. Mueller reminded her of her own mother who had emigrated from Germany when she was a young unmarried woman.

Emily's eyes lit up. "How lovely! By all means, show him in. Nellie, please fix the tea." Emily's southern upbringing had pre-pared her to be the perfect hostess. She stood up, and Nellie went to get hot water for tea. Ernest opened the tent flap and Reverend Mueller entered. He looked momentarily surprised at the fine rug on the ground and the two chairs carefully placed next to a small ornately carved table, but he quickly hid his expression and smiled warmly. He was always taken aback at the beauty of Miss Emily. She wasn't your average pioneer woman.

"Reverend Mueller, how kind of you to visit." Emily held out her hand and Reverend Mueller took it, bowing slightly.

"Miss Emily, it is a pleasure to see you again."

"Please sit down, Reverend." Emily indicated one of the chairs next to the table. Reverend Mueller sat in one chair, and Emily sat in the other. Ernest made his apologies and exited the tent, on his way to discuss business with Abel Brown. Emily smoothed her dress carefully and smiled at the odd little man. He was short and slight, and his hair was on the long side, but he was clean-shaven and dressed neatly in spite of the dusty day they had just had.

"I declare, one more day like today and I will just dig a hole and burrow in like a rabbit until this wind stops." The wagons had been forced to converge into a single line at Robidoux's Pass and the going seemed much more slow.

"Yes, it was hard today; very windy. Perhaps the weather will improve for tomorrow."

"Tell me, Reverend Mueller, why this place is called Scott's Bluff. I have read many accounts of travelers stopping here for the night, but no one mentions why it is called what it is."

"I understand it was named for a fur trapper named Hiram Scott."

"So he named it for himself?"

"Not exactly, Miss Emily. The story goes that he was left for dead sixty miles away and crawled this far before he actually did die."

"How horrible!"

"Yes, there's no lack of tragic stories on this trail."

"That poor man. It must have taken a long time for him to crawl sixty miles."

Nellie brought in a teapot and poured each of them a cup. *No tin cups here*, Reverend Mueller noted. These were fine white china cups with small pink roses decorating their sides.

"How do you manage to keep these cups from breaking on this rough trail?"

Emily smiled and looked at Nellie. "Tell Reverend Mueller how you do it, Nellie."

Nellie blushed and said, "I put them into the flour, and I haven't had one break yet!"

"That's a good idea, Miss Nellie!"

The three of them laughed and sipped their tea in silence until Reverend Mueller spoke.

"I have a purpose for visiting tonight. Of course, I've wanted to visit with you both again. What with the busy days and nights, time slips away. But I also have a favor to ask of you, Miss Nellie."

Both women looked bemused.

"What is the favor, Reverend?" Nellie asked.

"As you know, my mother is traveling with me. Ever since my wife died of cholera some weeks past, my mother hasn't been herself."

Emily and Nellie expressed their condolences.

"Thank you kindly. This journey did not agree with Greta. She had been sick from one thing or another ever since we left Ohio. At one point, I suggested we turn around and go back, but she wouldn't hear of it. I miss her very much, and my mother misses her too. She especially misses the conversations they used to have in the mother tongue."

"The mother tongue?" Emily asked.

"Yes, they would converse in German. My mother speaks English, but she very much enjoys speaking her first language, and now…" he paused.

"Do you speak German, Reverend Mueller?" Nellie asked.

"No, I don't. My parents wanted me to speak only English. They would not speak German in front of me. They wanted me to be an American and not a German immigrant. I was so young when we came over from Germany, and as soon as I was old enough to go to school, my parents made sure I attended, and I picked up English quickly. They learned English too, and we spent long hours in the evenings practicing. My parents thought it would be best for me if I forgot the German I knew, and it didn't take long for that to happen."

"And the favor you are requesting?" Emily prompted.

"Yes. Miss Nellie, I understand you speak German. I was hoping, if you have the time," and he glanced at Emily, "that you would come to our wagon and visit with my mother. I think it would comfort her. She was sick a couple of weeks ago. I think it would do her a world of good to be able to carry on a conversation with you in German."

"I think that's a wonderful idea!" Emily said enthusiastically.

"Oh!" Nellie exclaimed. "Well, I haven't spoken the language for quite some time."

"I'm sure it would come back to you. Please, Miss Nellie. It would mean a lot to me."

Nellie looked at Reverend Mueller. He looked so sincere, and she wanted to help him and his mother.

"I'll come by tomorrow evening if it's convenient, Reverend Mueller."

"Thank you so much, Miss Nellie. I'll let my mother know we have a visitor coming. I know she'll be excited."

The three of them spent the remainder of the hour discussing the trials and tribulations of the journey west.

June 19

The next night they camped close to the Platte River. The trail had been good, but in spite of the lessening of the wind, it was dusty, and they had only made nine miles that day. Emily was in a bad temper, and she and Ernest were having another argument. As Nellie left and made her way to the Mueller wagon, she heard Emily accusing Ernest.

"Don't tell me you and Mr. Brown are discussing business again, Mr. Hinton. I don't want to hear that you have been playing cards!"

Nellie crossed to the other side of the circle of wagons, and after a little searching, she found the Muellers' camp. She felt instant irritation when she saw the Irish girl, Brenna, bent over the fire. She knew it was unreasonable, but she couldn't get past the fact that Brenna and her family were Irish, and she hated the

Irish. Brenna glanced up and was mystified at the look on Nellie's face when their eyes met.

"Good evening, Miss Nellie," Reverend Mueller called happily when he saw her.

Nellie quickly rearranged her face. "Good evening, Reverend."

"Please, come up and sit here by the fire. This is Brenna Flannigan, a neighbor. She's making us some tea."

"We've met, Reverend Mueller. Good evening, Miss Nellie," Brenna said.

Nellie inclined her head stiffly and sat by the fire next to the reverend's mother.

"Mother, you've met Miss Nellie. She's come to visit for a while."

"Good evening, dear, how nice of you to visit an old woman."

"Guten abend, Frau Mueller."

Mrs. Mueller's eyes opened wide. She smiled happily. "Sprechen sie Deutsch?" she asked excitedly.

"Yes, Mrs. Mueller, I speak German, but please be patient with me. I'm not sure how much I remember."

They spent the next hour happily conversing in German with only a few lapses into English by Nellie. She was pleased with how the language came back to her. Reverend Mueller sat with them for a while, but he couldn't join in, so he busied himself with small chores. At some point in the hour, Brenna bade them goodnight. Mrs. Mueller hugged her warmly, but Nellie barely acknowledged her.

Soon Nellie said it was time for her to go, and she promised to return the next evening. Mrs. Mueller thanked her profusely, her merry eyes glistening with tears.

"I'll walk you back to your wagon, Miss Nellie," Reverend Mueller said.

As they walked companionably back to the Hintons' wagon, Reverend Mueller covertly studied Nellie's profile. She was a small, fine-boned woman with a sharp nose and a pointy chin. *She looks almost fragile,* he thought. Her warm brown eyes softened her features and her smile warmed an otherwise pinched expression. *She's had sorrow in her life,* he mused.

"I think you've made my mother very happy," he said.

"I enjoyed talking to her. She's had a lot of experiences, and she tells a good story."

"Yes, she loves telling stories—both truth and fiction. Sometimes she entertains some of the children with fairy-tales. Even Brenna loves to hear those stories."

Nellie stiffened slightly with the mention of Brenna's name. Reverend Mueller noticed, but he made no comment.

"I hope you'll come back, Miss Nellie. My mother enjoyed your visit so much...and so did I."

Nellie felt her face warming and was glad it was dark. "I'd like that, Reverend Mueller, and please, just call me Nellie."

"I will, Nellie, if you will call me John." They wished each other a good night, and Reverend Mueller returned to his wagon.

He thought about Nellie before sleep came. She was a kind woman. What was it about Brenna that distressed her? Maybe they had quarreled over something. Oh well, he never claimed to understand women.

A Revelation

Chapter Nine

⸺⸺⸺⸺◄((◉))►⸺⸺⸺⸺

Fort Laramie
June 22, 1852
Mile 650

"My Goodness! I can't believe how high these prices are," Ruth Benson complained to her husband Thomas as they perused the goods for sale at the Fort Laramie trading post. The trading post was a small adobe building, like all the buildings at the fort, and it was situated inside the high walls of the palisade. All of the travelers were purchasing vital supplies that had dwindled over the past two months.

Kate Flannigan was holding eight pairs of Indian moccasins. "Our shoes are nearly worn out," she told Michael, who was balancing sacks of flour, beans, and tea.

Emily Hinton looked dismayed. "Oh, how I wish there was something different in the way of food! I'm so sick of biscuits, beans, and bacon!"

"Why don't we get these pickles? That's something different," Nellie said.

"Pickles!" Emily exclaimed happily.

Resupplying the food stores took most of the afternoon, and that evening people were in high spirits. Captain Wyatt had spoken to everyone and said he was very pleased to be on schedule. Many folks had made good trades with Indians and now had dried fish and buffalo meat. In spite of the rain that had followed them for a week, people were in good spirits.

Nellie had become a regular visitor to the Mueller wagon in the evenings. She and Mrs. Mueller became close friends, and she was becoming very fond of John. He was so attentive to his mother, and to her. The only thing that put a damper on the otherwise enjoyable evenings was the presence of Brenna. She was there every evening, cleaning up the dinner dishes and making the evening tea. It was becoming increasingly obvious to everyone how much Nellie disliked the girl. One evening, Nellie and Mrs. Mueller were visiting by the fire as usual. John had left to see about getting some nails from the Hanssons. Brenna was bringing the tea to the women when she stumbled and nearly fell. The tea spilled onto Nellie's dress, creating a large stain.

"Oh! Look what you've done, you clumsy girl!" Nellie exclaimed.

"I'm so sorry, Miss Nellie. Let me get some water to clean that up," Brenna said breathlessly.

"No! Don't come near me again! Next time you'll scald me! You've done enough damage." Nellie blotted at the wet stain with a rag Mrs. Mueller handed her. She didn't see Brenna's face, but Mrs. Mueller did.

"I'm sorry, Mrs. Mueller. I should go," Brenna said, and she turned and fled the camp.

Mrs. Mueller gave Nellie some baking soda to mix with water to help reduce the stain. Nellie worked on her dress, all the while grumbling about stupid, clumsy Irish girls. Mrs. Mueller listened silently until Nellie had finished and sat down again.

"You don't like the girl." It was not a question.

"She spilled tea all over me," Nellie said defensively.

"No, there's something else. I noticed it the first night you came to visit. What is it?" Mrs. Mueller's face was kind.

Nellie hadn't realized how obvious her dislike of Brenna had been. She sighed deeply.

"She's Irish, Mrs. Mueller."

"Yes, I've noticed that."

"I hate the Irish!" Nellie said vehemently. "They come to America and take away jobs from decent people because they'll work for almost nothing. They strut around like they own this country just because they speak English. And what kind of English is it? It's not proper English when you use that accent no one can understand. They're all drunkards and brawlers, and if anyone says anything against any of them, they'll kill you and never bat an eye."

Nellie was working herself into a state of frenzy. She stood up and paced in front of the small campfire. Her breath came in gasps and her eyes were wide as her tirade continued.

"They came to Columbus, Ohio where my husband and I lived and tried to take over the town. They built their churches and looked down on anyone who wasn't Catholic. Why, they would barely speak to the Germans, because if you were German, most likely you weren't Catholic, and if they spoke to a non-Catholic, they would have to confess their sin to their priest!" She spit the words out of her mouth in distaste.

"My husband had a good job until they came and offered to do his work for half the pay. He was let go, and he couldn't find another job unless he agreed to work for what the Irish were being paid. Who could live on that? We were poor enough as it was!"

Mrs. Mueller listened quietly, letting Nellie vent.

"One night while he was at the bar drowning his misery, a group of Irish men came in. They were already drunk. The bartender told them to get out. He was a good German, and he wouldn't serve the Irish. Those micks wouldn't leave. Things got rowdy, and soon there was a brawl. Everywhere the Irish went there was a brawl. My husband joined in, of course." Her face had a tortured look, and she was in another place and time.

"It was an even fight in numbers, but the Irish never fight fairly. One of them punched my husband repeatedly in the face and stomach. My husband couldn't defend himself against this man. He tried to get away, but the Irishman kept after him until my husband fell to the floor, hitting his head on the foot rail of the bar. After the fight was over and the Irish had left, they tried to revive my husband, but he was dead! Brain swelling from a skull fracture, they said. The man who killed him was a professional boxer. That's what they told me, Mrs. Mueller. Those micks were never arrested. They were never charged with the murder of my husband."

Nellie put her face in her hands and sobbed. "I hate them! I hate all of them!"

Mrs. Mueller waited silently for Nellie to get back her composure. Finally, Nellie sat down and accepted the handkerchief Mrs. Mueller offered.

"I'm very sorry about your husband, Nellie. I'm sure that must have been a hard blow." She patted Nellie gently on the shoulder.

"Thank you, Mrs. Mueller. I shouldn't have gone on about it. I don't like to talk about it. I've never told this story to anyone before. Not even to Emily."

"Your story is here in my heart, Nellie, and it will go nowhere else."

Nellie's eyes filled with tears again. "You're a good friend, Mrs. Mueller."

After a few minutes, Mrs. Mueller said, "Have I ever told you about my experience with the Irish in New York?"

"No, Mrs. Mueller. What happened?"

"Well, New York City was experiencing the same problems with the jobs. The Irish would work for next to nothing. Well, they had nothing when they came to America, and they came from nothing in Ireland, so any kind of pay was better than what they were used to. The Germans and the Italians didn't like the Irish—and neither did anyone else."

"I can understand that," Nellie said.

"We didn't live in the German community in New York. We lived in a tenement that was largely Irish."

"Why would you live with them, Mrs. Mueller?"

"My husband's brother was a Catholic priest, and he thought he could help mend the rift between the Germans and the Irish."

Nellie's face was incredulous. "Your husband was a Catholic?" She instantly regretted saying all those things about Catholics. "But your son is a minister!"

"Yes, and a good one. He abides by the rules, but he never compromises his principles, Nellie. We wanted John to choose his own path. He has always had a deep faith, but he explored different religions and he ultimately chose to become a Unitarian minister, thinking that he would be able to reach more people. Even here on the trail, he has people of all faiths come to his Saturday evening services. Do you think that would happen if he was a Catholic priest?"

"No!"

"He has often told me that religion tends to divide people. He's more interested in the common humanity that binds people together in love and faith."

This was almost too much for Nellie to take in, but she was listening intently.

"Anyway, my husband Frank, being a Catholic deacon and a German living in the Irish quarters, was not very popular with other Germans, and at first, he wasn't too popular with the Irish either. But no matter what the Irish think of you, they're always hospitable. So Frank would knock on doors and people would invite him in. After a short while, everyone knew him and liked him. His brother was pastor at St. Peter's, a neighboring parish, and some of our neighbors started going to Sunday mass at our church. The Germans didn't like it too much when the Irish started showing up."

"I can imagine!" Nellie said.

"It wasn't too long before the congregation was more Irish than German. Well, one night—it was Good Friday—we were at the church late. It was after the Stations of the Cross, and everyone but my Frank and I had left. Frank wanted to do some last minute things before Easter services. I was in the back offices, and I didn't hear anyone come in, but I did hear a commotion, and when I went into the sanctuary to investigate, there was a man kneeling over my husband with a knife! All I heard the man say was, 'Today is your last day, deacon,' and then he stabbed my husband!"

Nellie gasped in shock.

"I screamed and ran at him. I had a candlestick in my hand that I had been polishing, and I began to beat him with it, but I was no match for him. I guess my screams attracted the attention of someone outside who ran in and overpowered the man. The police came and arrested him, and he hanged for the murder of my husband."

"Oh, no! I'm so sorry, Mrs. Mueller. Where was John?"

"John was in seminary school, and when he heard the news he was devastated. He and his father were very close."

"Was it an Irishman who killed your husband, Mrs. Mueller? Did he want to rob the church?" Nellie asked, sure that she knew what the answer would be.

"No, it wasn't. The man was German, and he spoke in German. He thought my husband was wrong to allow the Irish into the church."

Nellie sucked in her breath. It couldn't be true!

"And the man who came to my rescue and saved my life was an Irishman."

Nellie's head was spinning. This was wrong. Maybe Mrs. Mueller had gotten confused and mixed up the murderer with the hero.

"That can't be true!"

"Nellie, you're not angry with the Irish. You're not even angry with the man who beat your husband."

Nellie started to protest, but Mrs. Mueller continued.

"The Irish and the Germans are all the same, Nellie. We create the differences in hopes of placing blame for the bad things that happen to us. Really, no one is to blame. It's just the way it is. I loved my husband, but I hold no animosity for the man who killed him. He mistakenly thought he was doing the right thing. My husband used to say we are all here for a reason, and it has nothing to do with power and hatred, but everything to do with love. I'm sorry for what happened to your husband, but you can't let that ruin your life."

"But it has ruined my life!" Nellie cried.

"Only because you have allowed it to." Mrs. Mueller took Nellie's hand. "All you have to do to have a better life is to quit living in the past and appreciate what you have now."

"The past is all I have, Mrs. Mueller," Nellie whispered.

"No. The past is nothing. You have a life now and people who care about you. We have all had difficult times in our lives. We can't let those difficulties drag us down."

"But your husband…you loved him and he was murdered! How can you ever forget that?"

"Oh, I'll never forget it, Nellie. I will always love my husband. I miss him and think about him every day. But what happened in the past will not determine how I live my life today. If it did, I don't think I could go on."

As Nellie walked back to the Hintons' wagon, she contemplated all that Mrs. Mueller had said. All of these years she had nursed a hatred for the Irish because of what had happened to her husband. Mrs. Mueller's husband had been murdered also, and yet she had forgiven the man who killed him. Nellie wanted to think of her life differently. She wanted to put the past behind her.

Lost in her thoughts, she suddenly found herself near the Flannigan's wagon. Kate Flannigan was bent over the fire, and the others were talking quietly. Nellie remembered what Mrs. Mueller had said about Irish hospitality. If she was going to think of her life differently, she needed to change her thinking about the Irish. Before she thought about how she was going to do that, she took a deep breath and stepped into the light from the fire. They all looked up. Brenna's face was apprehensive, but she didn't say anything.

"Hello," Nellie said.

"Good evening, Miss Nellie," Kate said. "Please come and join us for a cup of tea. The water is just boiling."

Nellie smiled and moved close to the fire. Conor got up and offered her his seat.

"I was just talking to Conor and Brenna about some of the inscriptions we've seen on Register Cliff today."

"One of them is A.H. Unthank. That's a strange name!" Conor said.

"That one was just inscribed two years ago," Michael added.

"Maybe we'll meet him in Oregon City."

"It's possible, son."

Nellie smiled at Conor. She spent the next minutes in conversation with the Flannigans. When she got up to leave, she looked at them solemnly.

"This has been nice. You are all so kind, and I haven't been civil to you. I want to apologize for my behavior, especially to you, Brenna. I hope that things will be different between us from now on."

"Please visit us anytime. We've enjoyed your company," Kate said.

Nellie walked into the darkness. She was amazed at what had just happened. She could hardly believe what she had done. She marveled at her boldness. What had gotten into her? And yet, look what had come about. She and the Flannigans had carried on like old friends. And they were decent people, too. She felt light—like a heavy weight had been lifted from her shoulders. Maybe Mrs. Mueller was right. Maybe she could change her life. She made a resolution to try. *What have I got to lose?* She thought. And maybe there was everything to gain.

The Legacy

Chapter Ten

⸺⸺⸺◈⸺⸺⸺

Independence Rock
July 4, 1852
Mile 815

Conor Flannigan ambled through the wagons pulled up for the afternoon meal and rest. The wagon train had made its goal of reaching Independence Rock by the fourth of July. Later, there would be celebrations and a much-needed lay by. He didn't feel like celebrating. He was angry with his father and with Brenna. His father had lost patience with him when Conor was helping him unhitch the team.

"Conor, watch what you're about. All I need is for you to get stepped on by one of these beasts."

Then Brenna had irritably told him to go amuse himself some-where else when he accidentally kicked over the frying pan that the bacon for the noon meal had been sizzling in just minutes before. As he walked past the wagons, everyone was occupied with chores except for the small children who chased after each other. The other boys his age were helping their fathers, and they glanced at him as he passed. Conor scowled. *They're probably wondering why I'm not helping my Da*, he thought. He was small for his eleven years, but he was already developing the wiry muscular frame of his father.

Two younger boys ran past him, laughing. These children and their games seemed frivolous. Just a couple of months earlier he would have joined them, but now he wanted desperately to be of help to his father. Conor kicked a stone vigorously and it flew through the air and landed on the flank of an ox still hitched to a wagon. The beast jerked in the yoke and bellowed loudly. A young man looked around from the back of the wagon.

"Hey, what did you do that for?"

"Sorry," Conor mumbled miserably. Even strangers were angry with him. He couldn't do anything right today.

The tall young man walked up to him, eyeing him curiously. His dark hair fell over his eyes. "Good thing old Dobb's a calm one or he'd be halfway back to Missouri by now." Conor looked at the ox who was now calmly chewing his cud. He heaved a huge sigh.

"I wasn't trying to hit him—I didn't even see him."

"That's alright. No harm done. Name's Ezra Meeker," the young man said, extending his hand.

"I'm Conor Flannigan."

"Happy to make your acquaintance, Conor. As long as you're here, why don't you give me a hand? I need to water these oxen and my mule Doris. She's tied to the back of the wagon. My hired hand has been in bed all day so he's no help to me."

"Sure!" Conor brightened. He wanted to show this man that he wasn't a silly boy and that he knew his way around livestock.

"Now, if you'll take old Dobb, I'll grab Burns, and we can get them to the river. Then we'll come back for the other two." Half an hour later, they were hitching the oxen back to the wagon again.

"Doris is a good mule, but she can be stubborn. I don't think she'll give us any trouble, though. I'm sure she's thirsty," Ezra stated. Conor followed him and Doris to the shallow bank of the river. They sat on the grass while Doris drank greedily.

"Who're you traveling with, Conor?"

"My family—we're about twelve wagons up. My Ma, my Da, and my sister Brenna." Conor hesitated, unsure whether to confide in this stranger, but the morning's events weighed heavily on him. "They're all mad at me." He scowled again, remembering.

"Oh, well, you probably deserve it!" Ezra said with a chuckle.

"I just try to help, and I get in trouble," Conor complained, picking at the long grass.

"Well, you're learning, so you're bound to make mistakes. Don't be so hard on yourself. You're probably more upset than they are."

Conor watched Ezra. The young man was loosely holding the rope that was knotted around Doris's neck, allowing her to eat the rich grass growing along the riverbank. Ezra turned and looked at him. "I'll bet you're a great help to your Da. Look how much you helped me just now."

"I try to help, but I can't do anything right."

"Now you're feeling sorry for yourself." Ezra smiled at the scowling youth. "Your father needs you. Try to see it from his eyes."

Conor was silent for a moment, thinking about how he had stormed off like a child when his father seemed impatient with his awkward handling of the oxen. His anger left him suddenly, and he sighed deeply.

"My da has a lot on his mind. I guess I shouldn't have lost my temper."

"It's easy to do. I have my moments, but when I lose my temper, I lose respect—my self-respect and the respect of others." Conor looked at Ezra's kindly face and sincere eyes. Ezra smiled at him, and Conor smiled back. He had made a friend, and he knew Ezra would be someone he could talk to.

"Why are you going west?" Conor asked.

"Oh, I couldn't pass up the opportunity to settle in a new land, uncivilized, untamed. The trip alone is the most exciting thing I've ever done. Is your family going all the way to Oregon?"

"Yes, my da's a farmer. He wants to claim a half-section. He says the land is rich and fertile in Oregon."

"That's what I hear," Ezra replied. They both turned at the sound of someone approaching. A young willowy woman walked up carrying a small baby swaddled in a blanket. She carefully lowered herself to the grass next to Ezra and put the baby in his lap.

"Ah! Here's my hired hand. As you can see, Conor, he's not quite up to the task yet."

Conor looked at the small baby and laughed.

"Your son is fed, dry, and ready for his mid-day nap," the woman said in a melodic voice. The chubby baby gazed up at his father and cooed contentedly from his blanket.

Conor looked at Ezra's wife. She was a delicately beautiful woman. Her heart-shaped face was framed by auburn hair pulled back into a loose braid. Light smiling eyes regarded him, and her cheeks dimpled when Ezra leaned over and kissed her forehead affectionately.

"Conor, this is my wife Eliza Jane, and my son, Marion," Ezra said. "Conor helped me water the oxen," he explained to Eliza Jane as he played with the infant.

"Pleased to meet you, ma'am."

"It's my pleasure, Conor," Eliza Jane replied with a sweet smile. "Will you stay and have lunch with us?"

"Thank you, ma'am, but I have to get back to my family. My da needs my help," Conor said, glancing at Ezra.

"Yes, Conor's a big help," Ezra said. He leaned over and tickled the baby's stomach. "Someday you'll be a help to me like Conor is to his father." The baby gurgled and grabbed Ezra's finger. Conor blushed with the praise.

"I have something to send with you for your family," Eliza Jane said.

Conor carried the pie to his camp where his family was eating their mid-day meal. Apple pie was an unusual item to find on the trail. They hadn't had anything so grand since they left Missouri. They all exclaimed over the rare treat, and Conor described the Meeker family's hospitality as he ate his bread and bacon and drank his tea.

"Ezra said he could use my help from time to time," Conor said, holding his breath and looking at his da.

Michael Flannigan regarded his son. "As long as your chores are done, there's nothing wrong with helping a neighbor. I'm sure

Mr. Meeker could use your help. You're a good hand." Conor let his breath out and smiled appreciatively at his da. A moment later he bowed his head, and his face reddened. "I'm sorry about leaving you with the chores. You're right—I need to learn patience."

Michael Flannigan let out a sigh and roughly tousled his son's dark hair.

"I could use a little of that meself," he said roughly. They all laughed as Conor's mother cut the pie and served it up.

That night in front of Independence Rock, Reverend Mueller led the travelers in a prayer. Afterwards he talked about the journey and the triumphs and losses they had had, and about how important it was for everyone to help each other. Conor listened as the reverend spoke of each person being a pioneer and making a mark on the world.

"Each of you is leaving a legacy for those who will follow. Each of you, through your actions and your words, are creating a small part of a larger history. Make sure your part matters."

Then, in celebration of Independence Day, they sang patriotic songs around the campfire. There was dancing to fiddle music and merrymaking long into the night. Many of the women had made special treats that were shared around the fire. Many of the men toasted the union with their tin cups full of whiskey. The wagon train would stay here another day so the travelers could rest. The men would make repairs, and the women would catch up on baking and laundry.

Conor sat atop the huge turtle-shaped rock that fur traders had named Independence Rock. It was over 125 feet high, and it had been a strenuous climb. The view from the top of the nearly two thousand-foot-long rock formation was spectacular. The full moon illuminated the scene below. The Sweetwater River was a silvery highway disappearing into the western horizon. He looked down at the camp and at all the people dancing and singing. Everyone was in high spirits. He ran his hand over an inscription carved into the rock. It was one of hundreds—maybe thousands.

"Jack Carson 1849"

So many had already passed by here on their way west. So many had left their marks on this rock. It was somehow comforting to him to see the evidence of those who had followed their dreams. He felt like he was their witness—like it was important for him to see their marks on this rock. He was suddenly overwhelmed with the enormity of the starry sky and with this journey.

These people who had gone before—they had faith that they would make it, Conor mused. *They carved their names into this rock so that we would see the inscriptions and know that we aren't alone—that others have gone before and have done what we are doing.*

It was still a long way to Oregon. Conor thought about all he had learned since leaving Missouri. What was in store for him in the months ahead? He thought of his family. He felt responsible for them—for their safety and well-being. Today he had acted like a child. He knew that whatever happened, he wouldn't storm off again. He had learned a lesson and made new friends, and he felt older and wiser.

He took his knife out of his pocket. He would leave his mark alongside those left by others. He would carve his name into this rock, and future travelers would see it and have faith that they, too, would finish their journey. He bent over the rock and dug the blade into the granite. A little bit of hope—that's what he would leave behind. A little hope that someone who would see his name would know that it was possible to travel two thousand miles across unknown country to a better life. A little hope that it could be done because others had gone before and had done it. He carefully scratched his name into the rock. Just a little hope—that would be his legacy.

Ben And The Indians

Chapter Eleven

July 6, 1852

"I'll replace this rim, Mr. Douglas. It's not usable now." Ben Hansson was surveying the damage and calculating how long it would take to fix the wheel. The hoop iron that went around the wheel was broken, and the wooden wheel wouldn't last long without it.

The wagon train had moved ahead without them, and Ben had stayed behind to help Mr. Douglas. He was annoyed that Mr. Douglas had waited until the last minute to mention the broken rim. The other wagons had been readied for departure, and Ben had volunteered to stay behind to help out.

Mr. Douglas's bleary red-rimmed eyes surveyed him. "I appreciate it, Ben. In all the celebration I forgot to take care of it."

Ben looked at him askance. Mr. Douglas had been celebrating since they made camp at Independence Rock. He had seen him numerous times stumbling around camp with his tin cup in one hand and his whiskey bottle in the other. Ben bit his tongue. Mr. Douglas enjoyed his whiskey. He was traveling alone, but he always had a friend or two join him for a drink in the evening after camp was made. Ben wondered how many bottles of whiskey he had brought with him.

"Well, your wagon isn't going anywhere with this broken hoop iron, Mr. Douglas."

It took a couple of hours to repair the wheel and a few more wagon parts that needed fixing, and Ben was just finishing up when they saw the Indians approaching. There were seven of them advancing at a gallop with their bows drawn. Terrible whoops and aggressive gestures indicated their displeasure. Some of them had guns.

"They don't look too happy, Ben," Mr. Douglas said nervously.

Ben had already surmised this and reached for his gun. Mr. Douglas had his gun drawn. When the Indians rode up on their horses and noticed the guns, they lowered their bows, dismounted, and extended their hands.

"Shake their hands, Mr. Douglas, and then get on the wagon and let's get out of here," Ben said under his breath.

They shook the hands of all the Indians, and Ben mounted his horse while Mr. Douglas climbed up into the seat of the wagon. Before he could encourage the oxen to move, however, an Indian grabbed the yoke of one of the beasts, preventing all of them from moving forward. Another Indian climbed on the wheel, grabbed Mr. Douglas, and pulled him from the wagon. Before Ben could do anything, an Indian grabbed the bridle of his horse, and Ben was forced to dismount.

"Don't do anything hasty, Mr. Douglas. There's more company coming," said Ben desperately as he watched another hundred or so Indians riding towards them.

One of the Indians seized their guns and made Ben and Mr. Douglas sit on the ground. Four of them guarded the prisoners as the large group of Indians arrived and dismounted. A few of the younger Indians began a sport of running past Ben and Mr. Douglas and hitting them with their bows or arrows.

"I don't like the looks of this, Ben. What do you think they have in mind?" Mr. Douglas queried breathlessly as another brave ran past and hit him on the back of the head with his bow.

There seemed to be a difference of opinion among the Indians, who were arguing animatedly and looking at their captives. Ben surmised that the argument was about what to do with him and Mr. Douglas. Meanwhile, some of the Indians were unloading the wagon. All of the dry goods were passed around; the pots and pans, tools, food, clothing—everything was taken out of the wagon. When the picture of his mother was handed around, Mr. Douglas jumped to his feet.

"Hey! That's my property!" he yelled. He was rewarded with a blow to the head from the butt of a rifle. He hit the dirt hard and moaned softly.

"Keep quiet, Mr. Douglas. Don't rile them any more than they already are." But Mr. Douglas was very quiet, and his head was bleeding where he had been hit with the rifle. Ben nervously looked at the hostile faces.

Just then, an elderly gray-haired Indian came forward and stopped the arguing. He appeared to be in charge, and he was accompanied by a slight young man who looked to be about Ben's age, and who Ben figured was a mixed-blood Indian. The two men came towards the prisoners. Ben extended his hand to the chief.

"How do you do?"

The chief took his hand readily and said something in the Indian language. Then Ben looked at the younger man.

"How do you do?" he asked, extending his hand again. The little man took Ben's hand and said in accented English, "How do you do?" He was short and thin, and he wore a black wide brimmed hat over his close-cropped black hair. Dark shrewd eyes with a hint of humor surveyed Ben.

"Do you speak English?"

"Oui, Yes. I am John LePointe. My father was Canadian and trapped game and traded with the Indians."

"Mr. LePointe, would you tell the chief that I would like to talk to everyone?" Ben was taking a gamble that he hoped would pay off. Mr. Douglas sat up and held a bandana to his bleeding head.

The little man addressed the chief in the Indian language. The chief looked at Ben and then nodded. He spoke loudly to all of the braves, and soon all were seated in a vast semi-circle around Ben, Mr. Douglas, the chief, and John LePointe. Ben stood up next to the chief.

"We are from the United States," he began. "We have been sent by our great father to the great waters—the Pacific—where we shall settle with our families and remain."

The little man translated to the chief and the braves sitting in the circle.

"We are friendly with all the red men and we wish to treat you kindly. It was reported to us by some Canadians at Fort Laramie that a story has spread that we are going to join with your enemy, the Blackfeet. This is a lie!"

Ben knew he had hit on the truth when the Indians looked to one another and murmured.

"We are traveling with our women and children. If we were going to make war with you, we would not have them with us. Like you, we do not bring our women and children in our war parties." Some of the Indians nodded at this.

"I invite you to come with us to our wagons where we will welcome you and trade with you and give you gifts."

After John LePoint translated, the chief addressed the group for a few minutes. One brave angrily said something and the chief rebuked him harshly. Then he appeared to issue an order. All of the Indians got up and mounted their horses. Ben was given his horse and his gun, and Mr. Douglas was permitted to get onto his wagon. The whole party proceeded in the direction of the wagon train. Ben, the chief, and most of the braves rode ahead while Mr. Douglas and a few Indians proceeded more slowly at the pace of the oxen.

It was evening when Ben spotted the wagon train circled by the river. As they drew nearer, he saw that the travelers were looking their way and milling about in an agitated manner.

"It would be best if your men waited here," Ben said to the chief, nodding to John LePoint to translate. "My friends do not understand why you are here. They may fire on you if all of your men try to come into camp."

The chief looked at the confusion in the camp and then at Ben. He said something to John.

"The chief says he will take six men with him. The rest will wait here."

"Good," Ben said with a look of relief on his face. He could only imagine what everyone would do if he brought a hundred Indians into the camp.

The chief quickly chose six braves and the small group extricated themselves from the others and rode slowly towards the wagons with Ben in the lead. Captain Wyatt rode out to meet them halfway.

"What's this all about, Ben?" he queried, looking from Ben to the chief, to the small mixed blood man.

"It seems these Indians thought we were in league with their enemy, the Blackfeet. Before they had a chance to take our scalps, I was able to persuade the chief that we are friendly and mean them no harm."

"How did you manage that?"

"Cap'n, this is John LePointe. He speaks English, and he translated for me." The captain looked at the little man, and a slow smile spread over his face.

"Well, I'll be! I never thought I'd see the likes of you again. You've grown a bit!" He moved his horse next to the younger man's and they shook hands enthusiastically.

"Ah, Captain, we meet again, my friend!"

"The last time I saw you, you were half drowned at Three Island Crossing."

"Yes, my father thought I could swim. He discovered I couldn't." Captain Wyatt laughed heartily and LePointe smiled. Captain Wyatt turned to Ben.

"I met John four years ago at Fort Laramie. I was leading a group west and he and his father were trading with the settlers. They traveled with us to Three Island Crossing. They were very helpful in communicating with the Indians and they assisted us in crossing the river." He looked at John LePointe. "Is your father with you?"

"Sadly, my father was killed in a hunting accident two years ago. I live with Chief Lone Bull, my mother's uncle," he said, indicating the chief.

"I'm sorry to hear about your father, John. He was a good man."

John made the introductions in the native language, and Captain Wyatt shook hands with the Chief. "Chief Lone Bull was invited to your camp by this man," John said, indicating Ben. "We were promised a warm welcome and gifts."

Captain Wyatt looked solemnly at Ben. Both he and Ben knew it would be a sacrifice for the travelers to have to let go of anything. "Of course! Just make sure the others keep their distance," Captain Wyatt said, looking at the large group half a mile away.

"They will remain where they are as long as everything is peaceful, Captain."

"Tell your chief that it is my honor to invite him to smoke with us. We have gifts for him and his men."

John translated to the chief, and the small party made their way to the wagons.

The Indians and the settlers sat around the campfire, and a pipe was passed around many times. Mr. Douglas had his wound tended to, and he sat quietly in the circle. Ben sat with Brenna, who seemed very happy that he had returned safely. She had insisted he tell her the whole story twice, and she marveled at his bravery. Occasionally they heard whoops and gunshots from the Indian camp, but John LePointe assured everyone there was nothing to worry about. The women brought food and drink to the Indians who seemed to enjoy the fare very much. Someone played the fiddle, which amazed the braves. They looked at it, inside of it, and at the strange bow, wondering how the sound was made. The musician allowed some of them to try it, and their efforts were greeted with loud laughter from everyone. Then gifts of food, clothing, and a few trinkets from various wagons were brought out for the chief's inspection. Someone donated a mirror, and all of the braves took turns looking at their reflections. Mary brought a cornhusk doll. The chief smiled at her and nodded his approval.

Captain Wyatt spoke to John LePointe.

"Tell Chief Lone Bull that Mr. Douglas's property must be returned. He is not a wealthy man, and that is all he has in the world."

John translated to the chief, who agreed to the condition.

"Chief Lone Bull will make sure everything is returned in the morning," said John.

Sometime later, the Indians left the camp and returned to the larger group a short distance away. They had enjoyed the evening immensely, and they were happy with the trades they had made and their gifts. Before they left, Captain Wyatt said goodbye.

"John, it was good to see you. I hope we meet up again someday. Please tell Chief Lone Bull that it was an honor to have his company."

"Farewell, my friend. I'm glad our meeting ended happily."

In the morning, when the contents of Mr. Douglas's wagon were returned, Mr. Douglas vehemently expressed his unhappiness. Half of his supplies were missing, and all of the whiskey was gone. Judging by the subdued state of the Indian party, it had been consumed the night before.

"You can thank your stars you got half of your supplies back," Captain Wyatt said tersely. "Next time pay attention to your wagon instead of to your whiskey." Then he turned on his heel and left Mr. Douglas staring at his back.

At the Flannigan camp Conor was quiet. They had passed many graves, most unmarked, but one of them near their camp had caught Conor's attention. The crude wooden marker read, "Alva Unthank."

"Da, that's A.H. Unthank from the inscription on Register Cliff!"

"It could be, Conor."

"I guess we won't be meeting him in Oregon City," he said sadly.

"No, Conor, I don't think so, but you can honor him by collecting a few of these wildflowers for his grave and saying a little prayer. Then when we meet his kin in Oregon City, you can tell them what you did."

Conor spent the next minutes doing just that. After he said his prayer, he felt better.

"Alva, if you're listening, I'll make sure your family knows you've been taken care of," he said aloud, and he placed the small bouquet of wildflowers in front of the marker.

Emily's Sacrifice

Chapter Twelve

꧁ ⚜ ꧂

July 22, 1852

Emily Hinton looked down at her shoes as she walked beside the wagon. They were so covered in trail dust she couldn't tell what their original color had been. After these shoes wore out, she had one pair left, and they were her dressier ones that she intended to save for Oregon City. She knew the shoes she was wearing wouldn't last another hundred miles, and then what would she do? She most likely would have to buy moccasins at Fort Hall. She shuddered at the thought of wearing the common-looking footwear, but many of the other women had purchased moccasins at Fort Laramie from the French traders and their Sioux wives.

The brim from her pretty yellow bonnet shielded Emily's face from the sun, and she wore dainty white gloves to protect her hands. Some of her gloves were useless now, after holding the ropes in an attempt at keeping the wagon from tumbling down

Windlass Hill. Two days ago, it had been overcast; she had not worn her hat and gloves, and her face and hands had gotten pink.

"Miss Emily, what were you thinking? You should always wear a hat and gloves when you're outside!" Nellie remonstrated, and then proceeded to blot Emily's face and hands with cold nettle tea.

Buster trotted happily next to Emily. He was her constant companion. He even slept with her—something Ernest didn't care for at all. She looked at Ernest leading the stock that pulled their wagon. A general feeling of unease crept into her body. She wasn't sure why she felt like this. She knew Ernest was keeping things from her. When she tried to find out what he wasn't telling her, he would become evasive. Last night they had quarreled again.

"I declare, Mr. Hinton, you spend more time with Mr. Brown than with me. What is it that you talk about?"

"Emily, it's men's business. None of your concern." Ernest was sanding the splintery handle of one of the shovels.

"What kind of business, Mr. Hinton?"

"The kind of business that most women don't worry about, Emily."

Emily looked at Ernest testily. "You're not playing cards are you, Mr. Hinton?"

Ernest sighed heavily. "We play occasionally, Emily. Nothing wrong with that. It's a gentlemen's game."

"I hear tell that Mr. Brown is a gambling man. Are these card games played for money?"

Ernest had slammed the shovel against the wagon. "Emily! I am your husband, and what I do with my money is my business!" His voice was loud "Now stop with these questions!"

Emily's face flushed and she stared at Ernest until he looked away and left the camp.

They hadn't spoken today, and Nellie had noticed and asked Emily what was wrong.

"I wish I knew, Nellie," Emily had replied.

Abel Brown came around often, and the more she got to know him, the more she distrusted him. He was too smooth. He always had the right words, but she felt like he was hiding behind a handsome façade. The few times she had tried to draw him out in conversation and talk about his past, he had shifted the topic to something impersonal. He was a mystery, and more than that, he was enamored with her. He made subtle advances when Ernest wasn't looking, and he flirted with her shamelessly, especially when he had been drinking. Finally, she confronted him.

"Mr. Brown, you are taking liberties with me and it's making me uncomfortable."

He laughed delightedly. "Why, Miss Emily, I apologize if I have done anything to cause you distress. Rest assured it will never happen again." But it did, many times, and she had even spoken to Ernest about him.

"Emily, that's just his way. His background is different from yours."

"Just what is his background, Mr. Hinton? I can't get him to talk about his past or his family at all."

"He's a very private person, Emily. He's not close with his family, and he doesn't like to talk about them. Best to just let it be." After that, Emily made it a point to avoid Abel Brown until one day when Ernest was busy trading with Indians and Abel had sauntered into camp.

"Good afternoon, Miss Emily. Beautiful day today, isn't it?" Abel tipped his hat and walked closer to where she was making biscuit dough. After a brief glance in his direction, she continued with her chore.

"Mr. Brown, Ernest is away at the moment. Why don't you try back in an hour? I'm sure he'll be back by then."

"It's you I came to see, Emily. Why don't you clean your hands and sit with me for a while." He took her hands out of the bowl and wiped them with her apron. She jerked her hands away and backed up a few paces.

"You shouldn't be here, Mr. Brown. I think you should leave now."

"Don't be rude, Emily. Where's that southern charm I've seen you display so many times? Come on, you can be nice to me."

He closed the distance between them until her back was against the wagon. Then he leaned towards her, his hands on either side of her. She could smell the whiskey on his breath. His eyes, a yellow brown, smoldered. She looked around frantically, but no one was in sight. Then he chuckled.

"It's just you and me, Emily, and it's time we got better acquainted." He pulled her to him roughly and covered her mouth with his. She struggled against him, but he was strong and his arms held her tightly. After what seemed an eternity, she was able to push him away. Then she slapped him as hard as she could. She felt gratified at the sight of her handprint on his cheek. She grabbed the pitchfork propped against the wagon and brandished it towards him.

"Get away from me, Mr. Brown, or I swear I'll kill you!"

Abel Brown stepped back quickly, holding his hand to his cheek. He had personal experience with angry women and he knew what they could do. "Settle down, Miss Emily. I'm just being friendly."

"I don't like your kind of friendly. Now get out!" She jabbed the pitchfork towards him.

Abel was slowly backing up, keeping a close eye on the pitchfork. "I think I should go, Miss Emily. It's been a pleasure." He tipped his hat, turned, and walked out of camp.

Emily watched him go, and suddenly she felt her knees begin to give out. She sat on the bench and realized she was shaking. Her first thought was to tell Ernest. She wanted him to beat Abel Brown to a pulp. Then she almost laughed aloud. Ernest wasn't a fighter. He would never last against the likes of someone like Abel Brown. Ernest had been raised to be a gentleman farmer.

There was something sinister about Abel Brown. The more she thought about it, the more certain she was that Abel would kill Ernest and call it self-defense. No, it was better to keep it to herself. She would just make sure that she was never alone again where Abel Brown could take advantage of her. She just had to be careful. Her fingers went to her swollen lips. Not for the first time she wished she was a big burly man. "I'd teach him a lesson he'd never forget," she said vehemently. For the next half hour, while she finished the biscuits, she imagined all the ways she would get back at Abel Brown.

Emily's hands clenched tightly as she recalled that afternoon. She had never mentioned it to Ernest, and Abel had kept his distance. The wagons were slowing down and pulling into a shady area by the river. It was time for the mid-day meal and watering of the stock. As Ernest guided the wagon into its place, she noticed Rebecca Benson walking around their wagon. She was barefoot and seemed to be limping. It wasn't uncommon to see women barefoot, and Rebecca certainly was sturdy, but Emily was sure something was wrong.

While Nellie prepared the meal, Emily walked to the Benson camp.

"Hi, Rebecca."

Rebecca started when she heard Emily behind her. She was sitting on a bench applying some ointment to a large blister on her right heel. "Oh, hello, Emily! You startled me!"

Emily chuckled. "Sorry. I didn't know I was so quiet. That's a nasty looking blister!"

"Yes, I was wearing Ma's shoes and they're too small for me. I should have just gone barefoot."

"Are your shoes worn out?"

"The last pair lasted a long time. When the sole got big holes, I put cloth inside, but eventually even that didn't work. Ma told me to wear hers since she's riding most of the time now with the baby so close." She dabbed at the large and swollen blister. "But Ma's feet are smaller than mine. I didn't realize I was getting such a large blister. James made up this ointment for me to apply. Sure hope it works!"

Emily looked closely at Rebecca's foot. "I may have a solution for you, Rebecca. I'll be right back!"

A few minutes later Rebecca was exclaiming over the beautiful shoes that Emily had presented to her.

"I can't accept these, Emily! They're beautiful, and they'll be ruined on the trail." She held one up, admiring its ivory kid leather and side laces.

"Nonsense! I expect they will be ruined, but better the shoes than your feet! Now try one on. I think we may wear the same size."

Rebecca slipped one on the foot that was not blistered. She laced it up and it went well past her ankle. Then she stood up and smiled broadly. "It fits! Emily, how can I ever thank you?"

The two women hugged warmly, and then Emily walked back to her wagon. Ernest was leading an ox back from the river. He looked at Emily and she smiled at him brightly. "Lunch should be almost ready, Mr. Hinton." He smiled back, relief spreading over his face. "I'm famished, Emily," he said, and they walked companionably back to their wagon.

The Lie

Chapter Thirteen

Fort Hall
August 1, 1852
Mile 1217

Sam Benson looked at his father's serious face. He knew he could be in deep trouble. Amber, their horse—their only horse—had been stolen from him by an Indian youth about thirteen—his own age. Sam had taken the mare up river to water her during their midday stop. It was a warm day, and he was resting against a tree when the redskin came up behind him.

Sam jumped up, still clutching Amber's lead rope in his hand. He was scared. Here was one of the bloody savages and he was defenseless. True, the savage was young and had no weapon either, but he looked so fierce that Sam was petrified. The Indian took a step forward and Sam stepped back against the tree. He looked wildly around for help, but no one was near. He had thought about yelling, but at that moment, the Indian did some fancy footwork and Sam was on the ground while the youth held the lead rope. Then he deftly leaped onto Amber's back, scowled at Sam, and rode off without a backwards glance. Sam scrambled to his feet and started to give chase, but the horse and rider quickly outdistanced him. Humiliated, Sam watched them disappear over a hill.

He wondered what to tell his Pa. Could he tell him that a boy with no weapons and no accomplices had taken the horse from him? Sam's cheeks burned with embarrassment. He had to think of a better story. Suddenly he had an idea. He would say that Amber had run off with some wild horses the scouts had first spotted a couple of days ago. Amber was in season, and the stallion had been calling to her.

Thomas Benson was angrily contemplating his son's story about how their only horse had run off. At the same time, he was working out how to get her back. Sam perched on the edge of the lie. He could go either way—deeper into the hole he had dug or up into the light. All he needed to say was, "that's not exactly the truth," as if truth could be measured on a scale from one to ten, with ten being totally true. Sam looked at his father, gauging what he thought he wanted to hear. He heard himself tell the lie again.

"It's true, Pa. I was watering Amber when Conor and his friends came crashing out of the bushes yelling and screaming. They were playing Indians. Amber was so frightened she reared up and jerked the rope from my hands. I tried to catch her, but she was too fast." Sam saw the resignation on his father's face.

"I can find her, Pa. I'll borrow the Flannigans' horse and go look for her." Sam watched his father carefully. He could see that his father believed him, and he began to relax. Sam had no qualms about stretching the truth if it served him. Many times he had invented stories to avoid consequences.

"No, Sam, you stay here. Next thing I'll have a lost horse and a lost son. I'll ask the scouts to be on the lookout for that wild band. When they're spotted, I'll get some help to catch her. Now go get Tom. I want you two to fetch some water for your mother." Sam ran off in search of his brother, secure in the knowledge that his story was believed and that he wouldn't have to face retribution, or worse, embarrassment for his carelessness.

Thomas Benson looked worriedly at the horizon. *I wonder how far that fool horse has got,* he thought. It would be a tremendous loss if they didn't get her back. Horses weren't cheap, and Amber was a good horse for riding and for plowing. Then there was the fact that she was in a halter, trailing a lead rope. She could get caught up in all kinds of things and not be able to free herself. *I should ride out and take a look,* he decided. *At least my mind will be eased that I did what I could to find her.* Once the decision was made, he told his wife and set off to the Flannigans' wagon to ask Michael for the loan of his horse.

He found Michael Flannigan bent over the foot of his horse. The mare had thrown a shoe, and Michael was attaching a replacement. He stood up as Thomas approached.

"You look like a man on a mission," Michael said, noting Thomas's furrowed brow.

"My horse ran off. I think she's after that band of wild horses the scouts spotted."

"I heard the stallion last night."

"And did you hear Amber calling back to him? She's in season, and she's been a handful. She got away from Sam, and I'm hoping she isn't far off."

"Tessa was answering the stallion, too," Michael said, indicating his mare. "The grass has been pretty good for a couple of days, so they should be close."

"I was hoping to borrow your horse to go look for Amber."

"I've just finished replacing Tessa's shoe. She should be fit to ride."

"Thanks," Thomas said, grabbing the blanket and saddle from the back of the wagon. When Tessa was saddled and bridled, Michael handed Thomas a lasso.

"Good luck. If you're not back, I'll help Sam get your wagon under way when we head out."

"I appreciate it," Thomas replied, and he and Tessa rode toward the horizon.

A little while later, Sam was surprised to see Michael Flannigan walking towards him.

"Hi, Mr. Flannigan. Have you seen my pa? We're about to leave."

"He's looking for your horse, Sam. I'm here to see that everything's okay for your departure. Have you checked the team?" Michael Flannigan's eyes roamed over the oxen and the harnesses, making sure everything was secure. If he had noticed Sam's face, he would have known that something was wrong. Sam's eyes were round and his face was pale. He knew his father would never find Amber, and he was out there alone. It was a dangerous situation with all the Indians around. What if something happened to him?

"Everything looks good, Sam. I'll let your ma know what's going on. You should get yourself ready to drive the team." Michael walked to the back of the wagon to talk to Ruth, Sam's mother. Rebecca and Tommy were busy dousing the fire and cleaning up the younger children after their midday meal. Sam's apprehension mounted when he realized he was responsible for the team.

"Mr. Flannigan, I've never driven the team by myself before. I don't think I can do it. Will you help me drive them?"

Michael noted Sam's fear and felt sorry for the boy. "I can't do that, Sam. Conor is laid up with a sprained ankle, so there's no one left to drive my team but me. I'll tell the captain to check up on you when he comes by. You'll be fine, and your pa should be back soon. Get Tom to help you." Sam watched Michael Flannigan walk away. A feeling of doom settled over him as he realized he was responsible for this. He should have told his father the truth. Even if he found the wild band, he wouldn't find Amber with them. Now it was too late. He hoped his father would return safely.

The afternoon was warm and dry, and the train made good time, but there was no sign of Thomas Benson when the wagons made their circle for the evening near Fort Hall. Sam was beside himself with worry. What if his father never returned? What if he had been captured by the Indians—or worse! He and Tommy unhitched the team and fed and watered them. As soon as he could, he ran to the Flannigans' camp. Michael Flannigan was busy with his stock and Conor wasn't able to help out while his ankle was on the mend. Brenna was helping her da as best she could.

"Where's my pa?" Sam asked frantically.

"He's not back yet," Michael replied gently. He could see the boy's agitation.

"Do you think something might have happened to him?"

"Give him a little more time, Sam," Michael replied.

"This is all my fault!" Sam cried.

Michael looked at the boy. He could see Sam's grief taking hold of him. "Don't blame yourself for this, Sam. Horses are strong. If they want to go somewhere, you can't hold them back."

"No, you don't understand!" Sam was near hysteria. "Amber didn't run off. She was stolen by an Indian and I didn't do anything to stop it!"

"What are you saying, Sam?" Michael asked incredulously.

Sam's voice was rising. "I'm telling you that my dad isn't going to find Amber. She's not with the wild horses. I lied to him." Sam hid his face in his hands and sobbed. "I didn't want to tell him that I let an Indian boy take Amber from me, so I made up a story."

Michael Flannigan looked at Sam, horrified. "You've done a terrible thing, boy. You've put your father in harm's way because of your pride. More than that, you've put your whole family in jeopardy. Now you go back to your wagon and tell your family what you've done. I'm going to look for your pa."

Sam stumbled back to his wagon trying to control his emotions. Twice he stopped to take deep breaths and compose himself. How could he tell his ma what he had done? She was already in a weakened state with the birth of the baby so close. What would they do without Pa? He had calmed himself considerably when he got to their camp. The family was sitting around the campfire, and Rebecca was cooking dinner. Everyone was strangely quiet, but Sam didn't notice. He walked up to his ma and knelt before her.

"Ma, I have something to tell you." His voice wavered, but he continued. "Pa isn't back. He went looking for Amber because I told him Amber ran off." Sam's voice was uneven and his mouth worked uncontrollably. He took a ragged breath. "That's not what happened, Ma. I lied to Pa because I was embarrassed about what really happened. Amber was taken from me." Sam bowed his head and his shoulders shook. He struggled to control his voice. "An Indian boy took her, and I didn't stop him. Now Pa is out there looking for Amber. He'll never find her, Ma. This is all my fault. I don't know what to do." Sam buried his face in his mother's lap, sobbing.

Ruth Benson gently lifted her son's face in her hands. She wiped his tears with her apron. "I reckon you've had enough heartache over this," she said tremulously. Sam looked at her sorrowfully. Ruth looked behind her and said, "Come on out here now." Thomas Benson walked out from behind the wagon. Sam's faced drained of color.

"Pa!"

Thomas walked up to Sam, and Sam stood up and faced his father. They looked solemnly at each other before Sam threw himself into his father's arms.

"Pa, I was so worried about you!" After a few moments, Thomas took hold of Sam's arms and held him away from him.

"I got back after the wagons had circled. I never found the horses. I thought something was odd when Michael was doing all the chores without a sign of Conor. While I was brushing Tessa down, I asked him about it and he said Conor had sprained his ankle pretty good yesterday and had been laid up all day. I thought to myself, how could Conor and his friends have scared Amber if he was laid up all day? I mentioned this to Michael, and that's when we saw you coming. I hid behind their wagon and listened to you tell Michael what had happened. I'll tell you, Sam, I am pretty disappointed."

Sam was calm now, but he couldn't look his father in the eye. He listened quietly, head bent.

"I'm not going to say I don't understand why you did what you did," Thomas said. "But a man would have told the truth, even if it meant he would look foolish. We're in a dire situation out here in the middle of nowhere. Every day we are somewhere none of us has been before. Anything can happen, and we all need to stick together. That means we have to put our own feelings to the side and think of the others first. Can you understand that?" Sam nodded dumbly.

"I need to know I can count on you, Sam."

Sam took a ragged breath and looked up. His gaze was steady, and he met his dad's eyes. "I'm sorry, Pa. You're right. I have been thinking of myself and it hasn't been fair to you or to anyone else." He looked around the campfire at his family. They were watching him solemnly.

"I want to earn your trust, Pa. I'm willing to do anything to get that back." Thomas Benson looked at his son. Sam seemed a little taller. His shoulders were slightly broader. *Hard lessons are best*, he thought. They helped grow a man. This had been a tough one, but everyone was still here. He knew his son was telling the truth. Without breaking eye contact, he dropped his right hand and extended it to Sam. Sam took it and clasped it tightly. Then they embraced warmly, and little Deborah and Annie came up and hugged both of their legs. Soon, the moment was over. They ate dinner together and got ready for the night.

Later, as Sam lay in his bedroll looking at the stars that stretched across the sky endlessly, he felt insignificant. *How could I have been so selfish?* he wondered. He looked at the big dipper with the North Star shining brightly. Every night it was there like a beacon, so dependable, so steadfast and true. *I need to be like that star*, he thought. *I need to be someone my family can depend on.* He closed his eyes and made a wish. For the rest of his life, he would remember that night and his wish, and he would be forever grateful that his wish did come true.

The next day the women did the washing and baking. The children played games of tag and keep-away. Some of the men went hunting for antelope. Others made repairs to their wagons and tended to stock. Many animals had died crossing the dry and sandy desert. Some died from lack of food or water, and some from sheer exhaustion. Ben Hansson had his lariat, and he was practicing roping a steer skull he had placed on a rock when Conor Flannigan walked up.

"What are you doing, Ben?"

"I'm roping this here steer."

Conor watched Ben deftly twirl his lasso with his right hand, and when he threw it, he let the coil in his left hand play out. The loop encircled the horns of the skull. It looked easy.

"Can I try?"

"Sure. Here, hold these coils in your left hand and twirl this loop in your right."

Conor tried to twirl the rope like Ben had done, but instead of making an open circle, the rope came together.

"Rotate your wrist like this." Ben showed him how to do it.

"Oh, I see." Conor tried again with no success.

"You're trying too hard, Conor." Ben showed Conor again, lassoing the horns easily. Keep the fingers of your left hand slightly open or the rope won't play out."

Conor tried many more times before it looked like he was making progress. They both turned when they heard Brenna's voice.

"Here you are! Conor, Da's been looking for you. He needs your help."

"Let me give you some rope so you can practice, Conor." Ben went to the back of his wagon and found a length of stiff rope. "Do what I told you, and I'll help you again in a few days."

"Thanks, Ben." Conor took the rope and ran off to find his da.

"You shouldn't encourage him, Ben. He has enough idle pastimes to lose himself in."

"This isn't an idle pastime, Brenna. This is a skill he'll need."

"A skill? Catching skulls with a rope?"

Ben laughed. "You are a city girl, aren't you? Haven't you ever seen anyone rope a steer?"

"Yes, in Independence I did, but it looked like a game to me."

"Sometimes it is a game, but it has a purpose. If a steer strays away, how are you going to get him back? Or if you want to brand one so you know it's yours, you have to catch him, don't you?"

"Brand? What do you mean?"

"Well, when cattle are out on pasture they may get mixed in with someone else's, so you have to brand the cattle with a red hot iron so you can identify yours from theirs."

"You burn them?" Brenna looked aghast.

"Yes, that's how branding works."

"That's barbaric!"

"That's the way it's done."

"Doesn't it hurt them?"

Ben sighed. He could see this was going nowhere. "Sure it hurts them, but they get over it."

"I think that's brutal!"

"Well, I suppose you have a better idea?"

Brenna looked thoughtful for a moment. "Why don't the farmers tie a colored string to their cows' horns or legs?"

Ben guffawed loudly. "Oh, that's a good one," and he laughed until tears ran down his cheeks. Brenna's face became stormy. She crossed her arms and angrily watched him. After a moment, she turned on her heel and stomped away. Before she got very far, Ben's lasso flew up and came down around her shoulders. He tightened the line and slowly drew her back.

"Ben! Let me go!"

"In a minute," he said. "First I want to apologize for laughing at you. I'm sorry, Brenna. That wasn't very nice."

Her anger disappeared. "Apology accepted. I still think it's a horrible way to treat the poor beasts."

Ben hugged her tightly. "I know. You're just a softie."

Later at the evening meal, Brenna asked her father, "Da, what do you think about branding?"

"Branding cattle? It's very important in the west where there are no fences."

"But it seems so cruel to the animals."

"Aye, well, it's the best method of keeping your cattle separate from another's. Losing even one steer can be a hardship to a rancher. The branding helps keep everyone honest, and if you find your neighbor's steer mixed in with yours, you can return it."

"Ben is teaching me to use the lasso so that I can help find lost steers and rope them and bring them home," Conor said.

"That's wonderful, Conor. Roping is an important skill that I need to learn also. Perhaps young Ben will take on another student."

"I'm going to practice every day so that I can be as good as Ben. He said he always keeps his lariat close by because you never know when you'll need it."

"Good idea," his father agreed. Brenna looked at her ma and they both smiled. Men and boys and their toys! What next?

Kate's Gift

Chapter Fourteen

<hr />

America Falls
Mile 1235

Kate Flannigan put her hand on the small of her back. This day had been exhausting and she was hoping they would make camp soon. The trail was rough, and the grass, which had been plentiful the day before, seemed to get scarcer the farther they traveled. Yesterday they crossed the Snake River, and if she never saw another river again, it would be too soon! How many river crossings had they done since they had left Independence? She was mentally adding them up when she became aware of the faint roar of the falls. That cheered her up because camp would be close now.

"Brenna, gather some wood for the fire when you see it," She called to her daughter. Minutes later, they were passing America Falls, and the spray from the fifty-foot drop was a welcomed relief from the heat of the day. Conor skipped back to his mother.

"Da says we'll be camping up a ways on Birch Creek."

"Conor, help your sister find firewood," Kate said, and she lifted the top of the bucket to check the cream that had been churning into butter all day. At least the rough trail was good for something! Satisfied, she trotted up to where her husband Michael was guiding the teams.

"How much farther before we stop, Michael?"

"Just a few minutes more, Kate."

"Do you think we'll have a lay-by?" Kate asked hopefully.

"No, there's not enough grass here. We'll be leaving in the early morning." He saw Kate's face fall. "But I hear it's a very nice creek. Maybe you can find some time to get a bath." After the dusty day, Michael knew many of the women would want a refreshing dip in the cool water of the creek. "I heard Captain Wyatt say we'll be having a lay-by soon."

Kate seemed to cheer up with the news, and soon the wagons were circling for the night. After dinner and chores, Kate and Brenna made their way to the creek. They had some laundry to do, and they planned to take a little swim. Some of the other women were already in the water when they got to the edge of the creek. The water looked to be about two feet deep in the middle. Kate and Brenna stripped to their linen undergarments and waded into the water.

"Oh! It's freezing!" Brenna exclaimed.

"It's wonderful!" Kate said, sitting in the creek bed. "Where's that soap, Brenna?"

They spent the following minutes washing their bodies and hair, and then put their attention to the laundry. All too soon, it was time to return to camp and turn in for the night. Then it would be a few short hours before they would awaken to do it all over again. Kate kept her mind on the promised lay-by. She needed rest. The days were too long and the nights too short. She looked over to the Bensons' wagon. Ruth, heavy with child, was washing the dinner dishes in the light of the campfire while Rebecca tended to the little girls. Kate suddenly felt ashamed. She was young and healthy. Her children didn't need much looking after. Why was she such a complainer? She walked the short distance to the Bensons' camp.

"It's a beautiful night for a dip in the creek, Ruth," Kate said.

Ruth looked at her and smiled ruefully. "I was hoping to get into the water, but it's getting pretty late now." Her eyes had dark circles underneath and her cheeks were hollow.

"Come on, I'll go with you. It's wonderfully refreshing."

"Go ahead, Ma. I'll finish up the dishes," Rebecca said.

Ruth looked longingly in the direction of the creek. "I need to get Annie and Deborah to bed," she said wistfully.

"Dad will help me, Ma. Go with Kate," Rebecca said.

Ruth needed no more persuading, and the two women walked arm and arm into the night.

Mile 1295

Almost a week later, they were camped on another creek, and the plan was to lay-by. The grass was abundant and there was plenty of water for the stock. Kate felt relief at finally having an extra day to catch up and to relax. The trail had been so dusty, and everyone was hoping for rain. She looked over to the Bensons' camp. She knew Ruth was having a hard time and had been riding a lot in the wagon. The baby was due to arrive any day now. James Cardell had been a big help. His knowledge of plants and herbs had proved to be invaluable, and he kept Ruth supplied with strengthening teas and herbal supplements.

"Let's make bread in the morning, Brenna, and don't we have some apples? We could make a pie for dinner."

"Sounds good, Ma," Brenna replied.

In the morning, Brenna gathered the ingredients for the bread and began mixing the dough while Kate peeled apples for the pie. James Cardell was walking by when he saw the women busily working.

"Looks like someone will be enjoying apple pie later today," he remarked.

"If we have enough apples, we'll make two pies," Kate replied.

"How would you like some raisins to add to the pie?" he asked.

"Do you have some to spare?"

"I'll be right back," and he turned and walked in the direction of his wagon. Soon he was back with a small bowl of raisins. "And there's some cinnamon in there if you'd like."

"Cinnamon! What a treat! Thank you, Mr. Cardell!"

"Please, call me James."

"What are the benefits of cinnamon, James?" Brenna asked.

"Oh, cinnamon has many qualities. For example, it helps with digestion."

"Is that so?" Kate replied.

"Yes, and it improves blood circulation. It's also a calming herb."

Kate put her nose into the bowl and inhaled deeply. The spicy aroma filled her nostrils. "I think this will be just the thing to make these pies special. Come by later and help us enjoy them."

"I will!" James tipped his hat and left in the direction of the Bensons' camp.

That evening before dinner, Kate finished baking the pies. The crust was delicately brown with a few slits in the top where the apples had bubbled up. She was thinking about what James Cardell had said about cinnamon being good for digestion and blood circulation. If anything plagued a heavily pregnant woman, it was indigestion, and she knew how important good blood circulation was at the end of a pregnancy. She looked over to the Bensons' camp and spied Ruth sitting near the fire stirring a large pot and talking to James Cardell. On impulse, she picked up one of the pies and carried it over. Ruth saw her coming and stood up.

"It looks like someone was productive today," she said.

"We were able to get two pies from our apples with the addition of James's raisins," Kate said, nodding at James. "This one is for you and your family, Ruth, and I want you to have an extra-large slice. James tells me the cinnamon in here will help with digestion." The blush on Ruth's cheeks told Kate that she was right about her digestive trouble.

"Thank you, Kate. I haven't had the time or the inclination to do any baking. We will all enjoy this tonight."

Later, Michael came around from the back of the wagon and noticed one pie was missing.

"What happened to the second pie?" he asked.

"I gave it away," Kate replied shortly.

"You gave it away?"

"Yes, I did." Kate looked at him defiantly. Michael walked over to her and wrapped his arms around her.

"Ah, Katie, I'll never be angry with your generosity. That's one of the things I love about you the most."

"Is that right, Michael," Kate asked coyly, arching her brows. "And what are the other things you love about me?"

Michael squeezed her tightly. "After dinner and chores, when everyone is asleep, I intend to show you."

To Michael's delight, Kate blushed deeply.

New Life

Chapter Fifteen

Salmon Falls
August 14, 1852
Mile 1372

A muffled cry came from the Benson wagon in the late evening, contrasting with the soft and steady rain. Ruth Benson had spent the day in labor and was now delivering her seventh child.

The wagon train had stopped near Salmon Falls for the night, and the roar of the eighteen-foot drop could be heard throughout the camp. It had been rough going. The terrain was unforgiving, and the only vegetation was sagebrush and thickset licorice plants. The falls were beautiful even through the rain. Many Indians were camped close to the river where they were catching and drying salmon. Most of the overlanders had traded with these Indians for fresh and dried fish. For many, it was their first taste of salmon.

"How much longer, Dad?" Mary asked her father nervously as another cry came from within the wagon. Her freckles stood out against her pale face. She hated hearing her mother in distress. She remembered Annie's birth almost two years earlier. It hadn't seemed to take as long. Today had dragged on forever as her mother labored to bring the new little one into the world.

"It's hard to say, Mary. Annie was pretty quick. Deborah took a lot longer." They were sitting next to the wagon. Thomas had rigged a makeshift tarp to shield them from the rain. Still, they were all in various stages of wet. On hearing her name, Deborah looked up from the intricate but unidentifiable drawing she was creating with a stick pencil in the mud. Her blue eyes were round.

"Is Mommy crying?"

Thomas shifted a sleeping Annie in his arms. "No, Deborah, she's just pushing the baby out. It won't be much longer."

"Can I go in the wagon?" the four-year-old pleaded.

"Not yet. There's no room for us in there."

Rebecca was in the cramped wagon with Ruth, and Kate Flannigan had been checking in every hour during the evening since they had made camp. Tommy and Sam were doing the evening chores, happy to be away from the drama playing out inside the wagon.

"Do you think it's a boy or a girl?" Mary asked.

"I want a baby brother," Deborah said petulantly. She still hadn't gotten over Annie's birth and all the attention her little sister had stolen from her.

"Your mother thinks it will be a girl, and she's been right every time."

"How does she know?" Mary queried.

Thomas yawned. "I have no idea. Women's intuition I guess."

"What's into....into...?" Deborah asked.

"Intuition," Thomas replied. "Hmm...it's when you know something without having the facts that tell you that it's true, and then it turns out to be true later."

"Like a mystery that solves itself?" Mary asked.

"No, not a mystery. It's like when you have a feeling something's going to happen and then your feeling is correct."

There was another cry from inside the wagon. They could hear Rebecca's voice gently encouraging.

"Like when I had a feeling I was going to be sick and then I was," Mary pronounced.

"No, it's not a physical feeling. It's a feeling in your head—your mind. Remember a couple of weeks ago when Tommy had a feeling about the rocks we were camped close to? He felt they weren't safe to climb on, and later the Harmon boy was bit by a rattlesnake?"

"Yes! I wanted to play on those rocks and Tommy wouldn't let me!"

"That's right, Mary. He had a feeling—an intuition—that something was wrong."

"But Tommy isn't a woman. How does he have intuition?"

Thomas chuckled. "Everybody has it sometimes. Women just listen to it more often."

Mary frowned. "They listen? Does it have a voice?"

"Shhh!" Deborah said. Her earnest mud-smeared face looked at them seriously. "I hear it. It's whispering."

Mary giggled. Her little sister looked so intense. "What's whispering, Deborah?"

"Into-ishen. It's telling me something. Shhh!" Her finger went to her lips to silence them.

A prolonged low cry came from the wagon followed by a lusty baby's protest mingled with Rebecca's excited voice. "It's a girl, Ma. Oh, she's beautiful!"

Thomas rested the back of his head against the wagon and closed his eyes.

"Thanks be to God for this healthy baby, and thank you Lord for taking care of Ruth."

"Can we see her now, Dad?" Mary asked excitedly.

"In a few minutes. Rebecca and your mother still have some work to do."

"What kind of work?"

"They have to get the baby and your ma cleaned up and ready for company."

At that moment, Kate Flannigan walked into camp. "Well, I guess I'm not needed here." The baby was crying lustily.

"It's a girl," Deborah said half-heartedly, her attention on her mud drawing again.

"Aren't you excited about your new little sister, Deborah?" Kate asked teasingly.

"I already have a little sister. I wanted a little brother. I don't have one of those yet." They all chuckled, relieved that Ruth's long labor was over.

"Thomas, let me take Annie to my camp. She can spend the night with us and it will be one less thing you'll have to worry about."

"Thank you, Kate." Thomas gratefully handed the sleeping child over.

"And Mary, you come too after you visit the new sister. Annie will be more comfortable if you are with her, and you can visit with Brenna and Conor." Kate turned to leave and paused. "Have you named the baby yet?"

"Mattie," Deborah said absently, applying finishing touches to her drawing.

Kate looked to Thomas for confirmation. "What a lovely name!"

Thomas shrugged and looked at the four-year-old. "Where did you hear that name, Deborah?"

Deborah stopped her drawing and put down her stick pencil. "My into-ishen told me," she replied solemnly.

Mary laughed along with Kate and Thomas. "I'm going to go and find Tommy and Sam. They'll want to see Mattie," Mary said giggling, and she skipped off in the light drizzle.

"Who wants to see the baby?" Rebecca called. Thomas jumped up and picked up Deborah. He, Deborah, and Kate, who was holding a sleeping Annie, looked through the canvas opening at mother and baby. The small and very pink newborn was quietly nursing.

"She's tiny but strong," Ruth said, smiling tenderly at the new little life.

"Her lungs are really strong," Thomas replied.

"Look at all of that lovely hair!" Kate exclaimed.

"She took a while to get here," Rebecca said, "but she's healthy and hungry!"

Thomas watched his wife gently cradling the new little baby. Rebecca leaned over and stroked the tiny head. "You were a big help, Rebecca," he said.

"I didn't really do anything. Ma did it all!"

Tommy, Sam, and Mary ran into camp, and Thomas and Kate stepped aside so they could see.

"Is it over? Are you okay, Ma?" Tommy asked breathlessly.

"Yes, son, everyone is fine."

"Please tell me it's a boy. There are too many girls around here," he said playfully with a sidelong look at Mary.

"You're outnumbered again, Tommy. It's a girl!" Mary said triumphantly.

Tommy didn't look too disappointed as he watched his newest little sister drifting off to sleep.

"What's her name, Ma?" Sam asked reverently.

"I'm going to name her Martha after my mother," Ruth said. "We'll call her Mattie."

Thomas and Kate looked from Ruth to Deborah incredulously.

"How? What?" Thomas blubbered.

"Don't ask, Dad," Mary said sagely, patting his shoulder indulgently. "It's just that old intuition at work again!"

Thomas laughed until tears ran down his cheeks. He felt like he had been holding his breath all day, and laughter was a welcomed release. Kate and Mary laughed with him while the others looked at each other, puzzled. Little Mattie was happily oblivious. The day, nearly over, seemed to cheer up too, and a soft rumble of distant thunder announced the end of the rain.

Wedding Day

Chapter Sixteen

The next day was a lay-by. Another wagon train had been following theirs, and mid-day it pulled in. There was a lot of visiting and storytelling between the two camps. Travelers traded with each other for supplies that were getting low. Captain Wyatt and Captain Burnett were old friends and they were happy to see each other.

"It's been a while, David."

"Yes it has." Captain Wyatt clapped his friend on the back. "I thought you were done with leading trains west, Joe."

"Well, I thought so too. Turns out my niece and her husband are on this train, and she begged me to captain it. I've always been partial to her, so I agreed."

"Do you think you'll stay in Oregon for a while, Joe?"

"No, I don't think so. I have a practice in St. Joseph, so I believe I'll head back next spring."

"Joe, I wonder if you would have a little time to spare this evening."

"What's on your mind, David?"

119

After they talked for a while, Captain Wyatt went in search of Reverend Mueller. He and John had become good friends, and they had spent more than a few evenings together talking around the campfire.

"John, Captain Burnett is an old friend of mine. He's a man of many talents. Besides leading wagon trains, he's been a farmer, a surveyor, a lawyer, and a judge. In fact, he still practices law and holds court in the states. I asked him if he would be willing to take the time to marry a couple of my people and he agreed. Now you go tell Miss Nellie, and this evening we'll have a quiet ceremony."

John stared at Captain Wyatt. "David, I don't know what to say!" he exclaimed excitedly.

"Don't say anything, John. Go tell your bride!" John was overjoyed! He and Nellie had confided in Captain Wyatt when John had asked Nellie to be his wife a couple of weeks ago. They had thought they would have to wait until they arrived in Oregon City. He could hardly believe sweet Nellie would be his bride tonight! He went to the Hintons' camp and found her busy with some mending. She saw him approaching and stood up, wondering what the look on his face could mean. He took her hands in his.

"Nellie, will you be my wife?"

She looked at John closely. Was he suffering from the heat? "John, I answered you two weeks ago. Do you remember?" Her face showed concern.

A chuckle escaped from John's mouth. "How about this evening, Nellie? Will you marry me this evening?"

"John, what are you saying?"

"The captain of the wagon train that pulled in is also a judge. He can perform legal ceremonies. Nellie, we don't have to wait for Oregon City!"

"Oh, John!" They embraced happily.

"After the evening meal, Captain Burnett will come over and perform the ceremony. Is that enough time for you to get ready?" He suddenly looked anxious, realizing that women liked to have a lot of time to prepare for things like weddings.

Nellie laughed. "Yes, John, that's enough time."

That evening in the half light, Captain Burnett joined Nellie and John in matrimony. Nellie looked like a younger version of herself. She had bathed and washed her hair and Emily had fixed it in an elegant coiffure. Emily had also given Nellie a beautiful peach colored dress to wear. They were nearly the same size, and a few nips and tucks had made it fit perfectly. Nellie's face was slightly flushed and shining. John's mother, Emily, and Ernest Hinton were the only attendees to the ceremony. It was short, and when it was over and John had kissed his bride, a loud cheer went up. Startled, John and Nellie looked behind them. The whole wagon train—every man, woman, and child—had witnessed their vows from a respectable distance and was cheering for them. After that, they could not avoid the party.

Mrs. Mueller took Nellie's hand. "I couldn't ask for a better daughter-in-law!"

Emily gave Nellie a hug. "I'm so happy for you, Nellie."

"Thank you, Emily. Our wagon will be next to yours the rest of the way to Oregon, and I intend to help you like I promised your daddy."

"Nellie, I can take care of myself and Ernest. You have a new family now."

"Nothing has changed, Emily. I am still responsible for you, and I want to help you. You have always been like a daughter to me."

The two women embraced tearfully. Soon, everyone came up and hugged the newlyweds and gave them their best wishes. There was music and dancing well into the night.

"John, these people love you," Nellie said later, after they had danced many dances.

"They love us, Nellie. I feel so honored. I can't believe word got around the camp so quickly. Are you happy?" John asked, looking into her radiant face.

"More happy than I feel I have a right to be."

"Nellie, you have the right to anything you want. I intend for us to be happy for the rest of our lives."

Nellie's heart was full. She had thought she could never love again, and she had been so wrong! She realized that love has no boundaries, and she had enough love to give to everyone. In fact, it felt like the more love she gave, the more she got back.

Hand in hand, they went to the Muellers' camp, Nellie's new home.

Three Island Crossing

Chapter Seventeen

Aug. 20, 1852
Mile 1398

James Cardell stood in the dawn light at the back of his wagon with a worried crease between his eyes. He was uneasy. It was August 20, and he had come nearly fifteen hundred miles with his fruit trees. Today would be a difficult crossing. The Snake River was never easy, and with all the recent rain, the river was full and the banks were muddy and slippery. It was divided by two islands into three branches at this point. It was fordable, but the last branch was over a half mile wide with a strong current. Yesterday several of the men had made numerous attempts to swim their cattle over, but none were successful, and several beasts were swept down river and drowned.

So far, he and his wagons had made every other river crossing, although there had been a few close calls. The wagon train had made camp yesterday afternoon, but most people decided to wait until today to cross the river in hopes that the mud would dry up a bit. He and Slim, his hired hand, had just finished checking the fruit trees, and he was pleased that they were thriving. He had nursed these trees for months, making sure they were watered and pest free. His hope was to duplicate the efforts of Henderson Luelling, who had made the same trip with his trees six years earlier in 1846. He had heard that Luelling's orchards in Oregon were doing very well.

James was a dentist by trade, but his passion was gardening, and when he heard the story of Henderson Luelling, he had been consumed with ideas of starting his own orchards in Oregon. He had apple, cherry, pear, plum, and black walnut trees in two wagons that were full of dirt. Most of the other travelers had been by to see the odd sight—some of his trees were sticking out of the sides. Many people were skeptical, but he knew they would change their minds once his orchards were planted.

His parents had been against his going west. He remembered his father's disappointment. "You're a dentist. You have a thriving practice. Why would you want to leave it all to go out west where you don't know anyone?"

"I can't explain it, Dad. It's a dream I have, and I have to go."

"I forbid you to go. Your mother and I sacrificed to send you to school. Your practice is only a few years old, and look how well you're doing. Forget this foolishness. If you want to grow fruit trees, you can grow them in the garden."

"It's not the same. I don't want to be just a gardener, Dad. I want to be a farmer."

James shook his head slightly, remembering the arguments. His father had encouraged him to become a dentist, and James had dutifully gone to school in Maryland, but it wasn't what was in his heart. He loved the earth, the rich black smell of it, and the feel of it in his hands when he dug into it. He had a green thumb, and ever since he was old enough to walk, he had spent the greater part of three seasons in the family's large garden. Everything he planted thrived. He learned when to plant the carrots, potatoes, onions, and turnips and when to harvest them for the best flavor. His mother spent most of the summer and fall putting up his harvest for winter rations. Her pantry was full of jars of pickles, beets, and beans.

He had studied flowers and had the most beautiful flower garden in all of Illinois. People would come from all over town to marvel at the different blooms and the glorious colors. Nothing gave him more pleasure than watching his garden grow and sharing the bounty with friends and neighbors.

He thought of his mother now. She had been as upset as his father had, but she didn't get angry—just quiet. At first, she had tried to reason with him.

"James, you're such a good dentist. Think of all the people who depend on you."

"There are other dentists, Mom, good dentists who love their work. I can't do this. I have to follow my heart."

When she realized his mind was made up, she resigned herself to the idea, even though he knew she didn't like it. He remembered when she looked at him sadly and said, "James, all your people are here." He had given up trying to explain what he finally came to understand was impossible to convey. How could you explain in words the fire inside of you? How could you explain why you would leave a thriving practice in a town where you knew everyone to travel across an unknown country and start fresh in a place you had never been? No, they didn't understand. Only one person really did.

He looked across the way to where the Benson wagon was parked. Most of the family was bustling around getting ready for the day. He spotted Rebecca bending over the fire, and his heart swelled. He could talk to her and she always listened attentively. She knew more about his dream than anyone else did, and she was supportive of him. He watched her stir the pot of porridge, stopping briefly to wipe the face of a small sister.

He had met the Bensons shortly after the wagon train left Independence. Rebecca had come looking for the dentist because her father had a terrible toothache.

"How long has the tooth been bothering him?" James asked the comely young woman who had come to find him.

"For a few days now, but the pain was pretty bad last night," she had replied.

"Let me get a few things together and I'll take a look."

James peered into Thomas's mouth and probed around with a long handled instrument.

"Argh!" Thomas said when James hit a sensitive area.

"You have an infected tooth, Mr. Benson. It needs to come out. Is there any whiskey?"

Rebecca looked at James, astonished. *Does he need a shot of whiskey to pull my Dad's tooth?* She was wondering.

James saw her look and smiled. "It's not for me, Rebecca. It's for your dad—to numb the pain a bit."

Rebecca blushed prettily and said, "Of course."

After Thomas Benson downed a few shots of whiskey to numb the pain, James made short work of the matter, deftly pulling the tooth with his ivory handled tooth key. Thomas looked very much relieved once the troublesome tooth was gone.

"Let me pay you, James," he said blurrily.

"No, Mr. Benson, there's no need. I'm happy I was able to help," James said, smiling at Rebecca.

"There must be some way I can repay your kindness," Thomas asked.

James thought briefly. "I could use your help at some of the river crossings, if that's agreeable to you." Thomas Benson readily agreed, and the two men shook hands.

Rebecca invited James to dinner shortly after that, and their friendship blossomed. James became a regular at the Benson wagon almost every evening, but he never came empty handed. He had dried and preserved fruits and vegetables that he was more than willing to share.

He was also knowledgeable about medicinal plants, and he had made a habit of collecting herbs and plants he found along the way. Mary Benson often tagged along with him, and she was full of questions. On one occasion, he had been making a strengthening tea for Ruth Benson, Mary's pregnant mother.

"What are you putting in the tea?" Mary asked inquisitively.

"Well, I'm adding a little slippery elm to this chamomile tea. It should help your mother to feel better."

"What about dandelion root?" Mary asked, remembering how James had added it to other teas.

James looked at Mary appreciatively. "That's a good idea, Mary. I think you have a head for herbs and medicines. You'll make a good nurse."

"I don't want to be a nurse. I want to be a doctor," Mary pronounced emphatically.

"A doctor, is it? Well, if anyone can become a doctor, I believe you can."

Now Ruth sipped tea that Mary had made from nettles and red clover flowers. James had shown Mary how to brew the strengthening tea that Ruth needed since the birth of Mary's little sister Mattie. The baby had been born almost a week ago, and both mother and daughter were doing fine. Rebecca had taken on most of the work her mother had been doing, with the help of Mary, Sam, and Tommy.

James liked the Bensons. They all pitched in when they needed to. Even the little sisters sensed that no foolishness would be tolerated, and they were on their best behavior. Little Annie and four-year-old Deborah missed their mother, and Ruth made sure to give them attention when the baby was asleep.

Rebecca Benson looked up from stirring her porridge and smiled when she saw James. Then she saw his face and knew he was worried about the crossing. She had tried to reassure him the day before, but in truth, she was worried too. This crossing had a reputation for being the most difficult of the river crossings along the trail.

After Rebecca made sure everyone had their breakfast, she took a bowl of porridge to James. He was finishing watering the oxen, and when he saw her walking towards him, his preoccupied look turned into a smile.

"I brought you some porridge, James."

"Thank you, Rebecca, it looks very nourishing. Fact is I'm not hungry at all."

"Eat it anyway, James."

James looked at her determined face and smiled. "Yes, Ma'am." He leaned against the wagon wheel and spooned porridge into his mouth. Rebecca was right. He would need all of his strength and wits to get his wagons and teams across the river today.

"Pa said we'll get your wagons across first, and then we'll take ours. He said you could hire Indian pilots if you want more help."

"No, I don't want to risk my trees to Indians. I think between Slim, me, and your pa we'll be okay."

The Indian pilots charged the travelers to help them across the river. James had heard about these pilots, and he figured they were good with stock, but he was pretty certain they had never attempted to get wagonloads of fruit trees across.

Rebecca's brow furrowed and she sighed. "James, don't take any chances. Your life is more important than those trees."

"I've brought my trees this far, and I'm going to get them all the way to Oregon. This crossing isn't much different than the Green River or the Platte." Even as he heard himself saying the words, he knew it wasn't the truth. He was trying to convince himself as much as he was Rebecca.

"Pa said to let him know whenever you're ready." She looked at James entreatingly. "Promise me you'll be safe."

He saw the concern in her eyes. "Don't worry, Rebecca. I'll be fine, and so will my trees." He hugged her warmly and then joined Slim to make preparations for the crossing.

The Loss

Chapter Eighteen

————※《◎》※————

A little more than an hour later, James' wagons were lined up and ready to go. Thomas Benson and Sam were there to help him, as well as his hand Slim, Michael and Conor Flannigan, and a few other men. They had just watched a cart and two mules get turned upside down while fording the last part of the river. Then the mules got entangled in the harness, and they would have drowned except for the desperate struggle of their owner and some of the other men. Some Indians were watching also. They were the pilots who could be hired for a fee to help with the crossings. James clenched his jaw and muttered under his breath. He knew this wouldn't be easy, but he was beginning to think it might be impossible.

James and Slim led the first team down the steep embankment. It wasn't as slippery as it had been the day before, but they still had a hard time. Thomas, Sam, Michael, and two other men pulled against ropes tied to the back of the wagon to keep it from running over the team.

"Easy. Don't pull on the ropes. Keep a steady pressure," Michael cautioned from his position. Finally, the team and wagon were at the river's edge.

"Sam and Conor, you all go up and help Slim hold the team while we bring the second one down," James called.

Again, with Thomas and the two other men straining against ropes to ease the wagon slowly downhill, the second team was soon at the river's edge. Now came the tricky part.

"Let's tie these ropes around the necks of the oxen and lead them into the river," James said. He and Michael waded in up to their chests and the current pushed against them. They got a good lead, and then they pulled on the ropes while Thomas, Slim, and the other men prodded the oxen from behind. The oxen bellowed loudly and fought against the ropes, but eventually they started across. Two of the men helped to stabilize the back of the wagon while it floated precariously against the current. They made it to the first island and took a short rest before starting for the second.

Rebecca and Brenna watched nervously from the top of the embankment.

"I wish James had hired the Indian pilots," Rebecca said nervously.

Brenna squeezed her arm. "I'm sure they'll make it across."

Other men and women were watching the wagon and the men trying to keep it stable while fighting the push of the current against them. They had made it to the second island and were starting across the widest part of the river. A half mile of rushing water lay between them and the far shore. Rebecca realized she had been holding her breath and she let it out in a rush. This was the same spot where the mules and the cart had tipped over.

"It looks like they're having a hard time balancing the wagon!" Rebecca exclaimed.

The wagon began to pitch in the turbulent water. The men trying to hold it steady were frantically struggling against the current, but the force was too strong and the wagon rolled onto its side. Thomas shouted to Sam, "Get out of the way! What are you trying to do?" when Sam attempted to get under the wagon to push it up.

The oxen bellowed loudly as the tipped wagon strained the harnesses and pulled the oxen under water. One of the men cut the harnesses to keep the oxen from drowning. Rebecca could hear wood splintering from her position on the bank and she screamed when she saw James yell something to Thomas and begin to swim to the wagon, but it was free of the harnesses and it was swept away swiftly. Some of the trees floated out of the wagon and were carried away or disappeared in the river.

To Rebecca's horror, James seemed to be carried away also, but he had knotted a rope around his waist, and it was still tied to one ox that was yoked to the other. When he got to the end of it, he was pulled back by Thomas and the other men. The oxen were trying to turn around to swim back to the bank they had left, and it took the efforts of all the men to get them across. Once on the other side, they rested for a short time.

"Oh, Brenna! This is terrible," Rebecca said, and Brenna put her arms around her friend.

Rebecca could see the men conferring, and then they forded back for the second wagon. She saw the disappointment and exhaustion on James's face. He kept looking down river as if he expected to see the wagon washed up on shore. Then he looked up the hill at Rebecca and his face was grim. Rebecca realized she must look terrified, and she struggled to keep her expression calm.

She watched the men discuss the best approach to getting the second team and wagon across. Clearly, a better plan was needed.

"Let's use Hansson's canoes to float the wagon. It's worked at other crossings," Michael suggested.

James thought for a moment. "Alright. I'm not sure it will work since my wagons are heavier than most and they can't be unloaded, but I can't think of what else to do."

Ben Hansson floated the canoes over to the men. He and his father had successfully gotten their wagon across the river earlier. They unhitched the team and six of them got the wagon onto the canoes and started across the river, each man in position to keep the canoes and wagon stable.

"I think they're going to make it over," Brenna said.

Everything seemed to be going well until the last stretch. The canoes were ungainly in the strong current, and one of them began to dip from side to side. The wagon began to pitch, and try as they might, the men couldn't keep it upright. This wagon, too, overturned, spilling its contents into the Snake. James frantically grabbed a wheel and tried in vain to hold the wagon, but the current quickly snatched it from him and the wagon rolled under water.

"James!" Rebecca screamed.

Thomas had grabbed a hold of James when James grabbed the wheel, and he pulled the distraught man to his feet. All the men were shouting, and the people watching from shore were exclaiming their dismay. A few men started wading into the river to give their aid if it was needed. There was nothing left for James and the others to do but return to shore. They were all exhausted and discouraged, but none more so than James. He collapsed onto his knees on the shore of the Snake River and put his head in his hands. Rebecca half ran and half slid down the embankment and threw her arms around him.

"James! James! You're safe! Thank God, you're safe! You almost drowned out there!"

"I wish I had!" he said breathlessly. He looked up at her, his face contorted with grief and dripping muddy water. "It's all gone! Every last tree is gone, Rebecca. All my hopes and dreams; everything I've worked for—gone. There's nothing left."

Rebecca swallowed hard. How could she console this man she had grown to love and admire? Her heart wrenched when she looked at him, and she put her hands on both sides of his face. "James, no! All you've lost is the trees! You still have everything else. You still have all your skills and talents. You can grow anything, James. You can get seeds and start a nursery. Mr. Luelling will give you cuttings from his trees. And you still have me, James. I'm going to be by your side every step of the way because I believe in you. Don't for one minute think there's nothing left."

James looked into Rebecca's eyes and saw the conviction of her words. Drawing on her strength, he took a ragged breath and stood up. They put their arms around each other and struggled up the muddy embankment. Fellow travelers helped them up the hill and gave James encouragement and offers of help for the remainder of the trip. Many told James that they were dubious about the trees at first, but after getting to know James, they had no doubts that he would do exactly as he said he would. They had great admiration for him and his ideals, and they hoped he would pursue his dreams in Oregon. James humbly thanked everyone. Thomas Benson and Michael Flannigan came up.

"We're going to hire the Indian pilots to ferry our wagons over, James. They'll take the stock over, too. The river is too treacherous, and they seem to know the best places to cross," Thomas said. "We'll get them to take your team across, too."

James nodded numbly.

The rest of the day was a blur of activity as one wagon after another crossed the Snake. The Indian pilots proved to be skillful and knowledgeable. Their experience after years of ferrying wagons to the other side was invaluable, but still some wagons and livestock were lost, and a young boy was swept away in the Snake. At the end of the long day, it was decided that James would travel with the Bensons the remainder of the way to Oregon. Slim was a good hand, and Captain Wyatt knew him well. He needed Slim since one of the scouts had died of cholera.

James and Rebecca were inseparable after the ordeal, and knowing looks would pass between them. James never spoke again of his lost fruit trees, but in the evenings, he and Rebecca made many plans about their future in Oregon, and it wasn't too long before his easy smile and good humor returned. The future was bright again, and when he looked into Rebecca's eyes, he saw his hope reflected back and he knew that together they could weather any storm.

Cholera!

Chapter Nineteen

August 23, 1852

"Ma! Da! Mr. Hinton is dead!" Brenna exclaimed breathlessly as she ran into camp. Michael and Kate Flannigan looked up in alarm from their evening tea.

"What? Brenna, are you sure?" Michael asked, getting up from his seat by the fire.

"I was at the Muellers', and Nellie had been with Miss Emily. Mr. Hinton had been sick all day. He got so dehydrated, and he couldn't keep anything down. And he had the most terrible thirst. Then a short while ago he collapsed, and no one could revive him. He's dead, Da! Reverend Mueller says it's cholera!"

"Who's with Miss Emily?" Kate asked.

"Nellie and Reverend Mueller are there, but Billy Walters just came and asked Reverend Mueller to come to their wagon because his wee sister is sick. Mrs. Baker and her youngest are very sick.

James Cardell is with them. Reverend Mueller thinks they have cholera, too!"

Michael's face was grim. They had seen countless graves along the trail, and although their company had lost a few people to the dread disease, he had hoped they would escape the worst of it.

"We'll go and see what we can do," Michael said. "Brenna, stay with Conor."

When Michael and Kate got to the Hinton's wagon, Reverend Mueller had already left to visit the Walters. Nellie was with Emily.

"Miss Emily, we just heard about Mr. Hinton. We are so sorry!" Kate said as she went up to Emily, who looked to be in shock. Buster sensed something was amiss, and he whined softly and circled Emily. Kate put her arms around the young woman's shoulders and led her to the fire.

"Where is Ernest's body?" Michael asked Nellie quietly.

"He's in the tent," Nellie answered. "A few of the men are digging graves." She indicated the direction the men had gone with their shovels. "Three so far; Mrs. Baker and one of her children will be buried with Ernest. I don't know what John will find at the Walters' wagon."

"I was hoping we would not have to deal with this," Michael said solemnly.

"Do you think it's contagious?" Nellie asked nervously.

"No, it seems to affect people at random. In Ireland, many people died from it, but not necessarily everyone from a family."

Nellie looked relieved. Her marriage was young and she couldn't bear the thought of losing John.

The news spread through the camp quickly. Soon other men and women came to the Hintons' wagon to offer condolences and help. All the children were ordered to stay close to their wagons. The captain came by and said they would bury the three deceased in an hour, and Reverend Mueller would provide a short service.

Everything was over and done with quickly. Three new graves covered with rocks barely disturbed the silent prairie. In the light cast from a few lanterns, Reverend Mueller gave eulogies and offered a prayer. Nellie had a supporting arm around Emily Hinton, who stared unseeingly at the gravesites. Mr. Baker and a grown daughter comforted two younger children who wept piteously.

After the short service, the captain spoke to the people congregated around the gravesites.

"I'm terribly sorry for your loss, Mrs. Hinton and Mr. Baker. I had been feeling hopeful that we would avoid more of this sickness." He paused. "We've all noticed the number of graves along the trail in the last month, and we all need to be extra careful in the days ahead. We will be leaving early in the morning. Miss Emily, Ben Hansson will drive your teams. I trust you all have inspected your wagons so that there will be no breakdowns."

The captain paused and looked at the anxious faces surrounding him. "Tonight say a prayer for young Hope Walters. It appears she has cholera. We'll leave at first light."

Everyone slowly made their way back to their wagons. Brenna and Ben stood a little ways off from the others.

"Will your father be all right driving your teams alone tomorrow?" Brenna asked.

"Oh, yeah," Ben assured her. "I just hope he doesn't have to do too many repairs to other wagons. Hopefully folks have fixed everything that needed attention."

"What about Miss Emily's wagon?"

"It was brand new when they left Independence. I've looked it over and it's in good shape."

"I feel so badly for her. She's all alone now."

"If we were closer to Independence, I think she would go back to her family, but she's going to have to go on with us to Oregon now."

"What will she do once we get to Oregon?"

"She can go home next spring, or maybe she'll find a new husband."

Brenna's brow furrowed as she thought about the prospects of a young widow alone in a frontier town. She didn't know how close the Hintons had been, but she couldn't imagine finding a new husband so soon. And yet, what other options did she have? Brenna drew her shawl closer against the night chill and shivered. Ben noticed and put his arm around her shoulders.

"Are you okay?"

"Yes, just chilly."

"Don't you go getting sick, now," he said huskily and tightened his hold as they walked to the Flannigan's wagon.

Two days later the wagons made camp next to a beautiful creek and close to some hot springs. Everyone was exhausted from pushing hard. Six more people had died from cholera since they had buried Ernest Hinton, the Bakers, and little Hope Walters. The captain had made the decision that the wagon train wouldn't stop when someone got sick. Usually if someone got cholera, he or she was dead within twenty-four hours. He appointed a watcher who would stay back with the sick traveler. After the person died, the watcher would dig the grave, bury the body, and then catch up with the wagon train.

Dinner had been quiet in the Benson camp.

"Thomas, the little ones are asleep. We'll be back shortly." Ruth gave her husband a peck on the cheek and she, Rebecca, and Mary headed in the direction of the hot springs. Some of the other women had the same idea and took their laundry. The day had been warm, but it was cooling off. The men knew to stay clear since some of the women had indicated that it would be a good place to get a bath—the first hot bath they'd had since leaving Independence. The hot springs looked inviting as the women dumped their belongings on the rocks.

"Mary, take everything off. Here's some soap. Scrub yourself good," Ruth Benson said as she stripped her grimy threadbare clothes from her body. She stepped gingerly into the steaming water. It was so hot it took a few minutes before she could sit down. Then when the warmth enveloped her, she sighed deeply and sank in up to her neck. Other women and girls were doing the same. No one spoke for a few minutes, and the evening prairie closed around them. Ruth felt the tension leaving her. All the stress of the last few days melted from her body as the water gently massaged her aching muscles.

"Mary, let me wash your hair," Rebecca's voice seemed to float up quietly from the watery depths. Ruth's eyes were heavy. She hadn't realized how tired she was. Tomorrow morning she would bring Annie and Deborah here and give the youngsters a bath.

But tonight she felt totally relaxed, and she didn't want to get out of the pool. What a luxury! What bliss! She was floating in a warm cocoon, weightless and unencumbered. Soft voices drifted around her, but she didn't want to join in any conversations. She felt gentle hands on her head, taking apart the braids.

"Your turn, Ma." Rebecca worked the soap into a lather in Ruth's hair.

"That feels so good. Thank you, Rebecca." The head massage was bringing Ruth back to the present. "I almost forgot how wonderful it is to be clean. I feel so much lighter!"

"Yes, I'm sure we've scrubbed off pounds of prairie dust," Rebecca replied.

"What's Mary doing?"

"She's washing the clothes."

"She's really growing up, isn't she?"

"She is. But I'd better help her or we may be missing some things in the morning." The two women chuckled. Mary was helpful, but not always thorough.

A few minutes later, Ruth sighed deeply and sat up. It was getting late. She would help the girls finish the laundry and then it would be time to get back to camp.

"It's done, Ma," Rebecca said.

"Thank you, girls. I lost track of the time."

"It's okay, Ma," Mary piped. "You looked so relaxed. We didn't want to make you get out."

The others were leaving the water and putting on dry clothes. They gathered their laundry and slowly walked back to camp, refreshed and clean. Thomas, the boys, and James were talking quietly around the fire. They looked up when the women and Mary walked into the camp.

"Wow! Mary looks three shades lighter," Sam said jokingly.

"That was heavenly," Ruth said.

"You look great," James said, staring appreciatively at Rebecca's rosy cheeks and shining chestnut hair.

"It was wonderful, James. I feel so refreshed. Will you walk with me?" The two linked arms and walked out of the firelight. Thomas and Ruth shared a knowing look.

"Stay close by now," Tommy called after them teasingly. "And no kissing!"

Sam guffawed loudly, and Tommy collapsed into giggles.

"You two can get yourselves a bath," Thomas said sternly, but he could barely contain the smile threatening to give him away. Mary went into the wagon to put things away and check on Mattie. Then it was just Ruth and Thomas left by the fire. Thomas drew his wife close and put his nose in her hair.

"You smell nice."

"I feel so relaxed."

"Soon we'll be in Oregon City and you can have a bath every night if you want."

Ruth sighed into Thomas's arms. "This is the first real bath I've had in months. I hope we camp by more hot springs."

"I don't want you getting spoiled now!" Thomas said gently, kissing the top of Ruth's damp head. She turned her face to look at Thomas.

"We've done the right thing, haven't we Thomas?" Her eyes searched his in the light from the fire. "We've done the right thing to leave Iowa."

Thomas cocked his head to the side. "What's troubling you, Ruth?"

"It's just that we have the largest family in the wagon train, and all of us are still here. I almost feel guilty when I look at the women who have lost children or husbands. We haven't lost anyone to cholera, Thomas. I feel like we're very lucky, or maybe we're just foolish to think that we will all make it to Oregon City." Ruth's voice was edgy.

"Shh," he put his finger on her lips. "Don't get yourself all riled up now. You've had a nice bath, and you're warm and clean." His arms tightened around her. "Don't you worry, Ruth. We're all going to walk into Oregon City together." His voice was quiet and confident. "I've taken care of this family just fine up till now, and nothing is going to change that."

Ruth snuggled into Thomas. She felt safe in his arms. She felt like he was telling her the truth. If anyone could protect this family, he would.

"Thank you, Thomas," she said softly.

Later when Rebecca and James walked back into camp, Ruth and Thomas were still nestled together, companionably watching the dying embers of the fire. Thomas stretched his arms and stood up.

"I think it's time to kick those boys out of the bath. Come on, James. Our turn." The two men walked into the night.

Rebecca sat next to her mother. After a few moments she sighed, and then she confided, "James and I are in love. He's going to ask me to marry him."

"It's taking him long enough," Ruth replied.

"Ma!"

Ruth laughed. "I'm kidding, Rebecca." She turned to her daughter and enfolded her in her arms. "I'm so happy for you. Your father and I both think James is the perfect match for you. We've known for a long time that you two would be married."

"Oh, Ma, James makes me happy. I love him so much!"

"He's a good man, Rebecca. When will he talk to your father?"

"Soon, Ma."

Ruth felt a deep sense of satisfaction as she leaned back against the wagon. She felt clean for the first time in months. Rebecca, her oldest, would soon be a wife and then a mother of her own babies. Her children were healthy. Soon they would be in Oregon, and a new chapter would begin. Life was good. She closed her eyes and smiled. The smile was still on her face when Thomas woke her from her sleep and helped her to their bed.

Bad News

Chapter Twenty

Mile 1427

Emily Hinton stared disbelievingly at Abel Brown from the chair where she was sitting. Her heart raced in her chest. What he was telling her couldn't be true!

"Emily, do you understand what I'm trying to tell you? Your father is dead. Ernest got word of it at Fort Kearney, but he wanted to wait to give you the news."

Emily shook her head as if to clear it. This was impossible. Ernest had just been buried, and now Abel was telling her that her father was dead? Her eyes welled with tears.

"You're lying!" she exclaimed, her voice breaking. Buster whined when he heard his mistress cry out. He stood on his hind legs and put his front paws on Emily's knees.

Abel reached into the breast pocket of his coat. "Here's the letter from your…mother, Emily."

Abel held out an envelope. Emily recognized her mother's precise script. She took the envelope with trembling hands.

"Emily, I'm sorry to burden you with this when you've only just buried your husband, but time is short, and decisions have to be made." His eyes looked at her intently, but she had barely heard what he had said.

"I'll leave you alone to read it, and then we need to talk." Abel turned and left the tent.

Emily stared at the envelope for a long moment. It was addressed to Mrs. Ernest Hinton, Independence, Missouri, April 13, 1852. Someone else had added, "Overland Trail to Oregon, Captain Wyatt's train," underneath the address. Her mind reeled as she realized she and Ernest had probably just missed the letter in Missouri. She hurriedly removed the two thin sheets of writing paper. Her mother's words blurred on the page, and she had to blink continuously to clear her eyes.

Dear Emily,

    I am sorry to have to bring you the news of your father's death. It was sudden and unexpected. He took a fall from his horse and hit his head. He never regained his senses, and he lingered for two days, delirious, until he slipped away in the early morning of March 22nd.

    Your father's lawyer, Mr. Pound, will read the will soon…I know everything has been left to me. Your father was happy with your marriage and confident that Ernest will take good care of you. I and your brothers will continue to run the farm until your brothers are of an age to take over. At that time, I will deed the farm to them and live on here until I join your father.

    There is another matter. There is no easy way to tell you this, so I shall just write it out and hope that you receive this letter somehow.

    I am not your mother. Your real mother died after your birth. She was one of your father's slaves in Virginia. She was a mulatto, and since you had such fair skin, your father decided to pass you off as white. He thought your life would be easier if you could avoid the scandal and live as a white woman.

He and I married a year later, and he made me promise to keep this secret and raise you as my own daughter. Shortly after our marriage, we moved to Ohio. All these years I have kept my promise, but now there is no point. I thought you should know the truth.

You and I were never close, Emily. I resented the way your father doted on you. Perhaps he was trying to make up for the fact that I could not be a real mother to you. I feel certain that I will never see you again. Now that your father is dead, there is no tie binding us together. You may consider this my last correspondence. Godspeed and good fortune to you and your husband in the west.

Sincerely,

Mrs. Henry Lawton

Emily could barely read the last paragraph. Her tears spilled from her eyes and wet the paper in her trembling hands. Her husband's death had numbed her, and this news was heartbreaking. Visions of her father filled her. He had been the most important person in her life, and she could not bear the thought of never seeing him again. On top of that, the woman she had always thought of as her mother was not related to her! The letter slipped to the ground, and she bent her head to her hands and sobbed. Buster licked her hands and whined.

The tent flap parted and Nellie rushed in.

"Emily, my dear, I'm so sorry! Mr. Brown just told me." She held Emily in her arms and rocked her like a little child. Emily cried piteously for a long while, and Nellie patted her back and made soft soothing sounds.

"My daddy's dead, Nellie."

"I know, Emily. I'm so sorry."

"He's gone, Nellie, gone forever!"

"Shhh, Emily. You just cry, honey. You've had quite a shock. Your daddy loved you more than anyone in this world. He told me once when you were real sick that if anything ever happened to you, he would die himself."

"I don't know what to do, Nellie." Emily's shoulders shook with her sobs.

"Well, you'll just have to go back to Ohio. I'm sure your mother will need your help. There's nothing and no one for you in Oregon."

Emily suddenly stopped crying. She sat up and looked at Nellie with red-rimmed eyes. Her cheeks were streaked with tears, and her hair, usually perfectly groomed, had come undone. It cascaded over her shoulders in frenzied tumultuous dark locks.

"You never knew?" she asked, hiccupping.

Nellie looked at her alarmed, searching her eyes. "Knew what, honey?" Emily bent down and retrieved the fallen letter. She handed it to Nellie. Nellie could barely tear her eyes from Emily's face. What she saw there frightened her. Emily sat rigidly in the chair as Nellie read the letter quickly and then again more slowly. Her knuckles were white where she gripped the thin paper.

"My God!" she whispered softly. "I never understood why your mother was so cold towards you. This explains it! I guess you won't be going back to Ohio."

Emily regarded Nellie soberly for a few moments. Suddenly she threw her head back and laughed. Her laughter was mirthless, and soon it escalated into a high-pitched wail. Nellie dropped the letter, grasped Emily's shoulders, and shook her.

"Stop it, Emily!"

Emily stopped laughing as suddenly as she had started, but when she spoke, her voice trembled. Her eyes were wide in her face. "Nellie, I'm a Negro. I'm a widow. I have no family to turn to. What will become of me?"

Nellie squeezed her eyes tightly shut. She had to think. If news of this got out, Emily would be ruined. She would no longer be accepted in white society. What would she do? Where would she go?

"Listen, Emily. No one is to know about this, do you hear me? This is between you and me." Nellie watched Emily's eyes—beautiful deep brown eyes. Her dark brows furrowed over them. Her nearly black hair contrasted against her creamy skin. Her full lips quivered slightly under a nose that was straight and slightly broad. Now that she knew Emily's mother was a Negress, she looked at her features intently. Nellie had always thought Emily was beautiful. Her looks were slightly exotic, and she looked nothing like her father. She looked like an aristocratic southern belle.

The tent flap parted and Abel Brown entered. He was tall and slender in the black pants and coat he always wore. It gave him a debonair look uncommon on the trail. He regarded the two women calmly.

"I believe I have a solution to your problem, Emily," Abel said confidently.

Emily and Nellie looked at him. Emily's expression was wary. Nellie looked expectant and hopeful.

"You and I will be married," he said matter-of-factly. He crossed his arms over his chest and smiled thinly. Nellie gasped, and Emily's mouth twitched. She looked precariously close to hysterical laughter again.

"That's hardly a solution to her problem, Mr. Brown," Nellie stated crossly. "She's just lost her husband and her father."

"Nevertheless, it's the only possible solution, and it will be beneficial to both of us. Emily needs a husband. She has no assets and no prospects. I need respectability. I've made a name for myself, but unfortunately, it's not a good one. As my wife, Emily will bring me credibility. She and I will enjoy social circles that wouldn't otherwise be open to me."

Emily looked at Abel's smug smile. His roguish good looks did not hide the feverish ambition that always played underneath the surface of his seemingly calm demeanor. Her palm itched to slap the smile from his face.

"I have plenty of money, Mr. Brown, and no thank you, I won't be needing a husband."

Abel's caramel colored eyes looked at her appraisingly. "You have no money, Emily. Everything your husband once owned is now mine. I have receipts and I.O.U.s to vouch for this. Ernest was very indebted to me. I'm afraid your husband was not a very good card player."

Emily's face paled. She remembered all the nights Ernest had spent with Abel Brown and some of the other men. Her husband had told her they were discussing plans for Oregon.

"Ernest wouldn't squander our savings!" she cried.

Abel laughed scornfully. "Oh, he always hoped to win it all back—and more. Every time we played he was confident, but he just got deeper in my debt."

Nellie put her arm around Emily's shoulders and looked at her earnestly. "Don't you worry, Emily. You're coming with me and Reverend Mueller. We'll sort everything out once we get to Oregon."

"I'm afraid that won't do, Mrs. Mueller," Abel interjected. "Like I said, my solution is the only workable one, and that's the way it's going to be."

Nellie started to protest, but Abel held up a hand and said conspiratorially, "The three of us are the only ones who know Emily's secret. We know what her fate will be if that ever gets out." His voice lowered and he looked at Emily. "Now I want the best for you, Emily, but who knows what will happen if I'm not around to protect you?"

Nellie noted the barely veiled threat in Abel's voice.

Emily gasped. "You read the letter! That's my private property!"

"I need to know everything about you, Emily. After all, you are going to be my wife. You will have no secrets from me." He bent over and picked up the letter from where it lay on the ground.

"That letter belongs to me, Mr. Brown." Emily put out her hand.

Abel ignored her. He folded the letter and put it in his breast pocket.

"This letter will be in my safe keeping. I'll take care of you, Emily—better than Ernest ever could." Then he smiled, tipped his hat, and exited the tent. The two women stared after him. Nellie could barely make herself look at Emily, afraid of what she would see. When she finally did, instead of defeat, she saw determination on Emily's face.

"Emily, I know that look. What are you thinking?"

Emily took a deep breath. She straightened her back and folded her hands calmly in her lap. She gazed at Nellie for an instant. "Go back to your wagon, Nellie, I'll be fine."

"Emily! No!"

Emily's generous mouth tightened. She reached up, gathered her riotous hair, and began to pin it up methodically. When she looked at Nellie again, her eyes were cold.

"I'm afraid Mr. Brown is right. There really is no other solution to my problem."

On the evening of September 1 at Fort Boise, almost four hundred miles to the end of their journey, Reverend Mueller conducted a short ceremony uniting Emily Hinton and Abel Brown in matrimony. Only a few of the travelers knew about the wedding and gathered around. Mary Benson had picked wildflowers and strewn them about.

"Here's a bouquet for you, Miss Emily," Mary said, handing her the yellow and gold blooms. Emily looked confused and preoccupied. Mary picked up Buster who had been underfoot, and he licked her face.

Emily frowned at the flowers in her hands. "Thank you, Mary; that was very thoughtful."

No one felt that Emily was remiss in not mourning her dead husband the proper length of time. Everyone understood that these were special conditions, and a single woman of Emily's caliber would not make it on the trail alone. No one except Nellie was aware of the drama that had unfolded a few nights before—not even Reverend Mueller. No one knew about the letter and its contents.

Nellie cried during the exchange of vows. Her husband, Reverend Mueller, thought it was tears of happiness for Emily. Abel held his right hand over his heart—a seemingly sincere gesture. He felt the letter in the breast pocket under his hand, and he smiled confidently. He always got what he wanted.

He looked down at his new bride. Her eyes were lowered and her dark lashes shadowed her cheeks, hiding her expression. She wasn't happy, he knew, but that didn't matter. He was a wealthy man, and now he would have a well-bred wife. It didn't matter to him that she was a Negress, as long as no one discovered her secret. He was already plotting their future in Oregon and California. Yes, things were looking up.

Dinner Invitation

Chapter Twenty-One

La Grande Ronde
Sept. 15, 1852
Mile 1530

"Here's some beef for our dinner, Kate," Michael Flannigan said as he walked into camp.

"Wonderful!" Kate exclaimed. Fresh beef was a luxury on the trail, where salt pork was the usual fare.

"The Cayuse were willing to trade buffalo meat for the fish hooks I fashioned a while back. Oh, and I've invited Emily and Abel Brown for dinner. I happened to run into them on my way here with the beef. I hope that's alright." It was unusual to have company for dinner, but since there was plenty of fresh beef, Kate readily agreed.

"Besides, I want to get to know them better," he said.

They were camped in La Grande Ronde, a beautiful valley. To the west were the Blue Mountains. They would have been more beautiful if the overlanders didn't have to cross them. As it was, they simply looked foreboding. Although the days were still warm, the nights were cold and everyone was hoping to cross the mountains before it snowed.

Kate was touched to see that Emily had taken pains to look her best for dinner. Her lustrous dark hair was beautifully coiffed, and her wine-colored dress was tailored perfectly to her slender curves. Abel was darkly handsome in his usual black attire. They made a striking couple, and Abel seemed aware of this fact. Buster tagged along, close to his mistress.

"Thank you so much for the invitation," Emily said, clasping Kate's hands. "It's so kind of you to invite us to dinner. I understand your husband traded with the Cayuse today."

"Yes! It's been awhile since we've had beef. I'm so glad you could come and share it with us. Plus, we haven't had a chance to properly acknowledge your marriage," Kate said to them both, carefully avoiding the subject of Emily's husband's death.

Brenna couldn't help comparing herself to Emily. They were a little over a year apart in age, but they were centuries apart in experience. She looked at Emily's perfect hair and dress and at her own simple homespun frock covered with the apron she wore most of the day. She quickly removed her apron and tried to smooth her curly hair. Emily turned to Brenna.

"It's so good to see you again, Brenna." Their eyes met, and Brenna could see that Emily was sincere. *She's changed*, Brenna thought.

"Thank you, Miss Emily. It's good to see you too."

They all arranged themselves on the makeshift benches while Brenna dished up the beef and bean stew. Seasoned with salt and the wild sage Kate had collected and dried, it was very tasty. There were the usual biscuits to go with it. Abel took a silver flask out of his pocket and offered it to Michael.

"Real Kentucky bourbon."

"No thanks, Mr. Brown, but you go ahead." Abel tilted the flask and took a long swallow.

"I do love beef," Michael said, diving into his stew. "I'm going to raise some cattle on our farm in Oregon."

"My daddy raised cattle," Emily volunteered. Then her eyes clouded over. "You may not know that he passed away six months ago."

"I'm so sorry, Emily," Kate said. "Was it sudden?"

"Yes, he took a fall from a horse and hit his head. I miss him more knowing that I will never see him again."

"Emily, we should talk about something else," Abel admonished. "You don't need to get yourself all upset now, do you?"

"Of course. I'm sorry." Emily's flawless complexion colored.

Kate looked embarrassed. "It's alright, Emily."

"What sort of trade will you have in Oregon, Mr. Brown?" Michael queried, changing the subject.

"I intend to deal in land, Mr. Flannigan. Emily and I will apply for our three hundred twenty acres, and then I will buy up all the land that so many of these small-time farmers don't have the means or the skills to keep." Abel had a self-satisfied look on his face. He did not disguise the contempt in his voice. The others were quiet.

Emily noticed the silence. "Mr. Brown, I don't believe..."

"Emily, don't pretend to know what I'm talking about," Abel interrupted. Then in a conciliatory tone to Michael he said, "I swear, the prettier they are the less they have up here," and he pointed to his head. Michael dared not look at Kate, but he did catch Brenna's dark look.

Abel smirked and took another drink from the flask. "Just because land is free doesn't mean that any man who gets it will know what to do with it! No, I believe that most of these so-called farmers will bite the dust—so to speak!" And he laughed at his small joke.

"Is it true, Da?" Conor asked. Michael put up his hand in Conor's direction. He leaned forward with his forearms on his knees and looked intently at Abel.

"What makes you think this will be an easy thing for you to do, Mr. Brown?" He asked coolly.

"Because I know human nature," Abel replied confidently. "I know how greedy men are. They see the word FREE and they can't wait to get it, whatever it is! How many of the people on this wagon train do you think are going to claim their one hundred sixty acres?"

"Most of them, I would say," Michael replied.

"And in a year's time, how many do you think will still have it or want it? Be honest now, Mr. Flannigan."

"I really couldn't say, Mr. Brown."

Emily was mortified by Abel's lack of manners in the dinner conversation and by the fact that he hadn't touched his stew. Instead, he kept his flask in his hand and took frequent swallows.

"I'll wager that fifty percent of these overlanders won't be able to make it. They don't know what they're doing! They don't know the first thing about farming. Look at Mr. Cardell. He's a dentist for God's sake. He should have stayed in Illinois pulling teeth. He'd be better off. And how about Clem Morris?" Abel guffawed loudly. "Do you seriously think he'll be able to manage or afford a farm—even when it's free?!" He chortled with glee.

"You might be surprised, Mr. Brown. Having the will to do something is half the battle."

"Have you ever heard the expression 'don't look a gift horse in the mouth'? It's an American expression, so I imagine you've never heard it before, being foreigners and all," Abel said smugly.

"Yes, I've heard the expression. How does that have anything to do with farming in Oregon?" Michael asked testily.

Abel spread his arms wide and said condescendingly, "Well, that's what all these folks are doing. The free land is the gift horse, don't you see? If they looked closely, they would see that this gift comes with more responsibility than they are prepared for. That's where I step in, Mr. Flannigan. For a fair price, I will take the land off their hands when they have realized their folly. It's a win-win proposition as I see it."

"And of course you wouldn't be of a mind to encourage them to sell, would you now, Mr. Brown?"

Abel's stew slipped off his lap and spilled in the dirt. Buster, who had been asleep, quickly awakened and wasted no time in wolfing it down.

"Oh, my!" Emily exclaimed.

Kate could see the direction the conversation was going and the tightening of Michael's jaw. She stood up quickly.

"It's alright. Don't fret about it, Emily. This is a fascinating conversation, but women's work is never done! Would you gentlemen excuse me while I do up these dishes? Brenna, Emily, I could use your help."

"That's right, ladies. I'm sure you're bored to death with this conversation. Next time we'll talk about sewing and doilies," Abel said, and he laughed aloud and clapped Michael on the back.

"Da, I'm going to help Mr. Meeker," Conor said, and left the campsite.

"Ezra Meeker—there's another one. I'll be buying his land from him next year!"

Kate took the hot water from the fire and stepped to the other side of the wagon. Brenna and Emily followed with the dirty dishes.

"Brenna, you wash. Emily, you dry. I'll put away." They busied themselves for a few minutes before Kate said, "Well. It sounds like Mr. Brown has your future planned out for you Emily."

Emily looked at Kate with large luminous eyes. "This is the first I've heard of these plans, Mrs. Flannigan. Abel doesn't share much with me."

"But it's your future too," Brenna said.

"If the truth be told, I haven't given much thought to my future."

"It's been hard to think of anything except surviving each day out here in the prairie, but when we get to Oregon City and civilization, things will change," Kate said.

Brenna cleared her throat. "Miss Emily, I understand you have some books with you. Would you consider lending one to me? I miss reading, and it would be nice to pass the time with a book."

"Of course!" Emily couldn't hide her pleasure. "Come by tomorrow and you can go through my box. I had to leave most of them in Independence, but I kept my favorites. And please call me Emily. I dare say you make me feel positively matronly." They laughed together easily.

The women finished the dishes in easy conversation, and then Emily and Abel took their leave.

"Thank you so much, Mrs. Flannigan. I hope we can return the invitation soon," Emily said graciously, and they walked in the direction of their wagon.

Kate turned to Brenna. "Will you get some water from the river for the morning?"

As Brenna left with the bucket, Kate looked at Michael. "Well! That was interesting!"

Michael released his pent-up emotions. "What a crook! I don't believe for one minute that he'll offer a fair price for land. He'll most likely swindle their land away from them in a poker game, and poor Emily. What will become of her?"

"I feel badly for her."

"He's got her under his thumb. She can't even think without his permission."

Kate looked worried. "I wish we had stepped forward and offered to help when Mr. Hinton died."

"She had offers, Kate. The Muellers were willing to take her in, but she declined. She told them Abel Brown had proposed and she had accepted. She has her reasons for the choices she's made."

"I guess it's not for us to judge her for what she felt she had to do."

Emily and Abel walked in silence to their camp. Emily retired to the tent and Abel joined Dan Christopher at his fire close by. Dan owed Abel a considerable amount of money in gambling debts, and he was working it off by doing chores for the Browns.

"So, Dan, tell me about this farm you're going to have in Oregon," Abel said, taking another swig from his silver flask.

The Promise

Chapter Twenty-Two

———⊃(⟨◦⟩)⊂———

Mile 1573

"I'm tired of you holding this over my head, Mr. Brown. How can you be so cruel?" Emily's voice came from inside the tent.

"Emily, you have no idea." Abel laughed coldly.

Brenna Flannigan stood outside the Browns' tent. She had finished her evening chores and had come to borrow a book. She hadn't meant to eavesdrop, but she stood frozen, listening to their harsh words.

"Sometimes I think I would be better off letting my secret out. Then at least I would be free of your unreasonable demands and restrictions." Emily's voice was strident.

"You could do that, Emily," Abel said coolly, "But you know what would happen, and I don't think that's what you want. Besides, you're my wife. You belong to me. You'll never be free of me, Emily."

"You're a monster!" Emily cried.

Abel's laugh followed Brenna as she hurried away from the tent. When she was close to her camp, Ben Hansson caught up to her.

"Hi, Brenna, I've been looking for you. What's wrong?" he asked when he saw her face.

"Nothing, Ben. I'm fine." Brenna knew she didn't look or sound fine. She just wanted to be alone so that she could sort out what she had just heard. She carefully composed her face and turned to Ben. In spite of her efforts, her voice was shaking. "Ma and I had a little quarrel, but we've patched it up. I have to help her now so I'll see you later." She turned and walked into her camp.

Ben watched her as she walked away. He was certain that Brenna was not fine, and that this was the first lie she had told him. A worried look crossed his features. What would cause her to be so deceptive? Maybe she didn't trust him like he thought she did.

Two days later, they were camped in a pine forest next to a creek. There had been no water for the past two days, so everyone was filling containers and boiling the water "to kill the wiggle tails," as Captain Wyatt had told them. Brenna hadn't talked to Ben since she had been so short with him, and she thought he was probably avoiding her. She regretted treating him so badly, but she was piqued that he wasn't more understanding.

She looked across the circle and saw Ben talking animatedly to Betty Stewart. Betty was a pretty blonde girl who was obviously enjoying the attention. Something he said made her laugh, and the sound of it carried over to the Flannigans' camp. Brenna scowled.

"Brenna, are you gathering the firewood?" her father asked as he walked up behind her. He followed her gaze across the circle to where Ben and Betty were conversing. "I see young Ben has another follower," he said cheerfully.

"Da, don't tease me," Brenna retorted.

"You're not worried about that one, are you now?" he queried.

Brenna was silent but her face told her father the truth. "Och, she's just a little diversion. Have you and Ben quarreled?"

Brenna sighed. "Yes. No. I don't know. We haven't spoken for two days."

"Well, you love him, am I right?"

Brenna's eyes filled with tears. "I do, Da."

"Then you have to fight for him. There's nothing a man loves more than to see a woman fight for him. But do it after you gather the firewood." With that, Michael Flannigan walked back to the campsite.

Later that night after dinner and chores, Brenna walked to the Hanssons' wagon. She found Ben sitting by the fire on a bench he had made with a board and two rocks. He was busily repairing a wagon part.

"Hi, Ben."

He looked up briefly and then down at his work again. "Hello, Brenna."

She stood watching him for a few moments.

"You haven't been around for a couple of days," she said.

"No, I haven't," he replied, applying oil to a metal piece.

"I saw you talking to Betty Stewart earlier."

Ben looked up at her. "Yes, I was doing some work for her father." He paused. "She's a nice girl. Real friendly." He looked down at his work and picked up a wrench.

Brenna sat on the long bench next to him. "What are you working on?"

"This is part of Mr. Stewart's wheel. It was coming apart so I've repaired it. I'll take it to him in the morning." Ben paused. "Maybe I'll have a chance to visit with Betty again," he said casually.

Brenna took a deep breath. "Ben, I want to apologize for my behavior the other night. I was upset. I shouldn't have been so short with you."

Ben stopped working and looked at Brenna. He could see her nervousness, and there was something else.

"You were upset about the quarrel with your mother?"

"Yes. No. There was no quarrel, Ben. I was upset about something else."

Ben waited patiently.

"I overheard something I shouldn't have. It was a conversation I wasn't privy to, and it upset me terribly. It was Emily and Mr. Brown. I don't think I should talk about it…" Brenna was crying softly.

Ben stood up and drew Brenna next to him. "Then don't. I don't need to know."

"I lied to you, Ben. I'm so sorry. And then when you didn't come around, I was angry at you for not being more understanding." She sniffed loudly. "I guess you couldn't very well be understanding when you didn't know what was wrong."

Ben hugged her to him. "Brenna, I want you to always feel like you can confide in me. But I want you to know that I will understand if there is something you can't tell me. You don't need to lie to me. Just tell me the truth and I promise I'll understand. And I will always be truthful to you, too."

"You will?"

"Yes, I will, Brenna."

"Then tell me something, Benjamin Hansson."

"What is it?"

"Are you attracted to Betty Stewart?"

Ben laughed softly. "Oh she's very friendly in a silly way." He lifted Brenna's chin and looked down at her earnest face. "No one could ever measure up to you. Don't you know how much I care for you?"

"How much, Ben?"

"Now you're teasing me," he said smiling.

Brenna didn't smile back. "No, I'm serious, Ben."

Ben's smile faded. He put his hands on the sides of her face. "I've loved you from the first time I saw you in Independence. I don't know what it is, Brenna. I can't describe it in words, but I can't imagine life without you in it. My day doesn't begin until I see you. I can't sleep at night if I haven't made sure you're all right. These last two days and nights have been agony. I want to protect you. I want to support you. I want to be in your life. Brenna, there isn't anything I wouldn't do for you." He bent his head and kissed her tenderly.

"Oh, Ben, I feel the same way."

"A-hem."

They both jumped and looked to where Hans, Ben's father, was standing.

"I'm sorry to interrupt," he said, trying to conceal a smile.

"It's okay, Dad. I was just going to walk Brenna back to her wagon." They left giggling into each other's arms.

Ben said good night to Brenna and Michael Flannigan, who was sitting at the fire enjoying the solitude.

"I'll see you in the morning, Brenna."

She took a seat next to her father. "Where's Ma and Conor?"

"They're at the Bensons'. I see you and Ben are thick as thieves again," Michael said cheerfully.

"I did what you said, Da. I decided to fight for him."

"That's my girl. I knew you would do the right thing."

"But why did it take me two days to do it?"

"Well, your head had to quiet down so you could hear what your heart was telling you."

"I wish I would have listened to my heart two days ago!"

Michael put his arm around Brenna's shoulders and hugged her. "Your head always thinks it knows best, but it doesn't always, does it?"

"No, Da, it doesn't. And Ben was so understanding."

"Aye, but don't forget, he has a bossy head, too. Maybe he needed the time to listen to what his heart was saying."

"How did you get so wise, Da?"

"Och, Brenna, by doing exactly what you and Ben are doing. It's easy to live a smooth life. But it's the rough patches that teach us the way to love and understanding. Here's your mother and Conor."

The Flannigans spent the following hour playing Conor's favorite game: twenty questions. They laughed uproariously when Conor was trying to get them to guess wiggle-tails. Then it was time for sleep. The Blue Mountains lay ahead, and they would need all their strength and resolve to cross them. Brenna fell fast asleep. She had slept poorly the previous two nights, but tonight her sleep was dreamless and deep, and the last thing on her mind was Ben and his promise to her.

Abel Brown walked up behind Mr. Douglas, who was eating beans by his campfire.

"Nice night," he said loudly, causing Mr. Douglas to spill his plate.

"Oh!" Mr. Douglas exclaimed. "I didn't hear you coming!"

"If I didn't know better, I'd think you were avoiding me."

Mr. Douglas laughed nervously as he picked up his spilled plate. "Now, Mr. Brown, I wouldn't do that!" he said, avoiding Abel Brown's eyes.

"I'm glad to hear that because we need to have a talk." He sat down on the chair Mr. Douglas had just vacated. "Sit, Mr. Douglas." Abel took a knife and a piece of wood from his coat pocket and began to whittle. "Do you remember you owe me some money? We've had some poker games and you've racked up quite a debt."

Mr. Douglas looked uneasy. "I haven't forgotten, Mr. Brown. It's just that I've had some hard times." His voice shook, and he couldn't take his eyes from the knife and the shavings of wood falling from the piece Abel was holding. Abel didn't take his eyes off the wood as he whittled away. "Remember the Indians a while back?" Mr. Douglas continued. "They stole most of my provisions!"

"I don't care to hear your sad story." Abel stopped whittling and looked hard at Mr. Douglas. "I want my money, and I want it now."

"But I don't have it right now."

Abel Brown jumped up and grabbed Mr. Douglas by his shirt collar, pulling him to his feet. His knife was inches from Mr. Douglas's face. "I don't take kindly to men who promise and don't deliver. Now I have your I.O.U.s, and you're going to stand behind them, aren't you Mr. Douglas?"

"Yes! Yes! Whatever you want!"

"I'll tell you what I want. When you get your land in Oregon City, you're going to deed it over to me."

When Mr. Douglas started to protest, Abel Brown deftly sliced one of his nostrils with his knife. Blood flowed freely from the cut and Mr. Douglas clapped his hands over his nose and bent over.

"I'm bleeding," he gasped.

Abel Brown leaned close to Mr. Douglas and threatened, "You'll bleed a lot more than that if you don't do as I say. Do I make myself clear?"

"Yes! I'll do it! Just leave me alone!"

Abel put his knife and piece of wood back in his pocket and smiled grimly. "Nice talking to you, Mr. Douglas. We'll have another chat as soon as we get to Oregon City," he said, and then he sauntered away from the campsite.

The Trade

Chapter Twenty-Three

━━━━━◦((◦))◦━━━━━

Mile 1628

"I think she looks pretty good. What do you think, Mr. Flannigan?"
James Cardell and Michael Flannigan looked at the sorrel mare
and her two-year-old colt tied to the back of the Cummings's wagon.
She looked sound, and the colt was calm. James had asked Michael
to help him with this trade since Michael was knowledgeable about
horses. Mr. Cummings was in need of a team of oxen since he had
lost his, and James wanted to trade two of his oxen for this mare
and her colt. It was a good trade for James—far better than he
would have gotten in Independence. Horses were more expensive
than oxen, but they were harder to feed on the trail. He wanted
to give the horses to Thomas for all of his kindness and support.

"I like the look of her, that's for sure. Her eyes are wide set. Her
ears are alert, and she's interested in us. The nostrils are round
and soft. I can tell she's been treated well," he said, nodding to Mr.
Cummings.

"Ah, yeah, she's a sweet mare, and the colt will be big and strong too," Mr. Cummings replied. "He's got his mother's temperament so he'll be easy to train."

"How much have you done with him?" Michael asked.

"Oh, very little. He'll lead and tie. I can pick up his feet and look in his mouth. But he'll be easy."

Michael picked up one of the mare's front feet and examined it carefully. James watched him press on the bottom of the foot. He carefully cleaned around the shoe and around the frog of the foot.

"Did Ben Olson shoe this horse?"

"Ah, yeah, he does a good job, that lad."

"You're spending a long time looking at those feet, Mr. Flannigan," James said.

"No foot no horse, James. It's an old saying, but it stands true. If this horse has a bad foot, she'll soon be lame and of no use to anyone."

Michael inspected every part of the foot before moving up the hoof and to the canon bone. Then he ran his hands expertly up the lower leg to the knee.

"The knee is another critical joint, James. I want to make sure there is no swelling here. The young one's knees won't be closed yet, but hers should be strong and well formed. She's an eight-year-old, Mr. Cummings?"

"Ah, yeah, I raised her from a baby."

When he was finished with the foreleg, Michael stretched it out to the front, holding onto the back of the mare's knee. She was docile and didn't seem to mind the examination. Then Michael bent her leg at the knee so the foot was up close to her body. He inspected each leg the same way.

"I want to make sure there is no stiffness or soreness here," he said.

"I had no idea this would be so involved, Mr. Flannigan. I thought you would just look the horse over and tell me if she looked sound."

Michael paused to look at James. "You can't always tell if a horse is sound by just looking her over, James. Some horses bear up under pain, and you might not know something is wrong until it's too late to do much about it. Now take her lead rope and trot her up a ways." He watched carefully as the mare trotted away from him and then back towards him a few times.

"I'm watching her action, James. She plants all four feet firmly, and she moves nicely. She looks comfortable, and she isn't favoring any of her legs." Then he put his head on the mare's side below her shoulder, listening carefully.

"Her heart sounds good, and her lungs are clear." He then put his head low on one side of her belly. "Stomach noises sound right. Let's take a look at her stool." He separated some of the horse apples with a stick. "I don't see any worms here. That's good. Let's have a look at her stifles."

After the lengthy inspection was over, Michael gave James the go-ahead, and James and Mr. Cummings made the trade.

Thomas Benson was overwhelmed with the gift. "I can't accept this, James. It's too much."

"I know it's been hard for you without a horse since you lost Amber, and I want to do this. You and your family have taken me in, and I can't thank you enough. Please accept this as a small token of my appreciation."

"James, you've been such a help to me and to some of the others. You don't need to give me a horse."

"I want to, Thomas. Please accept my gift."

The girls all had to sit on the mare. Even little Annie had a turn, and she squealed in delight. Sam and Tommy each had a ride bareback with just the halter. Then the children turned their attention to the colt and discovered that he liked his ears scratched.

"Can we ride this one, dad?" Mary asked.

"Not for a while, Mary. He hasn't been gentled yet."

"What does gentled mean?"

"It means he hasn't been taught to accept someone on his back yet."

"What are their names?"

"The mare is Molly," James said. "She seems to know her name, and she comes when she's called."

"Then we'll keep it Molly," Thomas replied happily. He was running his hands over the mare.

"I don't think the colt has a name yet."

"Well, we'll all have to think of a good name for him."

"Michael helped me examine her to make sure she's sound," James said.

"If Michael looked her over, I'm sure she is. Thank you, James. You don't know what this means to me." Thomas's eyes couldn't take in enough of the beautiful mare. Her shining coppery coat glistened in the sun, and her large soft eyes regarded him quietly.

Rebecca gave James a knowing look. He had told her his plan, and she had assured him it wasn't necessary, but he had been adamant. She had known her father would be thrilled. James smiled at her, and they left her father and the children with the horses and walked hand in hand towards the trees to collect firewood to cook the evening meal.

"You've made my dad a happy man, James."

"It's the least I can do, Rebecca. Besides, I want to get in his good graces. I have an important question to ask him."

"Oh, and what would that be?" she asked merrily, her eyes dancing.

"I want to ask him for your hand in marriage," he smiled crookedly at her.

"Do you think maybe you should be asking me first, James?" He heard the laughter in her voice, and his face flushed.

"Oh—I guess I just assumed...I mean we've talked so much about marriage and what our lives will be like in Oregon."

"You should never assume anything when it comes to women, James." She grew more serious. "I want to be asked properly—formally."

They were beneath the trees now, and the early evening light softened her features. The branches arched over them like the roof of a chapel. The stream gurgled around rocks and boulders. James took Rebecca's shoulders and turned her towards him. He slowly bent on one knee and took her hands in his. He looked up into the sweet face he had grown to love. Her warm eyes regarded him tenderly.

"Rebecca, I love you more than I ever thought it was possible to love anyone. I can't imagine my life without you in it. You have been my rock. I know that you could do so much better than me, but I hope that you will consent to accepting my hand in marriage." He looked so earnest, and his words were spoken with a sincerity that she knew was heartfelt.

Rebecca hardly noticed the tears streaming down her face when she nodded and said, "Yes, James. I will be your wife."

He rose and kissed her gently, his arms enfolding her.

"Please let me know when I act so stupidly again. I never want to take you for granted, Rebecca."

"Oh, don't worry, James. I'll keep you informed."

The Confidante

Chapter Twenty-Four

Mile 1635

Brenna Flannigan walked into The Browns' camp. She knew she wouldn't be intruding since she had seen Abel talking with the captain. She was excited about the prospect of borrowing one of Emily's books. Buster came running to her panting happily. She reached down to scratch his ears and then thought better of it when she smelled him.

"Where have you been, Buster? You smell like you've rolled in some kind of manure!"

"Brenna! I was hoping you would come by today. Would you like to take a look at my books?"

"I'd love to!" Brenna said with enthusiasm.

They went into the tent and over to where Emily had a crate of books. "These are the only ones left. I had to leave three other boxes in Independence." She giggled. "They are pretty heavy."

Brenna scanned the titles. There was a wide variety of subjects. "You have a little of everything here, Emily."

"Yes, I'm interested in lots of subjects. I loved grammar school and secondary school. I thought about going to college, but I foolishly married instead."

Brenna picked up one of the books and opened the cover. It was a book about modern science. She scanned the table of contents.

"How about you, Brenna? Did you go to school?"

Brenna looked up. "I went to school a little in Ireland. My mother and my grandmother taught me a lot. Then when we lived in New York I attended secondary school there." She put the science book down and picked up one on philosophy.

"What was New York like? I've never been there," Emily asked.

"I didn't see too much of it—mostly my little neighborhood. It was very different from Ireland because there are so many people who come from all over the world. Once we settled into our tenement, I mostly saw the same people all the time."

"Mostly other Irish?"

"Yes, people in New York tend to live with others like themselves, especially those who don't speak English. I think it makes them feel more comfortable. "

"You would think that after being on a boat in close quarters for months, people would want to spread out a bit."

Brenna looked at Emily, this girl her own age who had grown up safe and secure in a world of privilege. "Yes, Emily, there were hundreds of people on the boat. Everyone had left a life of deprivation and indescribable conditions. Each of us was leaving our homeland to make a new life in America. I can't describe the feelings at the end of the passage as we all stood on the deck of the ship and saw New York harbor. The silence was intense. Then the ship's horn blew and we all cheered."

"That must have been an incredible experience."

"Yes, it was. I'll never forget it."

"Do you ever wish you could go back to Ireland?"

Brenna paused. "Yes and no. We left family there who I miss very much. I would love to see them again. I think my parents miss Ireland. I don't though. When I was young, life was wonderful.

But when the troubles started, everything changed. That's mostly what I remember. This is my home now, and I can't imagine living in Ireland again. I like how this country is so open to everyone."

Emily frowned. "Everyone except the Negroes."

"Yes, I don't understand that at all. Negroes were free in New York, but many people didn't treat them like that."

Emily hesitated a moment. "Can I confide in you, Brenna?"

Brenna looked cautious. "What is it?"

Emily took a deep breath. "I recently found out that I am not the person I thought I was."

"What do you mean?"

Emily looked at Brenna carefully. "I got a letter at Fort Laramie from the woman I had always thought was my mother. She's actually my stepmother."

"How horrible!"

"Yes, but it's worse." Emily drew in a deep breath. "Brenna, my real mother was one of my father's slaves in Virginia."

Brenna gasped. "What?!"

"Nellie and Abel are the only ones who know the truth—and now you." Her eyes were entreating. "You'll keep my secret, won't you Brenna? I don't know why I told you except that I feel close to you and hope we can be friends."

"Of course I'll keep your secret, Emily. You're still the same person you've always been."

"No, I'm not. Everything has changed, Brenna. If people find out the truth about me, I will be ruined. Do you understand?"

Brenna looked at Emily, a beautiful young woman. "You mean if people knew your mother was a Negress they would shun you?"

"I would be shunned by white people and Negroes. No one would accept me, Brenna."

"That's not right!" Brenna exclaimed.

"No, it's not, and that's why you have to keep my secret."

Brenna leaned over and took Emily's hands. "Your secret is safe with me, Emily."

The young women spent a few more minutes looking over the books. Brenna picked up a heavy one. "How about this one?" The title said *Ancient History*.

"That's a great book! I think you'll like it. Keep it as long as you want. Do you want to take another?"

"No, thanks. I think this one will keep me busy for a while."

"Can I ask a favor while you're here?"

"Sure, Emily—what is it?"

Emily looked down at Buster, who cocked his head and looked back at her.

A few minutes later, they had Buster in the creek up to his ears. He squirmed and whined trying to escape, but Brenna held him firmly while Emily soaped him from head to tail. When Emily was scooping up water and rinsing him off, he gave a final effort.

"Oof. Don't let him go, Brenna!"

"I can't hold on to him!" Brenna exclaimed and then laughed.

"He's getting away!" Emily yelled. They tried to grab him, and Brenna ended up face first in the creek. Emily laughed until tears ran down her cheeks. Brenna climbed halfway out of the water, grabbed Emily's dress, and pulled her in. Both women were thoroughly soaked and laughing hysterically. Buster sat on the shore regarding them solemnly.

"I'm wet to the skin!" Emily gasped climbing out of the water. "At least we got the majority of the buffalo dung off of Buster."

Brenna followed her and sat on the creek bank catching her breath. "He smells better anyway."

Kate Flannigan looked at Brenna's bedraggled dress and dripping hair when she walked into camp minutes later. "You should undress to take a bath, Brenna."

They both laughed and Brenna explained her appearance. "That little dog is strong and slippery when he's soaking wet!" She watched Kate building up the fire. "Do you miss Ireland, Ma?"

Kate looked up, surprised. "Where is this coming from?"

"Emily and I were talking. I think she's had a pretty sheltered life. I started thinking about my life compared to hers—all the places I've been and things I've seen. I was just wondering if you ever miss Ireland."

Kate's face suddenly had a tortured look. "Oh, Brenna! I miss it terribly!" Her voice broke.

"Ma!" Brenna looked alarmed. "I'm sorry!"

"No, it's alright, Brenna. It's just that when you said you've seen a lot in your life, it made me think about how true that is. You've seen more than any girl your age should ever see—all the poverty, the brutality, the misery, and people dying before your eyes. No girl should see that." Kate wiped her eyes with her apron. "That part I don't miss at all. But I grew up in a different Ireland, Brenna. I was raised in the same place my parents and theirs were raised. I knew every family in the county. There were always celebrations and dances where everyone would get together. Even wakes. Everyone was like family."

Kate looked wistfully at Brenna. "That's where I met your father and where we were married. The whole county was at the wedding. It went on for three days! You and Conor were both born and baptized there. You might remember some of the good times we had when you were young."

Brenna nodded.

"And I miss the country: the green of it, and narrow lanes, small villages, the smell of the sea." Kate paused and blew her nose.

"I miss Aunt Chloe and Uncle Donald," Brenna said.

"Yes, I do too." Kate paused in thought. "It's hard to explain, Brenna. It's everything—the land, the people, the customs. But what I really miss is more than that, and it's something I don't have here in America."

"What is it, Ma?"

"It's home."

"A home?"

"No, not *a* home—it's the feeling of home. I don't have that here yet."

Brenna nodded sagely. "That's why Da wanted to come to Oregon, isn't it Ma? He wants to try to get that feeling back."

Kate smiled at her daughter. She was so wise! "Yes, Brenna. That's the truth."

Training

Chapter Twenty-Five

Before the Blue Mountains
Mile 1639

James Cardell found Michael Flannigan working on his wagon. "Hello, Mr. Flannigan. Hard at work as usual."

"Good morning, James."

The camp was having a lay-by in preparation for the trip over the Blue Mountains. They had heard that it was a difficult ascent through heavy timber. The deeply rutted and often muddy roads wound through outcroppings of rock. The descent on the other side was also treacherous. The men were making necessary repairs on the wagons. Some of them went hunting with the older boys for pheasant and prairie chickens. Others were dickering with a couple of Cayuse Indians for some beef.

"I want to thank you again for your help in the trade yesterday. Thomas is very happy with the horses."

"I'm glad I was able to help you, James."

"I was hoping you would be able to help gentle the colt, Mr. Flannigan. None of us has had much experience with that." James waited while Michael finished the repair on the tongue of the wagon.

Michael straightened and wiped his brow with his sleeve. "To be truthful, James, I don't have the time, and I'm not the best one for the job anyway. If you want someone who is really in tune with horses, you'll want to ask Brenna. She has a gift, and no one can gentle a horse like she can."

"Brenna?" James was surprised.

"Aye, I've never seen anyone like her with horses. They seem to know she means them no harm, and they always cooperate. She's the best horsewoman I've ever seen. Ask her." He went back to checking over the wagon.

James walked to the back of the wagon where Brenna and Kate were kneading dough to bake into bread.

"Good morning, Mrs. Flannigan. Morning, Brenna."

"Mr. Cardell, I heard you made a good trade yesterday." Kate smiled at him.

"Thanks to your husband."

"Michael knows horses, and that's the truth."

"I hear Brenna knows horses, too," he said, smiling at Brenna.

"Aye, that she does—in a different way. Michael knows the bones, joints, and muscles. Brenna knows the heart of the horse." Kate looked at Brenna, who flushed with pleasure. "I think she can talk to them, and they like it!" They all laughed.

"Brenna, your father thinks that maybe you would help gentle the colt. He can be a handful, and I'd like to see him gentled before he gets any bigger," James said. "All the children want to ride him, and I don't want anyone to get hurt."

Brenna smiled broadly. There was nothing she would rather do. It was true she had a knack with horses. She loved everything about them, and from the time she was a little child and had crawled up onto a fence and slid onto the back of a horse grazing in the pasture, she knew she was at home. She looked expectantly at her mother, and Kate smiled and said, "Go. You won't be any good to me if you have horses on your mind, now will you?"

"Thanks, Ma." Brenna gave her mother a quick hug and happily accompanied James to the Bensons' wagon.

Brenna looked at the colt standing in front of her from the end of his lead rope. He stared back at her expectantly. He seemed to know that this girl was going to ask something of him. She had already spent some time rubbing him all over with her hands. She paid attention to every part of his body. He seemed to like the attention, but when he went to playfully nip Brenna's arm, she reprimanded him quickly.

"He needs to know that I am not a horse. I am his boss, and he needs to respect me."

His ears were turned towards her, but when he heard the sound of a mule hee-hawing in a noisy protest behind him, his right ear swiveled to the back. When he determined that the mule was not a threat, he focused both ears back on Brenna.

"He's listening to me closely. He wants to be friends, but he wants to make sure that he can trust me first. He already figured out what was happening behind him."

"But he didn't turn his head around to look," Mary said.

All the Bensons were watching intently. Ben Hansson was there, too. He had seen Brenna and James Cardell walking purposefully toward the Bensons' wagon, and he wanted to find out what was going on. He marveled at Sweet Brenna, who had taken on a whole different demeanor as soon as she stepped in front of the colt. Now she stood resolutely before this large and untrained animal, loosely holding the lead rope that was attached to the rope halter around his head.

"He doesn't need to turn his head to see behind him. He can see all around himself because of where his eyes are on his head."

"Yes!" Mary exclaimed. "I see they're more on the sides of his head than ours are!"

Brenna took the slack out of the lead rope and put some pressure on it. Instantly the colt leaned back against the pressure. Brenna didn't pull on the rope, but held it steady. After a few moments, the colt shifted his weight subtly forward and Brenna instantly relaxed her hands on the lead rope.

"He doesn't like pressure, and when he figures out how to get away from it, he will because it's more comfortable for him."

"What do you mean by pressure, Brenna? You didn't even touch him," Sam asked.

"I'm keeping steady pressure on the lead rope. I'm not pulling on it, but there's no slack. When he leans away from me, he feels pressure from the halter on his head and he doesn't like that. As soon as he leans forward, the pressure releases. I want him to walk up to me, and eventually he will. He just has to figure out that that's what I want from him." Again, she took up the slack in the rope and tightened it. The colt again leaned back, but then he moved slightly forward, and Brenna released the pressure by relaxing her hands on the lead rope.

"Good boy," she said. The colt's ears and eyes were on Brenna.

"But he didn't do anything," Tommy said.

"Oh yes, he did a great thing, Tommy. He gave in to me. Just a little, but that's a start."

Brenna again took up the slack and put pressure on the lead rope. This time the colt did not move back. He seemed to be stubbornly holding his ground, but then he shifted his weight forward, and he moved his right front foot one small step. Brenna instantly released her hands on the rope and praised him.

"So you pressure him, and when he gives in a little you give him release," Thomas said.

"That's right, Mr. Benson. Horses like food, comfort, and companionship. The best way to train them so that they don't get resentful is to use pressure and release a little at a time. Once they understand what it is you want them to do, they will do it for you, but they have to trust you first."

Brenna showed Thomas how to hold the lead rope and how to ask for what he wanted from the colt. It wasn't too long before the colt was responding to the pressure on the lead rope by walking up to them. At one point, he got a little too enthusiastic and almost ran over them. Brenna showed Thomas how to encourage the colt to move back by vigorously shaking the lead rope from side to side.

"He doesn't like this action, and he will move away from it because it makes him uncomfortable."

Ben watched Brenna, transfixed. He had never seen her take charge so confidently. She obviously was very good with this colt. Better than he would have been, he realized. He tended to try to muscle horses into doing his bidding. Brenna's technique looked effortless, and the colt was listening to her intently.

"Now I am going to ask him to move backwards."

"That's easy. We've seen him move backwards," Tommy said.

"Oh yes, he can move backwards all right. But will he move backwards when I ask him to?"

Brenna walked up to the colt and stood a foot away. She rubbed his face gently with her hand, and then she placed her palm on his nose halfway between his nostrils and his eyes and under the halter. Slowly she squeezed her thumb and fingers on either side of the long bones of his nose creating pressure on the sides.

"I'm not squeezing hard, but he's very sensitive here. I'm also using steady backwards pressure and I'm focusing behind him now."

The colt jerked his head up but Brenna kept her hand on his nose. Then the colt jerked his head sideways. Brenna kept her hand in place, using her other hand on the lead rope to bring his head back to center and keep him from moving forward. When the colt leaned back from the pressure, Brenna instantly released. After a few moments, she again applied pressure to his nose. This time he took a small step back, and Brenna released the pressure. Soon he was taking five and six steps back with very light pressure before Brenna relaxed her fingers. She always praised him and rubbed his nose after each try.

"You want to always rub the spot where you were applying pressure. It lets him know you are friendly. He's beginning to understand me now. He knows that I won't harm him, but I won't let him get away with any shenanigans either. He's beginning to see me as the boss. Now you do it, Thomas."

They worked with the colt for another half hour, asking the colt to step back by shaking the lead rope like they did when he got too rambunctious. At first, the shaking was vigorous, but soon the colt was taking multiple steps backwards with just a hint of a shake on the rope. Then Brenna said it was time to stop.

"But he's doing so well. Can't you keep working with him some more?" Mary asked.

"It's very important to stop the training while he still feels good about it, Mary. If you push him too hard, he'll resent you for it. You want to keep it fun for him, too."

"Oh I get it," Mary said. "It's like when mom wants me to keep doing my sums when I am tired and I can't think straight." Everyone laughed.

"That's right, Mary. This colt is tired now. It's a good time to stop because he just did something right. He'll remember that next time we work with him, and we should work with him every day now, even if it's only for half an hour."

"Can I work with him tomorrow, please?" Mary implored.

"He needs to get to know all of you, but I think you should practice on Molly first. Remember, he's just a baby mentally, but he's big and strong like an adult horse. I may make it look easy, but until you learn how to work with him properly, it's best to let me and your father gentle this horse."

"Me too," Tommy said enthusiastically. "I want to learn how to do it."

"Both you and Sam should learn these techniques. We'll teach them to you using Molly."

Sam smiled happily. He loved this new colt and he wanted to spend a lot of time with him. He thought he could be as good with him as Brenna was. He had been watching every move she made, and he thought he would be able to duplicate her actions. He wanted to make this colt his. He rubbed the colt's ears and whispered in his ear, "We're going to be best friends," and the colt nickered and vigorously nodded his head up and down. Sam smiled delightedly.

"Dad, let's name him Rascal."

Thomas thought about it for a moment. "That's a fine name, Sam. Rascal it is!"

A Proper Suitor

Chapter Twenty-Six

Ben walked Brenna back to her wagon. He put his arm around her shoulder. "I didn't know you were such a hand with horses."

"You don't know everything about me, Ben Hansson."

"What else don't I know about you, Brenna?"

"Well…you don't know my middle name, do you?"

"Yes, I do." He looked at her solemnly.

Brenna looked surprised. "You do?"

"Of course I do. It's Brunhilda."

They both dissolved into giggles. Kate Flannigan watched her daughter and Ben Hansson approaching from where she was standing at the back of the Flannigans' wagon. She frowned slightly as Brenna gave Ben a playful shove and squealed in delight as he chased her. It wasn't that Kate didn't like Ben. He was a well-mannered young man, and he certainly had a good future ahead of him. But he wasn't a Catholic. She sighed as she checked on the bread baking in the Dutch oven. She heard Brenna laugh uproariously at something Ben said.

"Michael," Kate called. "We need to talk."

Later that evening Michael and Kate were enjoying a cup of tea in a rare moment of peace and quiet. Brenna was visiting the Muellers, and Conor was at the Meekers' camp helping Ezra with his chores. Kate broached the subject.

"Have you taken notice of your daughter and young Ben Hansson?"

Michael gave her a sideways look. "Aye, I notice them both every day."

Kate looked pointedly at Michael. "Have you noticed how they are together?"

"As opposed to how they are when they're apart?"

"Michael! You know what I mean!"

Michael smiled. "They seem to get along together well enough."

Kate jumped up. "Well enough! Is that all you can say, Michael Flannigan?"

Michael pulled her back down next to him. "Calm down, Kate. What's troubling you?"

"I can see the writing on the wall, Michael. He loves her, and I think she loves him too!"

"Well, and so?"

"Ben Hansson is a nice boy, but he's not a Catholic. I want Brenna to find a good Catholic man."

"Oh, I see." Michael looked thoughtful. After a minute when he hadn't responded, Kate exploded.

"Well, what do you think, Michael Flannigan?"

Michael looked at her quickly and put his thumb and index finger on his chin.

"Well, let's see now. Who could we find for Brenna? Well, now, there's Mr. Banks. He's a Catholic."

"What! Have you gone off your head?" Kate exclaimed when she pictured Mr. Banks, forty-five at least, with two missing front teeth and an affinity for whiskey.

"I guess he is a little old for Brenna."

"Humph."

184

"There must be someone else. Let's see." Michael paused, deep in thought. Suddenly he brightened. "How about Clem Morris? He's young. And he's Catholic, too."

"Argh!" Kate groaned. Clem was a little older than Brenna. He chewed tobacco and had stains down the front of the only shirt he ever wore, and it looked like he hadn't washed since Independence. "That boy is allergic to soap and water, and he's not too bright, either."

"Aye, but he's Catholic!" Michael exclaimed happily.

"I see what you're about, Michael Flannigan," Kate said testily.

"What do you mean?" he said innocently.

"You're baiting me, Michael, and I'm trying to have a serious conversation with you about our daughter."

Michael sighed then. "Katie, if we were back in Ireland, things would be different. But we're not. What do you want for Brenna? Do you want her to grow into a spinster waiting for the right Catholic man to come along?"

"No, Michael, of course not, but…"

"She and Ben make each other happy. He's a good and kind man. Isn't that enough given where we are and where we're going?" Michael paused. "Besides, I've had a talk with him. He's willing to convert."

Kate's eyes grew large. "You talked to him? And you didn't tell me?" She threw herself at Michael tipping him off balance, and they both ended up on the ground laughing like children. When Brenna walked into the camp, that's what she saw.

"Ma, Da, why are you rolling around on the ground laughing?"

"Never mind, Brenna. I'm just teaching your mother patience and charity."

"Oh, I never…" Kate said as she attempted to get up.

"Och, the lesson isn't over yet my girl," and he pulled her back down and the two of them collapsed into each other giggling.

Very strange, Brenna thought, shaking her head. Sometimes her parents didn't make any sense.

Bear Encounter

Chapter Twenty-Seven

Crossing the Blue Mountains

Emily looked at her hands. They were red, raw, and blistered. "Mr. Hinton used to say I had the prettiest hands he'd ever seen. Now look at them!"

The ascent of the Blue Mountains had been very difficult in places. The trail was rocky and heavily timbered, and the thirty-four wagons that were left in the wagon train proceeded one at a time. At one point, the whole wagon train was held up for hours while the men removed a large tree that had fallen across the trail. Today they had begun the steep descent. All of the adults helped each other get the wagons down to more level ground. Emily and Abel, with the aid of a few others, had strained against the ropes tied to the back of the wagon, trying to keep it from hurtling downhill.

"Mr. Brown?" Emily held out her palms.

Abel Brown paid no attention to Emily. He was bent over a notebook he kept with notations and sums. He was trying to collect on the I.O.U.s he had accumulated from many of the men who had joined one or more of his poker games over the course of the last months. Some of them were able to pay. Some claimed their money was gone. When Abel exerted a little pressure, a few of those would manage to scrounge up the money, or some of it. A few who owed him considerable amounts were going to repay him by deeding their newly acquired Oregon land to him after they made their claims.

"Are you listening to me, Mr. Brown?" Emily asked. "I cannot do another day with those ropes. All my gloves are ruined. Look at my hands!" she exclaimed as she held them out for Abel's scrutiny.

Abel looked up from his notebook. "Yes, I see your hands, Emily. What do you want me to do about it?" He snapped. The qualities he had originally found charming in Emily were now annoying. She seemed to be always complaining about one thing or another.

"I'm your wife. I expect you to take care of me!"

Abel sighed loudly. He knew he would have no rest until Emily had an answer she was happy with. "Okay, okay, Emily. What do you want me to do?" He was attempting to keep his voice calm.

"I want you to hire one more man to help us besides Dan Christopher." Dan had lost his wagon and stock in a river crossing. Abel decided Dan should help them in return for payment of his gambling debt. He figured that since Dan had lost everything, he would never see any money from Christopher, so he may as well use him as much as he could.

"What other man? Everyone has their own wagons to worry about," Abel said crossly.

"Hire Clem Morris. He's been freeloading off of people since he lost everything in that fire."

Abel groaned under his breath. Clem Morris was an unkempt young man who didn't seem to have any skills. His wagon had gone up in flames one night a few weeks back when he built his campfire too close. He had said he was using the wagon as a windbreak so his fire wouldn't go out. Clem never joined the poker games, so

Abel would have to pay him, and he was loathe to part with any of his money. But he could think of no one else who didn't have his hands full. Abel sighed again. Emily's hands were ruined. He knew she wouldn't be able to manage the ropes again and they still had a ways to go to get down from these mountains. He cursed under his breath.

"All right, Emily. I'll talk to Clem in the morning."

The wagon train was camped in a circular valley surrounded by pine, cedar, and fir trees. While everyone attended to chores, the younger children amused themselves in a game of keep-away. Shouts and squeals of delight came from the meadow. Kate and Brenna Flannigan were making bread and discussing Emily Brown.

"Did you see her today? She was working very hard to keep their wagon from tumbling downhill. I've never seen her work like that before," Brenna remarked. She and Emily had become friends and shared conversations about the books Brenna was borrowing from her.

"Yes, things have changed for her since Mr. Hinton passed," Kate said. "I think Mr. Brown is hard on her. I know she's spoiled, but Mr. Brown could help her out a little. He seems to have a lot of money."

"I wish Miss Nellie was still with her," Brenna said. She would look after her and make sure she was treated kindly."

"You don't think Mr. Brown is abusive?" Kate asked.

Brenna was thoughtful for a moment. She hadn't told anyone what Emily had confided to her. "Not physically, but there are other ways a man can be hard on a woman. He seems to have an advantage over her. If he wants something, she jumps, and that's not like Emily."

"Why did she marry Mr. Brown?"

Brenna carefully worded her reply. "From what she's told me, he proposed and she felt that she didn't have any options. She's beautiful, a young widow with no family, and little money. She feels she doesn't have anyone to turn to or any place to go. Mr. Brown seems to have plenty of money, so he can take care of her."

"Someone said he's very good at cards, and many men owe him money from their losses. I wonder if Ernest Hinton owed him money. Get me a little more milk, Brenna."

Suddenly there was an urgent shout from the direction of the meadow. Shrill screams followed, and Brenna and Kate ran around the wagon to see what was happening. Brenna gasped when she saw a large bear on all fours running through the meadow towards the children. She was amazed at how quickly the bear closed the gap between itself and one of the boys whose red hair was streaming back as he ran as fast as he could. His skinny legs and arms were pumping furiously, but he was no match for the speed and power of the bear. Brenna screamed when the bear crashed into the boy sending him sprawling, and she heard her mother scream, "Tommy!" At the same time, a shot rang out. Brenna looked in the direction of the sound and saw Ben Hansson kneeling at the edge of the meadow loading his rifle again. The bear roared and stood up on its hind legs looking in the direction from where the sound of the report had come. Bright red blood poured from its shoulder. The boy was lying lifeless, his small frame swallowed in the grass. Ben took aim and fired his gun again. The bullet tore into the bear's neck and its angry roar filled the meadow. It looked at Ben, and even from a distance, Brenna could see the menace in its small eyes. It then dropped on all fours and ran towards Ben at a furious pace.

"Ben!" Brenna screamed.

Ben was loading his rifle calmly. He raised it, took careful aim, and fired when the bear was twenty feet away. Another shot followed closely behind Ben's, and the bear fell heavily to the earth, sliding in the dirt and ending up ten feet from where Ben still knelt in the grass.

"Ben! Ben!" Brenna screamed as she ran to him. Others were running towards the children. It had all happened so suddenly. A few of the men were standing close to the bear with their guns pointed at it when Brenna ran up and threw her arms around Ben. She was overcome with emotion, and she couldn't speak, but her tears flowed freely.

"It's okay, Brenna. I'm okay." His arm went around her and she felt him shaking.

"That's a big bear you brought down, Ben," one of the men said. "I do believe it's dead!"

Captain Wyatt rode up on his horse. He still had his rifle drawn, and it was his gun that had fired right after Ben's.

"That's a grizzly bear, Ben. They can be pretty mean and aggressive. That was a brave thing you did."

Then everyone's attention turned toward the meadow. Thomas Benson was picking up the limp form of his youngest son, Tommy, whose red hair was bright in the sunset.

"Oh no! Not Tommy!" Brenna cried.

Everyone made their way to where Thomas stood holding Tommy who, miraculously, was stirring.

"He's had the wind knocked out of him, but I think he'll be okay," Thomas said shakily. Tommy was coming around and he looked groggily at everyone. Ruth and Mary Benson ran up, and Ruth threw her arms around the thin boy.

"Tommy! Are you all right?" she cried.

"My head hurts," Tommy replied.

"That's what you get for wrestling with a bear!" Mary piped, and some of the men laughed with relief.

Hans Hansson walked up and clapped his son on the back. "You've been a crack shot since you were twelve. Good shooting, son." Everyone congratulated Ben, who was still shaken by the whole thing. Brenna would not let go of him. She was trembling. Just a few moments ago, she was helping her mother make bread. It could have gone differently.

Captain Wyatt spoke from his horse. "We need to be extra careful in this heavy timber. This bear attack was unusual, and I don't want to scare anyone more than they already are, but this is grizzly country. There's other wild animals too—black bear, mountain lions, bobcats. Just be vigilant." He turned his attention back to Ben. "When did you see the bear?"

"I was working from the back of the wagon and watching the youngsters playing when I saw him come out of those trees over yonder," Ben said indicating the dark trees to the left. I shouted at the children to warn them, and they screamed and scattered when it growled. I guess that attracted the bear and he chased after them. My Sharps was in the back of the wagon and it was loaded, so I took aim and shot him, but I must have missed."

"You didn't miss, son. You hit him but you didn't kill him," Captain Wyatt said. "You did get his attention, though. It was your third shot that killed him. Mine was just extra." Everyone chuckled.

"Ben, I don't know how to thank you," Thomas Benson said. "If it hadn't been for you, Tommy might..." His voice trailed off.

"Thanks, Ben," Tommy said tremulously.

Ben ruffled Tommy's hair. "You were running pretty fast, Tommy. I think you could've outrun him if your legs were a few inches longer." Everyone laughed as they headed back to their wagons with their children safely in their arms.

Brenna still clung to Ben's arm. She couldn't stop shaking. He turned to her and brushed the hair from her eyes. He regarded her solemnly.

"I'm alright, Brenna."

"Yes. Yes, I know that," she said, her tears flowing again.

"Then what is it?"

Her intense blue eyes looked into his. "I was making bread five minutes ago," she said. Her voice had an urgency that he didn't understand. Ben tilted his head and looked at her, trying to understand her. The meadow was empty except for the two of them. The last rays of the sun created a halo behind her riotous dark hair. "That's how quickly things can change. What if you hadn't been working at the back of your wagon? What if you hadn't had your rifle right there?" She was gripping his arm tightly. "What if you hadn't been able to load your gun the third time?"

"But I did, Brenna," Ben said quietly.

"Yes, I know that!" she cried. "But will it happen this way the next time?" Her face was streaked with tears. Ben folded her in his arms.

"Brenna, we can't think like that. If we do, we'll never have the courage to do anything."

"Marry me, Ben." Her words were muffled in his shirt, but he heard what she said. He pushed her at arm's length and looked at her closely. She noted the characteristic twinkle in the corners of his eyes. He smiled broadly then, his eyes slanting upwards.

"I think I'm supposed to ask that question of you," he said sweetly.

"I don't care, Ben. I just know that I want to be with you always. I want to be your wife and have your children," Brenna said passionately.

"Whoa! Let's not have children just yet." He suddenly grew serious. "For now, let's say we're engaged, and if you still feel the same way about me when we get to Oregon City, I'll ask you properly."

He bent his head and gently kissed Brenna. It was the seal on a verbal contract that she had every intention of holding him to in Oregon City.

Medicine Bag

Chapter Twenty-Eight

Umatilla
September 24, 1852
Mile 1769

The wagon train was on a much-needed lay-by after crossing the Blue Mountains. The ascent had been difficult, with everyone having to help each other get the wagons up the steep and rocky trail. Then the descent had been treacherous. Ropes had been tied to the backs of wagons to keep them from hurtling downhill. People and stock were exhausted. When Captain Wyatt announced the lay-by, a few of the travelers objected.

"We're so close. I say we push on through!" one man said vehemently. Others were agreeing.

"This is not a vote, Mr. Peters," Captain Wyatt said evenly. "We'll spend a day here and rest up for the final leg of this journey. We're still two weeks from The Dalles. Then we'll either float down the

Columbia River to Fort Vancouver or take the Barlow pass over the mountains. We've had it easy compared to what's up ahead."

Everyone looked nervously at one another. They had grown to respect Captain Wyatt, and no one said another word of objection.

In the Benson's camp, Ruth was nursing baby Mattie and keeping a watchful eye on the pot bubbling over the fire. Deborah wanted attention from her mother, but Ruth was trying to prepare dinner and take care of the fretful infant. "Deborah, stop pestering me! Can't you see I'm busy? Now go and find Tommy."

"My head hurts, and I hurt my biggest toe…see?" Ruth barely glanced at the petulant girl. This had been a regular scenario since Mattie was born. Every day Deborah had a new complaint. Ruth was amazed at how many problems a four-year-old could come up with. If it wasn't a physical ailment, it was boredom, or Tommy was teasing her, or the horse had looked at her funny.

She had expected two-year-old Annie to be the one to protest the new addition to the family, but Annie had turned into her mother's little helper, wanting to be close to Mattie, her new sister. Ruth was pleased that Annie was so enamored with the baby, but it was frustrating to have her underfoot all day long, insisting on helping with all of the baby tasks and keeping up a steady stream of mostly indecipherable conversation. Mattie was colicky, and although Rebecca and Mary were helpful, Ruth was the only one who could feed her, and it seemed like this baby wanted to be fed every waking moment.

"Deborah, go and find Tommy or Mary. They can look at your toe and wash it for you."

Deborah shook her head, her blond curls bobbing. "Mary's not here. I don't want my toe washed. That will hurt. I need some medicine," Deborah whined.

"Don't be silly, child. You don't need medicine. Tell Rebecca to come and take the baby. I have to get dinner ready." Ruth frowned at the stormy face of her third youngest. It had been a long day, and there were still many chores to do before she would be able to catch a few hours of sleep. She was in no mood for Deborah's theatrics.

Deborah opened her mouth to protest, but Ruth was quicker. "Go, Deborah. Find Rebecca."

Deborah stuck her lower lip out as far as she could, but her mother wasn't looking. She turned and left the campsite, shoulders sagging, small feet dragging in the dirt.

She found Rebecca with James Cardell, Sam, and her father. They were all attempting to settle the colt so that Thomas could doctor its foot.

"Hold that can closer, Sam," Thomas said. He had the colt's foreleg bent in his arms. James had mixed a concoction of herbs, camphor, and neat's-foot oil to dry out the foot and hoof. The wet weather had been hard on the stock, and the colt had been favoring his foot for a few days.

"Rebecca, my toe hurts," Deborah said when she got close to her big sister.

The colt struggled, and James and Rebecca tried to hold him steady while Thomas cleaned the foot.

"Deborah, get back!" Rebecca yelled. Deborah stepped back a few paces. She was a little frightened of the big animal that now looked menacing. His eyes were wild and his nostrils flared with the smell of the unfamiliar unguent. He snorted loudly while he attempted to free his leg, but Thomas held on.

"Rebecca, Mommy needs you!"

"Hold his head, Rebecca," Thomas yelled.

"I'm trying, Dad—he's very strong!"

"James, pick up his rear leg on the other side. Sam, be quick now. As soon as I finish cleaning out the foot, paint the stuff all over the inside, and then get the hoof. Ready everyone?"

"Rebecca, did you hear me?" shouted Deborah. She watched the four of them struggling with the colt, and that made her even more fearful of the animal. She backed up a few more paces. If four big people were having such a hard time with the horse, he must be very powerful. She momentarily forgot about her toe while she watched the struggle.

"Okay—let him go, James," Thomas gasped. "Let's take a break for a minute before we try again. Sam, you have to be quicker."

"Dad, I'm trying, but he won't stand still!" Sam's frustration showed on his face.

"Rebecca, my biggest toe is hurting." Deborah began to cry piteously. "Mommy won't give me medicine. No one is listening to me! My head hurts, too!" Her voice rose to a high-pitched squeal.

"Deborah, go tell your mother that Rebecca will help her in a few minutes. Stop your crying now. Can't you see we're busy?" Thomas said sternly, wiping the back of his head with his neckerchief. Sweat dripped down his face. He looked at the colt that now stood calmly.

"Okay, let's talk this through before we try again."

Deborah walked dejectedly back to their wagon. It was hard for the four-year-old to understand why no one was paying attention to her when her head and her toe hurt. Everyone was too busy. She leaned against the back of the wagon and considered what she could do to help herself. Sometimes Mommy put a wet rag on her forehead when she wasn't feeling good. She climbed into the back of the wagon to find a cloth to use. There on the shelf was the medicine bag. She had seen Mommy use medicines from the bag many times. Once she had taken the bag off the shelf to look inside, and Mommy had taken it from her and told her not to touch it. Maybe there was something in it that would make her feel better. Her small fingers closed around the little bottle of laudanum. It was a powerful narcotic that had many uses to pioneers. In moderation, it could mask pain and calm nerves. Deborah unscrewed the cap. It was medicine, so it would help her toe feel better.

An hour later, everyone was gathered at the campfire for the evening meal. Rebecca was dishing up the biscuits and gravy and the wild onions Mary and Tommy had dug. Mattie was in her usual place, sound asleep in a makeshift sling around Ruth's chest.

"Sorry I couldn't come and help you, Ma," Rebecca said. "Deborah told me you needed me, but I had to help Dad with the colt."

"Yeah, that horse is really strong and stubborn!" Sam added.

"Where is Deborah?" Ruth queried, looking around at all the faces.

"She's sound asleep in the back of the wagon," Tommy quipped.

"Thank goodness for that," Sam said. "She was really crabby." They all chuckled, recalling Deborah's latest drama.

"I asked her to help us dig onions, but she said her toe hurt," Mary added.

"She's had a rough time of it with the new sister," Thomas said, getting to his feet. "I'll go see if she's hungry." He walked towards the back of the wagon as Sam began to tell the story of how they finally got the medicine on the colt's foot.

Suddenly there was a strangled scream from the wagon. Sam stopped talking. All heads turned towards the sound. The scream came again, and Ruth jumped to her feet spilling her plate. A terrible sense of dread came over her.

"Thomas! Thomas, what's wrong!" She rushed to the wagon. The rest of them jumped up. Plates of food and cups of tea spilled into the dirt. Thomas stepped from the wagon with the limp body of Deborah in his arms. His face contorted in pain as he looked at his wife.

"She's not breathing!" He bent his head to the little bundle and sobbed.

Ruth screamed and took Deborah's face between her hands. "Wake up! Deborah, baby, wake up!" But the little head fell softly against her father's chest.

"Thomas, give her to me!" James cried, and he laid the limp little girl on the ground and put his head on her chest, hoping for a heartbeat. He placed two fingers on her neck but there was no pulse. He lifted the eyelids, and blue eyes rolled back into the small head. The little body was cold. He looked from Thomas to Ruth and shook his head.

"I'm sorry," he whispered.

"No!" Ruth screamed. She flung herself on the ground, gathering up her daughter. Mattie, awake in her sling, cried fitfully, suffocating under the weight of her older sister. "She was just fine. How could this happen? She was just fine!"

Thomas knelt down and took Deborah from Ruth. His face was tortured and he could barely get the words out.

"I found the medicine bag and the empty bottle of laudanum next to her in the wagon."

For a moment, there was shocked silence from the little group hovering over Thomas, Ruth, and Deborah. Then realization set in, and Ruth, head back, eyes squeezed shut, opened her mouth in a silent scream.

The sound that finally came from deep within Ruth was a sound none of them would ever forget. It echoed off the canyon walls and penetrated the darkness. It was the sound of a mother grieving for her lost child. It was the sound that sorrow would make if it had a voice.

Grief

Chapter Twenty-Nine

Much later, the Benson camp was quiet. All the children were finally asleep. Next to Ruth, Thomas was still, but she knew he was awake. There were no more tears, and no words—only an emptiness along with exhaustion. She was more tired than she had ever been, but she knew she would not sleep. She heard one of the horses whinny, and another answer from a wagon close by. An owl hooted softly in the distance. The sound brought back a memory of a night not long ago when Deborah had come to her in the early morning hours, afraid of the owl sound.

"It's just a bird, Deborah. It's an owl. They sleep during the day and they're awake at night."

"It doesn't sound like a bird." She rubbed her eyes with her small fists and crawled next to her mother. Ruth remembered the warmth of her little body snuggled close. "Why doesn't it say 'chirp-chirp' like the other birds?"

"I guess it wants to talk differently, but it's still a bird."

Deborah was quiet, thinking about what her mother said. Suddenly her face brightened. "Like Mrs. Mueller! She talks funny, but she's a lady like you, mommy." Ruth chuckled, telling Deborah that Mrs. Mueller was from Germany, a country far away, and that she had an accent. "That's why she sounds different from us."

Ruth felt her throat closing as her mind flooded with memories of Deborah. Then the last memory came rushing in.

"Mommy, my biggest toe hurts." What had she done? In her mind's eye, she saw herself as a monster, shrieking at her daughter to go away! Ruth's eyes were wide, staring unseeing into the darkness as she relived Deborah's last minutes. She remembered frowning at her daughter, and telling her to find Rebecca. *What would have happened if I had taken the few seconds to look at her toe, hug her, and tell her she would be all right?* she asked herself silently. A heavy weight settled on her chest, and she could barely breathe. Why hadn't she put the medicine bag out of reach? She was responsible for Deborah's death. It was her fault. Her hands went to the ache in her throat.

"Thomas! Thomas, I'm so sorry," she croaked, hardly able to speak. Her hand searched for Thomas in the darkness, but when she found him, he turned away from her.

James and Rebecca sat together in the darkness, the campfire reduced to coals, the only sounds from crickets and the occasional night bird. Rebecca had finally fallen asleep, her head lying heavily on James's chest. His arms encircled her protectively. She had always been so strong—his rock. Tonight she had been inconsolable, and he had been there for her. But he wasn't feeling very strong now. Within the quiet came the heavy sadness.

He had grown so close to the Benson family, and little Deborah had been a joy to him. He thought about her quick smile and bubbling giggles; her endearing habit of taking his hand when she wanted attention; the way she pouted when she wasn't happy about something. She had been a bright light in his life, so quickly extinguished. He pressed his cheek against the top of Rebecca's head and realized his face was wet with tears. From inside the wagon, he heard Mattie cry. Poor Ruth. The demands of an infant wouldn't wait for grief. Rebecca stirred in his arms.

"Mattie. Ma. I should help her," she mumbled.

"Shh. Your mother has her. You need to rest, Rebecca."

Rebecca closed her eyes, but Deborah's angelic face floated in her mind. She remembered her little sister's constant questions. She usually had patience with the child, but not earlier today. "Deborah, get back!" she had yelled, ignoring the girl's crying. Now her sister was gone. What had she done? Why couldn't she have been more understanding? More tears made their way down her face. She would never forgive herself.

Mary had cried herself to sleep, but now she was awake again. She could hardly comprehend the meaning of her sister's death. She had never had anyone close to her die before, and she felt helpless and alone. Part of her feeling of isolation was because of the lie. She hadn't meant to lie. She just hadn't told the truth, and now she never could tell anyone what had really happened. Her mind went back to earlier in the day. She and Tommy had been sent with a bucket to dig wild onions for dinner. It would be fun, and Mary had made a game of it.

"I bet I can dig more onions than you, Tommy," she said, as they left the campsite.

"We'll see about that!" Tommy replied. "I'll go back and get another bucket so we can keep our onions separate."

"Where are you going, Mary?" Deborah asked, running up breathlessly.

Mary frowned at the little girl. "I thought your toe was sore, Deborah."

"It's better now!" Deborah exclaimed happily. "See?" She stuck her foot out for Mary's inspection. Mary looked at the toe and could see nothing wrong with it.

"That's funny. You were just complaining about how much it hurt."

"But it's better, now. Can I go with you and Tommy?"

"You'd better stay here, Deborah. You're too little for this game."

"No I'm not! I'm not little! Please, Mary. Please let me come!"

"No, Deborah!" Mary said as she saw Tommy returning with his bucket. "Don't follow us! Come on, Tommy." They ran off quickly, laughing, leaving her behind. Mary glanced back once to make sure the little sister wasn't following them, and she saw Deborah's crushed face. She remembered thinking they had outsmarted her. Then later at dinner, she told everyone that Deborah didn't want to go along with them because of her sore toe.

Her tears ran freely again. Deborah was gone. She had died because of Mary's meanness. If only she had let her tag along, Deborah would still be here! The burden of her lie rested on the eleven-year-old's heart. As she drifted off to sleep again, Mary swore to herself she would never tell anyone what she had done. She was too ashamed.

Tommy could hear Mary tossing and turning. He didn't want to talk to her. He didn't want to talk to anyone. He kept seeing Deborah asleep in the back of the wagon. He hadn't suspected that anything was wrong. He was happy she was sleeping so that he wouldn't be told to watch her. He purposely walked away quietly so he wouldn't wake her up, and he didn't tell anyone where she was. She had been a real problem for him lately. Ever since Mattie had been born she was always whining, and he was tired of being asked to amuse her. He had been happy to find her fast asleep. He hadn't known she had drunk the medicine. He hadn't known she would never wake up. The realization slowly came to him that if he had told someone where she was when he first saw her, maybe they could have helped her. Maybe she would still be alive. The convulsive sobs welled up and out of him, and he turned his face into his blanket to hide them. *"It's too late now,"* Tommy said to himself. *"You could have saved her if you hadn't been so selfish!"*

Thomas felt Ruth reach for him and he turned away from his wife. He couldn't take her sympathy now. His grief was a live thing inside of him, and he could barely control it. Deborah, his little flower, his bright little star, was gone, and the last thing he had said to her had been an admonishment, showing his annoyance with her. He remembered her sweet face. She had looked so sad before she turned and walked away. He had been busy with the colt, and he hadn't given her a second thought.

He remembered all the other nights. Before she fell asleep, she had to have a hug and kiss from Daddy. She had told him she couldn't go to sleep without his hug and kiss. He had always humored her because she was so sweet. Deborah had a way with him that melted his heart, and she usually was able to get what she wanted from him. She had learned how to wink when she was just two years old, and sometimes she would tell him a "secret" and wink at him like it was something just between the two of them.

Thomas felt vulnerable and this frightened him. It was an alien emotion, and he didn't know what to do or where to turn. He couldn't remember ever having to ask for help, and he wouldn't know how to go about it if he did. He felt responsible for Deborah's death, and he thought Ruth looked at him accusingly. He was supposed to keep this family together, and now they were torn apart. Ruth had reached out to him, but he couldn't accept her sympathy. He couldn't give in to any more emotion. It was too painful. It would be better to just keep it all to himself; better for everyone. He would deal with it sometime later.

A cold wind came out of the north and blew through the camp. People snuggled more deeply into their bedrolls. The chill descended on the Benson camp. It settled into the space between Ruth and Thomas. It seeped into blankets and there was no getting warm. James carried Rebecca to her bedroll and covered her gently. He stood up and breathed deeply. The promise of winter was in the air, and the warm autumn days were over. Deborah was gone, and things would never be the same. He could feel it. He just hoped this family would survive.

Confessions

Chapter Thirty

Mile 1788

James Cardell handed the basket of dried apples to Nellie.

"Thank you so much, James. I know John will appreciate the apple cobbler I'll make from these. He has such a sweet tooth! Here's the flour I promised you."

"Thanks, Nellie. This will help tide us over till we get to Oregon City."

"How is everyone doing, James? I haven't seen much of Ruth or Thomas lately. I know Deborah's death was a hard blow. How are they coping with it?"

James was startled by the question and hardly knew how to respond. No one in the Benson family was talking about Deborah. He sighed heavily, and then he said, "I don't know, Nellie. The Bensons are very polite and helpful towards each other, but something is wrong. I can't quite put my finger on what it is. It's like they are all too careful and cautious with each other—even Mary and Tommy. I know they are still privately grieving. I don't know what to do to help them."

Nellie looked concerned. The Benson family had always been so vibrant and the center of the wagon train community.

"James, sometimes these things take time to work out. I know they appreciate your presence and support. Give it a little more time, and I'm sure things will change."

"I hope so, Nellie. Right now the family is broken, and I feel helpless watching each of them suffer. Even Rebecca is different. She's serious all of the time, and she has a look on her face that doesn't invite conversation. I'm trying to be understanding, but I feel like I'm in the way a lot of the time."

Nellie remembered how she had felt after her husband had died. She hadn't known how to talk to anyone about her feelings, and it had taken her a long time to come to terms with life without him. She looked at James's careworn expression. "Death is never easy for the survivors, James. Rebecca just needs her space right now, and time to heal. I know she and Deborah were very close."

"Yes, Rebecca became a second mother to Deborah and Annie when Ruth was struggling with her pregnancy with Mattie. Then when Mattie was born, it took all of Ruth's strength to take care of her. She hasn't been an easy baby."

"Don't give up, James. This family has always been strong and supportive of one another. They need you now."

Later Nellie discussed James Cardell's dilemma with her husband Reverend John. "He feels helpless, John. The Bensons mean so much to him, and he doesn't know how to help them. Is there anything we can do?"

John looked thoughtful. "Nellie, this family has to accept their grief and allow each other to mourn. I'll visit them. Maybe I can help them."

That evening Ruth Benson made dinner while Rebecca amused Mattie and Annie. Ruth called everyone to come and eat, and they had just settled around the fire when Reverend John walked into the firelight. Thomas looked startled but quickly covered it and rose to greet him.

"Good evening, Reverend. Have you eaten? We'd be honored if you would join us."

Reverend John extended his hand and shook Thomas's. "Thank you, Thomas. I would like to join you, but I haven't come empty handed." He handed Thomas a stollen his mother, Mrs. Mueller, had made. "It's a recipe from the old country."

"Ah, smells wonderful!"

Rebecca quickly got up and poured Reverend John a cup of tea. John looked around the campfire at the faces of the Bensons— faces that looked pleasant but strained. Ruth passed around the plates of beans, biscuits, and stewed buffalo meat.

"Would it be alright if we say grace?" Reverend John asked.

Eyes lowered to the ground, and even in the flickering fire-light, John could see Thomas's face redden.

"Please do, Reverend. We haven't said grace for a little while now." His voice faltered.

Reverend John nodded at Thomas and lowered his head.

"Bless this food, Lord, and provide us with your bounty in the days ahead as our journey comes to an end. And bless this family, who you have smiled upon again with little Mattie. We are forever grateful for your abundant blessings. And as we remember dear Deborah, safe in your arms now, we ask for your infinite love and understanding with each other. We miss Deborah terribly, but we know that she is happy and alive in your eternal kingdom. Amen."

"Amen," came from a few voices, and silence from others. A choked sob came from Mary.

"What is it, child? What troubles you?" Reverend John asked gently.

Mary's tears flowed freely now. She could not control her sobs as her grief opened up and spilled out of her. The rest of the Bensons looked with dread at Mary. This was territory they had been avoiding.

"I know she is with God, and I know she is happy, but I miss her and I wish she was still here," Mary cried as she wiped her face on her sleeve. "Sometimes it feels like she is still here. Sometimes I think about the day she died, and it's like it's happening all over again, and I think that if I had done things differently she wouldn't be dead now. Like maybe it's been a dream and I've woken up and Deborah is sleeping next to me."

Rebecca gasped from across the campfire. "I've had a dream like that, too. I dreamt that I listened to Deborah when she told me her toe hurt. I gave her a big hug, kissed her cheek, and promised to look at it when we finished with the horse. When I woke up, it took me a few minutes to realize that I had been dreaming and Deborah was still gone." Tears trickled down Rebecca's cheeks. She hadn't shared this with anyone, and she was amazed with herself that she was talking about it. She reached for James, and he wrapped his arms around her.

"But she would still be here if it wasn't for me!" Mary cried. "I lied to you about Deborah." She looked from her mother to her father. Ruth and Thomas looked aghast. Mary continued. "She wanted to come with me and Tommy to dig onions, but I told her she couldn't. I sent her back to the wagon and we ran away from her! I laughed about leaving her here! Now she's gone forever!" Mary's voice had reached a fever pitch and she stood and covered her face with her hands.

Ruth looked incredulous. She could hardly take it in. Mary had been blaming herself. She stood up, walked across the campfire to where Mary huddled within herself, and took the small girl in her arms. "Mary, don't do this. It's not your fault. It's my fault. I sent Deborah away because I was busy—too busy to pay attention to her. You didn't do anything wrong, Mary."

Tommy had been trying to keep himself in control, but watching his mother comfort Mary was too much. He stood up. His face was tortured. "I saw her sleeping in the back of the wagon," he cried. "I snuck away so I wouldn't have to put up with her whining. I didn't tell anyone where she was, and she died. She would still be here if I had told you where she was. There would have been time to save her!"

Thomas watched his family falling apart before his eyes. He looked from one to the other, feeling their pain and his own. His wife clung to Mary, and Rebecca had taken Tommy in her arms. Tommy was crying softly.

"What have you done, Reverend?" Thomas's voice was angry. "Why did you have to bring up Deborah? We were getting over her and now you've stirred everything up again."

Before Reverend John could reply, Ruth turned on Thomas.

"How dare you! You've kept this family quiet and desperate because you haven't wanted to talk about Deborah, and we have all needed to talk. I've felt responsible for Deborah's death, and now I find out that these children have kept their guilt within them since she died. What is the point, Thomas? Why?"

Thomas looked stricken. He felt like an outsider as he watched his family comfort one another. He had never heard such harsh words from his wife. "Ruth, I thought you blamed me. I thought you all did," Thomas looked at his family. "No one did anything with Deborah that we hadn't done a hundred times over. I don't know why she died. I should have prevented it somehow. I promised you I would keep this family safe and I've let you down."

Ruth's face filled with compassion as she heard the tortured words from her husband. She walked over to where Thomas was standing. He looked lost and vulnerable. She took his hand in hers and said softly, "Thomas, you are the head of this family, but that doesn't mean you can do everything. We have to help each other now. You don't have to try to be strong anymore. We know you're strong. We need you to grieve with us."

"Dad." It was thirteen-year-old Sam, who had been very quiet since Deborah's death. "Dad, you told me once to not be so hard on myself, and now you're doing it. I haven't been able to talk to you about anything lately—or to anyone else. Everyone has been so closed up. All of you have been blaming yourselves for Deborah." He looked around at his family. "It was an accident, Dad." Sam's eyes searched his father's.

"I'm so sorry, Sam." Thomas's voice broke. He hugged his oldest son. "I thought it would be easier if we didn't talk about Deborah. It hurts so much to talk about her." Thomas looked at Reverend John. "I don't know where to begin, Reverend."

Reverend John looked around the campfire at the grieving faces of this family. There was a lot of work to do, but he knew they were strong enough and loved each other enough to do it.

"Thomas, I'm going to leave you to your family and your dinner. If it's agreeable to all of you, I would like to come back tomorrow evening and we can talk some more."

"Thank you, Reverend. I think we would all appreciate that," Thomas said as he looked at his family. Ruth's eyes were hopeful and more alive than they had been since Deborah's death. Rebecca and James stood together, arms around each other, and Mary, Tommy, and Sam looked relieved.

Thomas realized that he was indeed the keeper of this family. They had all been silent because he had wanted it that way. Reverend John extended his hand to Thomas, and Thomas took it, drew the Reverend into his arms, and embraced him. He felt something let go inside of him—a hardness that he had been carefully nurturing, and in its place, his tears finally came and he didn't try to hide them or stop them. The two men stood for a few moments holding each other. When they parted, Reverend John said, "You're going to be alright," and Thomas believed it was true.

Mile 1819

A few days later, Tommy and Mary Benson were walking next to the wagon. Sam and Thomas were driving the team, and Ruth was in the wagon with Mattie. The baby had been fretting all morning.

"I wonder why Mattie's so upset," Tommy said.

"Ma thinks it's just colic and she'll get over it when she gets a little older," Mary replied.

"Do all babies get colic?"

"All the babies I've ever seen have had it."

"I don't remember Annie being so crabby. Did she have colic?"

"Yes, and Deborah did, too. I remember Ma wondering if Deborah would ever stop crying."

They both paused. They hadn't mentioned Deborah in any conversation except when they purposefully discussed her death with Reverend John and the family.

"Tommy! I just talked about Deborah and it didn't hurt!"

Tommy looked at his sister. She was smiling but tears rolled down her face.

"Why are you crying then?"

"Because I'm happy, Tommy. Don't you see?" Mary said excitedly. "I want to talk about Deborah because that way she will always be close to me. It's hurt so much to talk about her and think about her, but just now, I didn't think about the sadness. I was just remembering her, and that makes me happy."

Tommy looked at his sister doubtfully. How could someone cry and be happy? Maybe this is what Dad meant when he said he never would pretend to understand women.

Inside the wagon, little Mattie had finally fallen asleep. Ruth had overheard Mary and Tommy's conversation, and she cried softly. Someday she hoped she would be at the place where Mary was. For now, she followed Reverend John's advice and just took every day as it came. She tried not to look back or look ahead. What had he said? She searched her memory.

"The past is gone and the future doesn't exist. All we have is right here and now."

It had taken her awhile to wrap her head around that thought. She understood the first part. She knew she couldn't change the past, but the wisdom of the second part eluded her. She remembered when Sam had objected to Reverend John's statement.

"But there's always a future. We're living in yesterday's future."

That had seemed to make sense, and Ruth had looked at Sam with admiration. He was such a smart boy!

Reverend John had smiled. "I know it seems that way, Sam, but yesterday you didn't know you would cut your finger with your knife today, did you?"

"No," Sam agreed, looking at the cut on his index finger wrapped with a bit of cloth.

"The future is not a place or a thing. It's nothing except what we make of it, and so it's different for everyone. The only thing that is real is right now. Do you understand?"

"I'm trying, Reverend John."

"Just try to remember that the only time you can do anything about is right now."

Ruth looked down at her sleeping infant. Mattie looked angelic. She smiled in her sleep and Ruth's heart melted. She suddenly realized the truth of Reverend John's statement. Just a few moments ago, Mattie was crying and Ruth felt frustrated. How quickly she had forgotten her frustration when she was just now watching her daughter smile so sweetly. The past was just a memory. What happens in the next moment, hour, or day doesn't exist yet. She felt lighter. What could she do right now? She could love her daughter and enjoy holding her small body next to hers, and that was a great comfort to Ruth.

Shivaree

Chapter Thirty-One

September 30, 1852
Mile 1833

The night was softly falling when Reverend John took Rebecca Benson's hand and placed it in James Cardell's. For a moment, the only sounds were the cricket songs and the lowing of a cow in the distance. Rebecca looked into James's eyes. He looked so serious. She smiled at him and squeezed his hand lightly, and he visibly relaxed. He thought she had never looked so lovely. The sun had set behind her and the prairie sky was a palate of reds and oranges. It lit her chestnut hair on fire. Mary had made her a wreath of wild flowers to wear in her hair, and the yellows and golds framed Rebecca's young face. Her dress was fresh and her moccasins new.

"Dearly beloved," Reverend John began. There was an almost audible sigh of relaxation from the onlookers. As the stars appeared one by one, all seemed right in the universe. Everyone present had watched the love blossom between James and Rebecca. Though hardship and tragedy had visited often, the two young lovers had supported each other, and now everyone had gathered to support them.

The ceremony was short, and night had settled in when Reverend John said, "You may kiss your bride." Tears glistened on Ruth's cheeks. Thomas squeezed her shoulders and kissed the top of her head. She was so happy for Rebecca.

Everyone cheered as James complied with the pastor's request. Then there were many well wishes, a few small gifts, and much singing, dancing, eating, and merry making. Emily hugged Rebecca warmly. "You and James are perfect for each other, Rebecca. I know you'll be so happy."

Brenna and Ben came up, grabbed the two newlyweds, and engaged them in a lively dance. They finally collapsed in laughter and exhaustion.

"Let's get out of here," James whispered into Rebecca's ear a little while later. Rebecca giggled as they sneaked off into the shadows and made their way to their tent. They stopped at the entry and James swooped Rebecca up into his arms. She squealed delightedly. He stood holding her for a few moments.

"I wish this was a proper house."

"Wherever you are is the only home I need," Rebecca replied softly.

James ducked through the entry, carrying her into the tent. Once inside, they both drew in a breath. Someone had gone to great lengths to make the meager tent look like something out of *The Arabian Nights*. Dark tapestries and lengths of fabric hung around the interior. Candles of various sizes cast warm shadows from their flickering lights. There was even an oriental carpet spread out on the ground.

"Oh! It's so beautiful!" Rebecca exclaimed with pleasure.

James looked from the decorations to Rebecca's face. "It's nice," he said, smiling, "but you're beautiful."

"I'm so happy, James."

He set her down gently and put his hands on her shoulders. "You are the best thing that's ever happened to me, Rebecca. I promise I will always take care of you. I love you so much." He bent to kiss her tenderly when a great racket commenced from outside the tent. They both jumped at the raucous noise, which then was joined by many voices singing boisterously.

"What in the world…" Rebecca said.

James drew back the tent flap and saw what appeared to be fifty people all banging pots, pans, and various tools together. He and Rebecca stepped outside the tent and the noise stopped. Everyone grinned at the newlyweds.

"What's going on here," James said, laughing.

"Why, we're giving you two a proper shivaree," Old man Tucker said gleefully.

"Back home it's called a serenade," Mrs. Markham said, and with that, they all commenced to singing and banging on their makeshift instruments again. After one bawdy song, James said, "I thank you all, now if you will please…" Someone started up another song and when that one was finished, yet another was sung, all accompanied by their makeshift instruments. By this time, folks were so tickled with the exasperation on James's face and the patience on Rebecca's that they couldn't help but giggle, and the song dissolved into laughter.

"Now it's time to kidnap the groom," someone said. Then James went into action. He picked up a pitchfork that was leaning against the tent and brandished it at the crowd.

"Oh, no, you don't," he said. "Your songs have been real nice. Now it's time for all of you to go get some sleep and leave me and my bride to our rest."

"Ha! Your rest, you say?" Came a voice from the back, and the crowd laughed uproariously. James's face wore a menacing smile, and although people thought he was joking, no one wanted to test the new groom.

"Alright, son. We'll leave you two be. We couldn't let the night go by without a shivaree to celebrate your marriage," Old man Tucker said.

James stood the pitchfork up next to him but he kept his hand on it. "Well, we thank you all kindly. I must say you are in fine voice tonight."

Everyone laughed.

"And whoever decorated our tent," Rebecca said, "it's beautiful. Thank you."

Then there were handshakes and hugs, and soon the newlyweds were alone again.

"Did you know they were going to do that?" James asked as they returned to the tent.

"I had no idea!" Rebecca said, laughing. "It's very sweet, though."

James looked thoughtful. "These people all mean a lot to me. This is a night that I will always remember."

Rebecca took his hands in hers. "You mean a lot to them. That's why they did this for us."

He looked at her a long moment. "I thought I left my family back east, but I've gained a new family. When your folks took me in after I lost all my trees in the Snake, I thought that was very kind of them. But it's become more than kindness. It's bigger than that." He took a long breath and let it out. "After everything that's happened, I feel like we all have a bond that goes deeper than kindness. We've been through things no one should have to experience. So much pain and loss, and so much joy, too. It's hard to describe, but I would do anything for them."

"Yes," Rebecca said, drawing him into her embrace. "Yes, you're right, James, but it's not hard to describe. It's simply love." She kissed him sweetly.

"Why don't you blow out the candles," she whispered, and James happily carried out the first request from his new bride. As he put out each candle, he made little promises to himself, and they all included love, kindness, and joy.

Birthday Gift

Chapter Thirty-Two

Mile 1842

The rain had been steady for two days and they hadn't made good time. Captain Wyatt was encouraging everyone to push on. He rode up alongside the Browns' wagon. Abel was in the driver's seat. Emily was inside the wagon with Buster, sheltered from the rain. Dan Christopher and Clem Morris were leading the oxen.

"Mr. Brown, your stock would move more easily if you got down and helped them along." He had to raise his voice above the rain.

"Christopher and Morris are helping."

"Your weight is an extra burden, Mr. Brown."

"Those oxen are strong, Captain. I'm fine where I am."

"Those beasts are nearly played out, Mr. Brown."

"They only need to last a little longer, Captain, just until we get to The Dalles. Then I'll trade them in for a guide to take us down river."

Captain Wyatt looked long and hard at Abel Brown before he turned his horse and rode off. He wasn't a fool. He knew what Abel had been up to with his card games masquerading as business meetings, but there wasn't a thing he could do about it now. Maybe he could make something happen in Oregon City. Time would tell.

He found the Muellers a few wagons back. Mrs. Mueller was inside the wagon, and Nellie and John were leading the teams. Nellie looked exhausted.

"John, we're going to stop up here in another mile. We'll rest for a couple of hours before we move on."

"Alright, Captain. I think the rest will be very welcomed," John said, glancing at his wife.

Captain Wyatt moved through the train informing the families of his plan. He knew some of them wanted to stop for the night, but he couldn't let that happen. They were a little behind schedule, and he was worried about snow. He had been caught once before three years back. The wagon train had taken the Barlow Road and hadn't gotten very far when a snowstorm had stopped them. Two days later, when the storm passed, they had had to backtrack and take the river route. He didn't care for the river route. There were always mishaps, and invariably, someone drowned—a bitter end to a long and hard journey.

He drew up next to the Hanssons' wagon. "Hans, Mr. Rowe could use your help when we stop in an hour. One of his wheels is coming apart."

"Alright, Captain, I'll take a look at it."

Both Ben and Hans helped anyone in need whether they would get paid or not. Usually if they weren't paid in money, they were compensated with a hot meal or a trade of another sort. Their skills with wagons and stock were invaluable, and they were the only overlanders who were actually making money on this trip.

Except for Mr. Brown, the Captain thought darkly. *He's making a lot of money.*

Two days later the rain had stopped and the sun shone brightly. The air was crisp with the smell of autumn, and the trees wore brilliant hues of reds and golds. Everyone was in good spirits antic-ipating the end of the long journey.

Rebecca was putting finishing touches on Tommy's birthday cake. There had been other birthdays in the past months that had gone uncelebrated in the daily toil of the trail, but Mary had begged Rebecca to make Tommy a birthday cake. She had had to borrow sugar from Emily and eggs from Nellie. The little cake looked forlorn without icing, but she knew it would still be a wel-comed treat. Sam had carefully whittled small sticks to use as can-dles, and these Rebecca spaced evenly around the top of the cake. Then Sam used a torch from the fire to light them.

"Okay, everyone," Rebecca said as she walked to the campfire with the cake.

Little Annie spun in circles clapping, delighted with the cel-ebration. Even Mattie seemed happy and content. Tommy leaned over the small cake and blew out all the candles, and everyone cheered.

"Give us a speech, Tommy," Mary teased.

Tommy stood up, smiling, happy to be the center of attention. He bowed deeply.

"Thank you all for coming to my party," he said. "And thank you, Rebecca, for making this fine birthday cake!" He looked around imploringly at the faces of his family. "Do I have to share it?"

"Cake!" Annie exclaimed, clapping her hands. Everyone laughed.

"Okay," Tommy said with mock resignation. "I guess I'll share."

Rebecca cut the small cake into tiny pieces and passed them around.

"It's really good, Rebecca," Sam said. He had finished his piece in two bites. "Is there any left?"

"No, Sam! You don't get any more. If there's any left, it's Tommy's," Mary said indignantly.

"Who made you queen of the world," Sam said cuttingly.

"Tommy, someone has brought you a gift," Thomas said stand-ing up. He went to the back of the wagon and returned carrying a large and heavy rolled bundle. "Mr. Ames tanned this hide for you.

He thought you might like it." Thomas unrolled the hide and they all looked in silence for a few moments. There was the hide and head of the bear that had chased Tommy in the meadow. It was now a bearskin rug. Its teeth were bared and the eyes were pieces of black stone.

"Wow!" Tommy said. "Is it really mine, Dad?"

Annie crawled into Rebecca's lap, not sure what the mean looking animal would do.

"Yes, it's all yours!"

"You're so lucky!" Sam exclaimed. "Look at those teeth! They almost chomped you, Tommy!"

"That's scary!" Mary said.

Ruth and Rebecca exchanged looks. "That is not going in the house," Ruth said adamantly.

"Ma! It would look so great on the floor in front of the fireplace," Sam said, feeling one of the long incisors.

Ruth looked at Thomas threateningly.

"It's okay, Ma," Tommy said. "I'll put it in my room."

Ruth let the discussion end for now, but there was no way that bear was ever going to have a place in her home. Never!

Sam, Mary, and Tommy were closely examining the head of the bear. Thomas looked at his wife from across the fire. He recognized the determined jaw set on Ruth's face. He smiled to himself. *The bear might end up in the barn*, he thought. That would be the closest Ruth would ever let it get to her family. It had gotten too close when it was alive.

Lost And Found

Chapter Thirty-Three

October 5, 1852
Mile 1883

The wagon train had crossed the Des Chute River and was stopped for the mid-day meal when James Cardell told his wife Rebecca that two oxen were missing.

"Missing? Where could they be?" she replied.

"They can't have gone far. I looked close by but I didn't see them."

"James, we have to find them!"

"Sam and Thomas are helping me look. Thomas saddled Molly and is riding out a ways." James looked worried. They were so close to The Dalles now, and to lose two oxen would be devastating. But they weren't on the prairie, and visibility was compromised by the trees and brush.

"James, what about asking the Indians to help us?" Rebecca asked. When they had made camp, there were a few Indians camped close by.

James looked reluctant, but then he remembered losing his trees in the Snake River because he hadn't asked the Indians for help. He sighed heavily. "Alright, Rebecca, I'll ask them."

James and thirteen-year-old Sam walked over to the Indian camp. Two of the four men stood up when they approached. "Speak English?" James asked.

One of them nodded.

"I've lost two oxen and I could use your help."

The English-speaking Indian turned to the other and spoke in his native language. The other man looked at James and Sam and then back to his friend. He nodded.

"We will help," the first man said, and the two Indians turned and walked to their horses that were tied close by.

James breathed a sigh and he and Sam walked back to camp.

"Why are we asking the Indians for help? Why can't we find them ourselves?" Sam asked.

"Because the Indians know this place. They've lived here a long time, and they know where animals will go."

Sam was thoughtful for a few minutes. "I guess you're right, James. How did you get so smart?"

"Your sister Rebecca is the smart one, Sam. I've had to learn the hard way."

A short while later the two Indians rode into camp leading the oxen with a rope. Thomas had returned disappointed that he hadn't found the beasts. James jumped up from his seat at the campfire and smiled broadly. "You found them!" he exclaimed.

The English-speaking native gestured in the direction from where the oxen had wandered. Sam grabbed the ropes and led the beasts to the front of the wagon.

"How can I pay you?" James asked the men.

The one who could speak English looked around the camp. He saw two of James's shirts hanging from the back of the wagon to dry from Rebecca's washing the night before. He gestured at the shirts.

James looked to where the man was pointing. "You want those shirts?" he asked.

Rebecca was already removing the shirts from the wagon. She walked up to the Indian and handed him the shirts. "Thank you so much," she said, smiling.

The Indian accepted the shirts and smiled back at her. Then they turned their horses and left.

"I was going to bargain with them, Rebecca. Those were my last two shirts!"

"It's worth it, James. They've done us a huge service." She looked at the disappointment on his face. One of the shirts was still in very good condition and he had worn it on their wedding night. "I'll make you a new shirt, James. It will be better than those." She hugged him warmly and he smiled at her.

"I could use some help here," Sam called, and James went to help him with the oxen.

Later that night, snuggled next to Rebecca in their bedroll, James reflected on the day. He hadn't trusted the natives. He had heard so many stories about their treachery before he left Independence on the wagon train. So many friends had warned him that the Indians were thieves and cutthroats. He remembered Mrs. Dougherty, one of his dental patients.

"Be careful, James," she had said, her blue eyes round. "I know a man whose cousins were ambushed by Indians and killed for a cow! They're very sneaky, James. Don't turn your back on them!"

Mr. Fenton, another patient, had related stories of war parties and terrible atrocities from the friend of a friend who had traveled the Oregon Trail two years earlier. Much of the talk around the dinner table in the weeks before he had left had centered on the "savage" Indians. He had been fearful and mistrusting, he realized, and now he knew that it had cost him dearly. He believed now that if he had trusted the native guides at the Snake, he would still have his fruit trees. He sighed loudly and Rebecca stirred.

"What's wrong, James?"

"Nothing, Rebecca, go back to sleep."

She sat up on one elbow. "Not until you tell me what's troubling you."

James could see her eyes shining in the dark, and he knew she was wide-awake now. "I was just thinking about my trees. I was thinking that if I had trusted the Indian guides at the Snake, I might still have them today."

Rebecca paused a long moment. "James, why are you putting so much energy into thinking about what's already happened? You lost the trees. Maybe the Indians could have gotten them safely across the river, and maybe not. It doesn't do any good to keep thinking about it. Think about today instead. You asked the Indians for help and they found the oxen. Now we can make it up the Barlow Road and over the mountain to Oregon City."

"I know, Rebecca, and I'm very grateful. I just wish I hadn't been so fearful of the Indians. I guess I believed all the stories I heard about them."

"We believe what we hear from people we respect, but sometimes they're wrong, James. And just because we hear a story more than once doesn't mean it's true. Often people talk from a place of fear, and fear can be very convincing."

"I wouldn't have believed that earlier, Rebecca, but I do now. I've seen so many examples of kindnesses from the natives. They've shared with us the little they have. Some of them have learned our language, and they've taught us hunting and trapping skills. Many of them are so poor. They're trying to do the best they can, just like us. I guess when I think about my trees, I'm feeling regret. If I could do it over again, I would hire the native pilots."

"You did what you did, James, and it's brought you to where you are now." She wrapped her arms around him. "I don't want you to regret the past, James. We have so much to live for today."

James knew she was right. He felt the truth of it somewhere inside. He resolved then and there to never look back again. He felt himself get lighter. A weight seemed to be lifted from him, and he easily fell asleep in Rebecca's arms.

Down River

Chapter Thirty-Four

———————»《①》«———————

The Dalles
October 8, 1852

"The Barlow Road has been closed due to early snow. For those of you who had planned to take that route, you'll be taking the Columbia River with the rest of us." Captain Wyatt made his pronouncement and left the campfire. Earlier he had briefed everyone on what to expect. Many people were uneasy about the risky Columbia River route, but now they had no choice. The Barlow Road was also treacherous and difficult. It had been opened in 1846 and allowed wagons to skirt the south shoulder of Mount Hood.

Michael Flannigan looked grim. The river crossings had been rough, but he knew this would be far different. It wasn't a crossing; it was a float down river on unwieldy rafts and wagons, and part of it would be done in fast-moving rapids with eddies and unpredictable whirlpools. But it was the only way now.

"What are we going to do, Da?" Conor asked.

"We're going to float down this river, Conor."

"Are we going to build a raft?"

"We have a raft, son. Our wagon is watertight and it will float us down."

Conor looked skeptical. "How will we all fit?" Even though their provisions were greatly diminished, the wagon was still full of everything else they had brought with them, not to mention the buckets, boxes, and utensils hanging off the sides.

"We'll make it work, Conor. We may have to leave some things behind."

The next days were spent readying the wagons they would ride down the river. Everything was unloaded and the insides were caulked with tallow and tar. The wheels and tongues were removed and put inside the wagons. Everything was loaded and balanced, and if a family had one, the featherbed mattress was placed on top. This is where they would ride. Thomas Benson crafted a long pole from a pine log to use to help guide the wagon.

They were all camped close to the fort, and some of the travelers bought or traded for food and provisions. These last hundred miles would be hard, and everyone needed to keep strong for the river trip. The men who were driving the stock overland on the pack trail had left. They would travel over Lolo Pass and the northwest shoulder of Mt. Hood to Eagle Creek and on to Oregon City. Theirs would be a difficult journey also.

The Bensons' large family wouldn't all fit in their wagon, so they spent some time building a raft from pine logs. Some of them would ride in the wagon, and the rest would be guided down by an Indian navigator in the log raft. Thomas traded the last two oxen to the Indian who would be their guide.

Emily and Abel Brown, the Muellers, and some of the others who still had money hired Indians to steer them in canoes downriver. Other Indians would bring their wagons and belongings on rafts. Abel traded his tired oxen for their transport.

A town was growing up around Fort Dalles, and a few of the families decided to stay at the fort over the winter rather than brave the rapids. Work was done at a fever pitch as the overlanders felt the cold fingers of winter sweeping down off the Cascade Mountains.

The morning arrived when most of the travelers would put in to the river. Emily Brown was so nervous she could barely function. "Let's go, Emily. It's time," Abel said as he took her arm and led her to the canoe. Buster dutifully followed his mistress. A tall Indian stood ready to take his position as their guide.

"Mr. Brown," Emily said breathlessly, "I can't breathe!" She was hyperventilating and feeling faint.

Abel took one look at her white face, swooped her up, and put her into the canoe. He gestured to the guide to push off. Buster jumped in and Emily fell backwards in a swoon.

Captain Wyatt had proposed that the Indian guided boats and rafts leave first and the others follow. The Indians were familiar with the rocks and boulders that poked up from under the surface or lay hidden beneath the churning water. They would lead the way and the others would try to keep the same path.

The place where each wagon, raft, and boat put in was calm. One by one they followed each other downriver. Ruth Benson sat in the middle of the raft holding baby Mattie. Mary and Tommy were next to her, and Thomas and the Indian guide steered. Following them was their wagon navigated by James Cardell and Sam, with Rebecca holding on to Annie on top of the featherbed. The children were enjoying this easy float, unaware of the dangers that lay ahead.

"This is fun!" shouted Tommy excitedly.

"It's better than walking!" Sam shouted from the wagon behind the raft.

"At least you have shoes," said Mary, who had worn out her last pair walking to The Dalles. She too was enthralled with the smooth and gently moving watery highway.

Behind them, Michael Flannigan maneuvered his wagon in the water. Kate, Brenna, and Conor were sitting comfortably atop the featherbed mattress.

"Hey, Ben, try and catch up!" Conor yelled to the wagon floating behind theirs.

"Why don't you slow down," Ben yelled back laughing.

After hours floating down river, they pulled into a willow thicket and camped for the night. The children had enjoyed the day immensely. It was like a picnic on the water. They were in high spirits and couldn't understand why the adults were so somber.

The next two days were a repeat of the first day on the river, except the wind had picked up and it was cooler. That evening as they gathered around the campfire, Captain Wyatt spoke to them.

"Tomorrow we will be coming to the narrow part of the gorge where the Columbia River cuts through the Cascade Mountains. It's going to be treacherous, and there will be many rapids, whirlpools, and eddies. Keep the children close. If someone falls overboard, there's little that can be done."

"How far are we from Fort Vancouver?" someone asked.

"We're still over fifty miles away, but some of those miles will go quickly. After the narrows, we'll float downriver to the fort. The chief factor is John McLoughlin. He's a good man and he'll make sure everyone has a roof over their heads and a good meal."

"Where is Oregon City from there?"

"It's another fifteen miles downriver. There's a man named Robert Moore who owns a company called Robin's Nest. He operates a ferry that will take you across the river to Oregon City."

Everyone turned in for the night with mixed emotions: excitement because the end of their long journey was so close at hand and dread over what they would find on the water the next day. Brenna and Ben sat up watching the fire long after everyone else had gone to bed.

"Are you worried about tomorrow?" Ben asked Brenna, putting his arm over her shoulders.

"A little," she admitted. "I wish you could be with me on our wagon."

"Why don't you come on our wagon?" Ben asked.

"I need to help Conor and Ma."

"They'll be alright, Brenna. I really want you to be with me."

Brenna looked at Ben and saw his worry. "I promise to be safe, Ben."

"I'm going to keep you close, Brenna. If you need me, I'll be there."

Rapids

Chapter Thirty-Five

—————⟫(◉)⟪—————

The next morning, the wind was screaming through the canyon. Everyone had a quick meal, and then the men proceeded to load the rafts and wagons. Emily Brown hadn't done well on the river. She was pale and bedraggled, and she didn't care how she looked. Buster shivered next to her. He knew something was wrong with his mistress. She wasn't giving him the attention she usually lavished on him. Abel Brown barely paid any attention to Emily. He knew she would rally when they got to Oregon City.

Rebecca tried to get Emily to drink water and eat something, but Emily turned green at the sight or smell of food, and she could barely keep water in her stomach. James made Emily some herbal tea and that seemed to help. She sipped at the tea and watched the other women hug each other and wish each other well. *I'm going to die*, she thought. *No one will ever find my body, and no one will care.* She felt light-headed and her vision was blurry. She hardly had the strength to get up and move to the canoe when it was time. Buster curled up in her lap and whined softly.

The procession of boats, canoes, and rafts proceeded down the now swiftly moving river. It didn't take long before the gorge narrowed. The cliffs alongside were high and rocky. The river was running faster the further they went. There was a roar ahead, and Emily vaguely wondered if the sound was a monster that would swallow her whole.

Soon, the lead boats rounded a bend and the overlanders saw the source of the loud roar. The rapids stretched ahead of them cascading downward over boulders and around outcroppings of rock. Many of the women screamed at the sight and clutched their children closely. The canoes with Indian guides were in the lead. They deftly avoided the whirlpools and large rocks. The others followed as closely as they could. Emily swooned at the sight of the rapids, and Abel cursed as he tried to balance himself and hold on to her.

"Emily, wake up!" he yelled, but his plea landed on deaf ears.

Ruth Benson clutched a screaming Mattie who was wrapped tightly in her sling around Ruth's body. Mary and Tommy clung to their mother, while Thomas tried to help the Indian guide with the raft, which pitched in the churning water.

In the wagon, Annie was terrified and howled loudly. Rebecca held on to her tightly. James and Sam tried to keep the same course as the raft ahead. Behind them, Michael Flannigan was having trouble with his wagon. It was not balancing properly, and it pitched erratically from side to side. He was trying desperately to keep the wagon on course, but at one point, it slid into a whirlpool and spun around.

"Hold on everyone!" Michael yelled as he tried to turn the wagon in the treacherous water. Just as he got the wagon turned around, it dropped into a hole and wedged against large boulders. Water was coming into the right side of the wagon.

"Get to the left side," Michael screamed. Everyone moved over causing the wagon to tip precariously on its side, but it stopped the water from rushing in. He was trying to think of how to dislodge it from the rocks.

Ben watched helplessly from behind. He saw the Flannigans' wagon dip into the whirlpool and knew they were in trouble. He wanted to jump in and help them, but he knew that was fool-hardy in these rapids. He could only watch in horror as the drama unfolded.

Michael yelled, "One by one, come up to the front if you can."

Conor made his way slowly to the front of the wagon. Then Kate followed. Just as Brenna started, the wagon lurched and freed itself, and Brenna flew over the side and into the freezing and churning water.

"Brenna!" Kate screamed.

Brenna surfaced swallowing a mouthful of water. She was diso-riented and the roiling water spun her around. She felt her knee painfully hit a rock. Through the frothy water, she saw her parents and Conor up ahead in the wagon. Kate's face was tortured look-ing back at her. Brenna wondered vaguely if this would be the last time she would see them.

"Brenna!" Someone was calling her name.

She was able to look behind her to see Ben and his father steer-ing their wagon towards her.

"Brenna! Grab this rope when we go by!" Ben had his lasso. The water was numbing and she wasn't sure she could move her arms. Her heavy skirt was dragging her down. The wagon was get-ting closer, and Ben was twirling the lasso above his head. He was staring at her intently.

"Get ready, Brenna! I know you can do this!" Brenna didn't answer for fear of swallowing more water.

Now they were nearly parallel to her and twenty feet away. Ben let the lasso fly at the critical moment. The loop flew up and out and landed in the water right in front of Brenna. She grabbed at it and caught it before it disappeared in the churning water. She quickly put it over her head and under her arms. Ben wasted no time in hauling on the rope. Soon, Brenna was alongside the wagon. While Hans steered, Ben reached over and grabbed Brenna's arm. He pulled her part way out of the water. Her wet clothing was very heavy and he felt her slipping.

"Ben!" She screamed.

"Hold on, Brenna! I've got you!" He wedged his feet under a cross board and leaned over the side of the wagon. Now that he had better purchase, he was able to use both his arms to pull her up and over the side of the wagon. She lay on top gasping for breath.

"Brenna, stay down until we get through these rapids," Ben yelled. Up ahead he could see Kate and Conor hugging each other while Michael steered the pitching wagon.

Rebecca had watched the whole thing happen, and her screams mingled with Annie's howls until she saw Ben pull Brenna into the wagon, and then she cried with relief.

Finally, they were through the worst of it. Gradually the rapids lessened and the wagons and rafts settled into calmer waters. The trip the rest of the way to Fort Vancouver was uneventful.

As the first canoes pulled into the fort, which was also a British trading post, the others followed suit, and they were greeted by many men and women on shore who helped the weary travelers off the boats, wagons, and rafts.

Emily had awakened in the calmer water only to succumb to a violent bout of seasickness. She had spent the last part of the river trip with her head over the side of the canoe. Buster whined and pulled on her sleeve with his teeth.

"Just let me die, Mr. Brown," she cried.

Abel was too disgusted to answer.

When the Hanssons' wagon came into shore, Michael Flannigan helped Brenna off. Kate hugged Brenna to her tightly and cried. "I thought we had lost you!"

Annie stopped crying the moment her feet were on land. "Mama!" she called out. Ruth handed Mattie to Rebecca and picked up the little girl. "You were very brave, Annie."

After they had all hugged each other, they heard the bad news. One of the rafts had dipped into a whirlpool and capsized. The family had all drowned. While they came together and mourned the loss of their friends, they felt comfort in each other's arms.

That night the overlanders ate at tables for the first time since leaving Independence. Ruth and Thomas Benson sat across from each other at a long plank table in the home of Frank and Viola Clark. This kind couple took the whole family in and gave them a hot meal of venison, green beans, and potatoes. As they sat together around the table with the steaming bowls of food in front of them, they joined hands and Thomas said grace.

"Lord, we thank you for this bountiful meal and these kind people. We give thanks for our safe landing here at Fort Vancouver. We pray that our new life in Oregon City is happy and prosperous. Amen."

"Amen," echoed around the table. The weary family enjoyed the meal and entertained their hosts with stories from their journey.

John McLoughlan, the Chief Factor of the fort, made sure that all the families had been taken in by settlers and immigrants who had established residency near the fort. That night, most people slept under a roof. A few of the overlanders were restless and carried their bedrolls outside under the stars, where they had no trouble falling asleep. The hardest part of the journey was over, and the relief spent itself in exhaustion and deep sleep.

The next day everyone went into the fort to buy supplies. Many were penniless but the Chief Factor extended them credit so they would have a start. The next day most of the travelers would continue south to Oregon City, the seat of the American Provisional Government, and the Willamette Valley.

Home

Chapter Thirty-Six

Oregon City
October 17, 1852

Oregon City was bustling with activity. There were dry goods stores, eateries, saloons, a millinery shop, a blacksmith, three grocers, a bank, and a land office. One of the hotels, the Oregon House, had a vacancy sign, and Emily and Abel Brown made their way over. The proprietor, Mr. Garcia, showed them to a clean room with a four-poster bed, a small desk and chair, a washstand and mirror, and a wardrobe. Emily sat down shakily on the chair. She hadn't felt well since the river trip.

"I'm going to locate our belongings and have them sent over here, Emily." Abel Brown looked at her dirty dress and disheveled hair. "I'll tell Mrs. Ortiz you'll be wanting a bath. When I get back I'll have one too." He left the room. Emily immediately went to the bed and instantly fell asleep with Buster curled up next to her.

Soon there was a knock on the door. "Mrs. Brown, your bath is ready." Emily sank into the steaming water and closed her eyes. As her aching muscles relaxed, she began to return to her senses. Her mind's eye saw the long journey anew. She relived the tearful departure from her childhood farm, the terrifying river crossings, Ernest's and her Father's deaths, and the letter from the woman she had always thought of as her mother. Everything had been such a blur. Her marriage to Abel Brown had been a nightmare. He was cold and demanding, and he didn't hesitate to use any means at his disposal to get what he wanted.

"If only he hadn't read the letter," she mused. Abel knew her secret and he wouldn't hesitate to use it against her if she ever crossed him. She sighed deeply. Life certainly had taken a turn.

She woke up some time later when the bath had cooled. Taking the bar of soap from the holder, she scrubbed her body, washed her hair, and quickly dried herself with the towel. She donned a clean chemise and dress from the bag Abel had had sent over with their other belongings, and then she returned to their room. She brushed her hair and let it hang loose to dry. It fell nearly to her waist in long, lustrous locks. She surveyed herself in the mirror. She was thin, which made her look older than her nineteen years. Her high cheekbones and generous mouth gave her an uncanny beauty. Her brows were like wings that defined eyes so dark they looked bottomless, eyes that had a knowing look of experience that was rarely found in one barely nineteen.

The door opened and Abel entered. He was taken aback by the figure of Emily before him. She looked young and vulnerable with her hair cascading around her shoulders, and he was struck again with her uncommon beauty.

"I see you've had your bath and a little rest," he queried.

"Yes, and I feel much better now," Emily said.

"Good. I'm going to get a bath and then we'll find a restaurant and have dinner. I have something to discuss with you."

The Bensons had a joyful reunion with Thomas's brother William, his wife Dorothy, and their three children. They had left Iowa three years earlier, and Thomas and Ruth had never seen the youngest boy, Louis. He was a sturdy three-year-old. Parker, seven, had grown. William and Dorothy hugged the children and exclaimed over Annie and Mattie.

"Deborah is no longer with us," Thomas said.

"Oh, no!" Dorothy exclaimed. "I'm so sorry," she said, hugging Ruth tightly. The women clung to each other briefly.

"She would have loved it here," Ruth said, her voice catching.

After a moment of silence, William cleared his throat.

"We were able to rent a house for you that recently was vacated. It's smaller than your Iowa house, but bigger than the wagon you've been living out of."

"Is it close to you?" Tommy asked, standing next to his cousin Robert who was the same age as he was.

"Yes, it's close. You boys will be neighbors."

The boys looked at each other and smiled. They had been inseparable when they lived in Iowa, and they had instantly renewed their friendship in Oregon City.

"Let's get your wagon and head on out," William said.

Molly the mare pulled Thomas's wagon and Rascal, her colt, followed behind. They traveled a few miles out of town with most of the children in William's wagon bed.

The house was a clapboard two-story painted white with a shingled roof. There was a broad porch at the front. A huge tree shaded the west side, and a lonely swing hung from a sturdy branch. Mary ran over to the swing and jumped on. Soon she was swinging high above the ground. A sparsely wooded glade stretched out in back behind a small barn.

"I think this should work out until you claim your land and build your new home," William said.

Thomas put his arm around William's shoulders. "Thank you, William. I think we'll be very comfortable here."

The children, with the adults following, ran up the three steps to the porch and entered through the front door. There was a short hallway with stairs leading to the second story. Tommy and Sam took the stairs two at a time. To the right of the hallway was the parlor with a small fireplace, and to the left, the kitchen with a white enamel sink and a cook stove. A small pie safe stood against one wall. At the back of the house were two small bedrooms.

"Mom, come up here!" Tommy shouted. Mary ran up the stairs, and Ruth and the others followed. Upstairs there were two small bedrooms. Each had a window that looked out over the landscape. The west window opened to branches from the large tree.

"I want this room so I can climb out to the tree," Tommy said.

"Don't give it to him, Ma. He'll fall out and crack his head," Mary said, looking down from the window to the ground.

"Will not," Tommy said indignantly.

Ruth laughed. "We'll sort out who sleeps where later. Let's go down and look at the barn.

The barn was two hundred yards behind the house. It was sturdily built and painted red. Inside, there were two stalls and a tool shed. Behind that was a room with a wide door for a buggy or carriage.

"Mom! Dad! Look at this!" Sam yelled from outside. They walked behind the barn and saw Sam standing beside a creek. "There's fish in here!"

"There's a pump house and the outhouse on the other side," William indicated, pointing to the east side of the house.

Ruth turned to William and Dorothy. "This is real nice." She smiled broadly. "It feels good to finally be home."

Reverend John, Nellie, and Mrs. Mueller breathed a sigh of relief when they arrived in Oregon City. The trip down the Columbia River had been harrowing, but surprisingly, Mrs. Mueller had found it exciting. "I've never had such a ride!" she exclaimed when they arrived at Fort Vancouver. She spent little time making the acquaintance of many of the older women who had settled with their families near the fort, and when they found out that John was a minister, they arranged for him to conduct a service the following morning. It was widely attended by the overlanders and the residents.

After the service, a plump gray-haired woman came up to John and handed him an envelope that had GEORGE WEISS printed in neat block letters on the front. She said, "This is the name of my nephew. He runs a dry goods store in Oregon City.

He'll make sure you get settled in. Please give him this letter from me."

In Oregon City, they found WEISS DRY GOODS and introduced themselves to George Weiss, a robust man with a handlebar moustache. They gave him the letter. He read it through and smiled wistfully. "My aunt is a good woman with a heart of gold. She helped me get started when I came from Pennsylvania three years ago." He looked at John. "This town needs a minister, Reverend Mueller. We've had a few preachers come through but no one who has stayed. I hope you'll like it here."

"Thank you, George. We intend to make this our home," John replied.

"I don't know if you have made arrangements for lodgings yet, but I have a couple of rooms above the store that you're welcome to use until you find something else. I used to live up there until recently. I've just built a little house a short distance from here. I won't charge you rent if you will help out in the store. What with all the wagons coming in, I get pretty busy."

"That's very kind of you, Mr. Weiss." John looked for approval to Nellie and his mother. "We'll take you up on your generous offer."

They quickly settled in to their new lodgings. Mrs. Mueller's room was small, but it had a bright east-facing window. John and Nellie's room was larger, and their window looked out at the hustle and bustle of Main Street. They stood with their arms around each other gazing outside.

"I have a good feeling about this town, Nellie."

"I do also, John. I think we're going to fit in here."

The Flannigans set up camp in a clearing where other overlanders were camped.

"This is temporary until I claim our land. Then we'll move to the farm and begin building our new home," Michael said.

"When will you do that, Da?" Conor asked.

"As soon as I can, Conor. I'm going to talk to folks and visit the land office and find out where available land is located, and we can rent a buggy and drive around and take a look. How does that sound?"

Kate hugged Michael and smiled. "We're here! I can hardly believe it!"

"We did it, Kate. We left Ireland and came across the Atlantic Ocean. We traveled three thousand miles from New York to Oregon over this vast country, and here we are near the Pacific Ocean in our new home. I couldn't have done it without you." He bent and kissed Kate soundly.

Brenna smiled at her parents, delighted with their happiness. She looked across the meadow at Ben Hansson and his father setting up their camp. Soon, she and Ben would be married. She hadn't forgotten his promise, and she reminded him of it frequently. It was only seven years since her family had left Ireland. Where would she be in the next seven years? She could hardly wait to find out.

Later at dinner, Abel and Emily were deep in conversation.

"I intend to make my claim for our land quickly," Abel said as he cut into his steak.

"What will we do with the land, Mr. Brown? I don't see you as a farmer."

"No, I will never be a farmer!" he said contemptuously. "I will hire some hands to clear some of it and plant something profitable and easy to grow. After it's harvested, I will use the money for another planting."

"And will we live on this land?"

"Yes, after the house is built. My house will be the biggest around, a large colonial with a barn for the horses."

"It sounds like you're becoming respectable, Mr. Brown."

He smiled cynically. "As far as appearances go, my dear, I will be very respectable. Money talks in a boomtown, and I intend to exert every effort to promote myself—with your help, of course. You will be my leading lady, and you will play your part to perfection."

"You must be planning to give up poker then."

"Not necessarily. There's nothing wrong with a gentlemen's game now and then. It's a very civilized game—or it can be. Is something wrong with your food?"

Emily had barely touched her dinner. "I'm not hungry."

"Eat, Emily. You're too thin."

A few days later, Abel took Emily and made his claim for three hundred twenty acres of land a couple of miles out of town. It was heavily wooded, which was why it was still available so close to town. Farmers would rather have meadowland even if it were farther out.

"I'll have the land cleared and sell the timber. I already talked to a man who wants to work for me. He'll hire a crew, and I won't have to do anything except count the money," he said with a satisfied smile.

"You're fortunate that you have the capital to hire help, Mr. Brown. Most of these farmers have little to nothing left."

"They're simple dirt farmers. Next year, I'll buy their land from them for a fraction of what it's worth, and they'll be happy to get rid of it."

Emily regarded Abel Brown's smug expression. She made no comment, but she wondered how long his hiatus would last. "What goes up must come down," her daddy used to say. *When will you come down, Mr. Brown?* she wondered.

The Card Game

Chapter Thirty-Seven

Oregon City
November, 1852

It had been over a month since they had arrived in Oregon City, and Abel Brown had been busy. He had not only secured his and Emily's three hundred twenty acres, but he had called in his I.O.U.s and was now in possession of an additional one thousand ten acres. The ones who were flat broke had claimed their land and signed the deeds over to him. Others had been able to borrow the money they owed from friends or relatives to pay him off. He laughed when he remembered the look of fury on Mrs. Warren's face when her husband deeded his land to Abel.

"You're a monster, Mr. Brown!"

"Everyone is entitled to their opinion, Mrs. Warren."

"What are we supposed to do now, after traveling all this way?"

"That is none of my concern," he replied, and turned and walked away. What did these people expect? He hadn't twisted anyone's arm when they joined his poker game. They came of their own free will. Now they had to pay the piper. He believed in consequences, and they simply had to face theirs. He gloated to Emily, who didn't share in his satisfaction.

"You've taken these people's hopes and dreams, Mr. Brown. How will they survive?"

"Come on, Emily, you don't think for one moment that they would make it farming, do you? You can't be that naïve."

"How can you be so sure?"

"I've studied people, Emily. I know how they think and why they do the things they do. I know what motivates them. I've found that people are really very selfish."

"And I suppose you're not?"

"Oh, I'm selfish, but at least I know that about myself. Most people are deluded. They want to believe they have high moral standards, but when it comes down to it, they're just as low as the rest of us. These people thought they were going to get something for nothing. Now they have what they deserve—nothing!" He laughed at his joke.

Emily stared at him. He was despicable. She liked nothing about him. She remembered a time when she thought he was handsome. Now that she saw who he truly was, there was nothing attractive about him.

"Emily, the logging on our property is turning a profit already. Some of the settlers who have claimed their land are buying timber from me to build their homes."

"What about the ones who have no money?"

"If the bank won't lend them the money, I'm lending it to them—for a price, of course."

"What kind of a price?"

"If they haven't paid it back within two years, they forfeit their deed to me. That's more than fair, I think."

"Two years! That's hardly time for them to plant a decent crop. How can you expect them to repay you in two short years?"

"They haven't thought as far ahead as you have, Emily. They're only thinking about getting a roof over their heads."

Later, they rented a buggy and drove out to their property. They watched the logging for a while, and then Abel drove her over to the site where the house would be built.

"The construction on our home will commence soon. No simple log home for us; I've had plans drawn up for a colonial style house. I expect it will be grander than your house was in Ohio."

Emily thought back to the home where she had grown up. It was a beautiful house with six bedrooms, a dining room, a library that was also a study, a sitting room, a parlor, an enclosed sun porch on the back, and a wraparound porch in the front. The large kitchen at the back of the house was her favorite room. Mrs. Harris the cook was always baking something delicious, and she always let Emily help her. Emily sighed. She most likely would never see her home again.

Abel looked out proudly at his land. By this time next year, he would be wealthy beyond his wildest dreams. He already had amassed a huge fortune in land and cash.

"This is indeed the land of milk and honey," he reflected.

Captain Wyatt looked at his cards. It was a good hand, but he wasn't sure it would be good enough.

"Call," he said. Jack Thompson looked at him from across the table and smiled. The others had folded, and it was just the two of them. Jack laid his cards on the table: a full house. Captain Wyatt looked at Jack for a moment and then placed his cards face up: two pair. Everyone laughed, and Jack scooped up the pot from the center of the table.

"That's it for me," the captain said. He had won a few dollars and knew when to quit. The others got up also. Captain Wyatt knew there was a time and place for everything. He wasn't opposed to gambling in moderation. He went to the bar and ordered a drink. Jack came up and sat beside him.

"That was a good game, Captain. Do you play often?"

"Only when I'm winning," Captain Wyatt replied.

Jack laughed. He had an easy manner, but underlying that was a man who knew what he was about.

"Where are you from?" the captain asked.

"Most recently from California."

"How long you been here?"

"I just got in this afternoon. I prefer California to Oregon in the winter, but I have a job to do and it's brought me here."

"What line of work are you in?" Captain Wyatt asked curiously.

"I'm a lawman, Captain. I'm looking for someone name of Chance Parker. Ever hear of him?"

Captain Wyatt thought for a moment. "I meet a lot of people on these trains. Been doing this for a few years now, but I don't believe I've ever heard the name."

"He also goes by an alias. Ever hear of Luke Patterson?"

"No, I've never heard of him."

"This man is a ruthless killer. He's wanted in a few states, most recently in Kentucky. He gunned a man down in cold blood." He reached into a pocket. "Here's his picture on this wanted poster."

Captain Wyatt stared at the picture. He looked at Jack Thompson. The name on the wanted poster said Chance Parker, but the picture was of Abel Brown. The captain smiled grimly. It looked like he had been in the right place, and it was the right time.

Reckoning

Chapter Thirty-Eight

⸺⸺⸺))(() ((⸺⸺⸺

The next morning, Abel Brown shaved, dressed, and left their room at the hotel. He didn't tell Emily where he was going. He wanted to get to the bank as soon as they opened and check over his deeds that were stored in a safe deposit box. When he arrived, one of the tellers showed him to the private room where he could look over the contents of the box. He took the deeds out and checked them over one by one. All but one had been signed over to Emily and notarized. The only one under the name Abel Brown was his claim of one hundred sixty acres. He hadn't wanted to put the deeds in Emily's name, but he was worried about having them in his name, which wasn't really his name. Abel Brown was an alias, and he didn't want that to catch up with him down the road. He clearly couldn't put the deeds in his real name, Chance Parker. No, having the deeds in Emily's name was best. She was his wife; what she owned was his legally, and she never needed to know.

He looked at the other document in the box. There was the precise script of Emily's so-called mother on the envelope addressed to "Mrs. Ernest Hinton." He smiled thinly. He had no fear that Emily would ever leave him. As long as he knew her secret, she would remain with him.

Emily made her way to one of the tables in the café of the hotel. It was a small room next to the lobby with five tables. Only one other table was occupied by a couple having a lively discussion.

Mrs. Ortiz brought Emily a steaming cup of coffee.

"Thank you, Mrs. Ortiz."

Emily took most of her meals here. The food was hot and nourishing, and Mrs. Ortiz was very kind to her.

"You're too thin, Miss Emily," she would say, and she would bring Emily a special treat she had baked.

Today Emily ordered biscuits and gravy instead of the usual eggs. While she waited for her food, she sipped her coffee and wondered what she would do today. Every day was much like the next. She spent her time reading her books and mending her clothes. All of her dresses were in various stages of ruin. She had bought yard goods at Mr. Weiss's store, but she hadn't had the motivation to begin a new frock. She couldn't think of one reason why she wanted a new dress, so the material lay in the corner of their rented room. Buster had taken to making it his bed, and every night he scratched at it until he fluffed it up, and then he circled three times before he settled down. It would have made Emily laugh if she had felt anything but tired. Mrs. Ortiz came over with a thick slice of cinnamon bread.

"Fresh out of the oven. Still warm!" She left the plate on the table, and Emily picked at it. It was probably delicious, but she couldn't taste it.

Soon, her food arrived, and Emily ate some of it. She was in the habit of taking what she didn't eat up to Buster. He enjoyed her choices immensely. Maybe she would go up to the room and take a nap. It was still morning but she felt exhausted.

Abel closed up the safe deposit box and indicated to the teller that he was finished. The teller put the box away, and Abel made his way out of the bank. It was a fine day, and he was going to rent a buggy and drive around to check out all of his new properties. Just as he stepped onto the boardwalk a voice said, "Hold it right there, Parker."

Abel froze at the sound of his real name. He turned towards the man who was holding a gun pointed at his chest. He saw a tall man with steel gray eyes under a wide brimmed black hat.

"You can put your hands up nice and slow. My name's Jack Thompson and I'm a United States Marshall."

"There must be some mistake. I don't know who this Parker fellow is. My name is Abel Brown." He was nervously watching Thompson who was handling his gun like he knew how to use it.

"Turn around Parker. Easy now. Put your hands on that hitching post and spread your legs," Thompson ordered. He quickly frisked Abel and found the small gun in his boot.

"You won't be needing this where you're going," Thompson said as he put Abel's gun in his pocket. "Let's go!" and he nudged Abel in the back with his revolver. He and Abel walked to the government offices, which served as a courthouse and a jail. There was a single cell, and this is where Abel would stay until Jack Thompson arranged their transportation back to California, and from there to Kentucky.

Captain Wyatt had watched the arrest from across the street. Today was a day of reckoning, he thought, and he made his way to the hotel to inform Miss Emily.

Emily was finished picking at her breakfast and had decided to return to her room when she saw Captain Wyatt from the window walking towards the hotel. She hadn't seen him in over a month, and she wondered what his business was. He walked through the front doors, and when he looked to the left and saw her, he came over to her table.

"Good morning, Miss Emily," he said, removing his hat. "May I join you?"

Emily tried to hide her surprise. He looked so serious! "Of course, Captain. What can I do for you?"

Captain Wyatt was a man of few words and he didn't mince them now. "Abel has just been arrested."

Emily gasped. "What? Why?"

"He's wanted in the States for murder. There's been a warrant for his arrest, and a United States Marshal has tracked him here. His real name is Chance Parker."

"Abel a murderer!" Emily clutched her throat.

"He's in the government building in a holding cell. The marshal will take him back to Kentucky where he will stand trial for murder, and most likely hang. I'm sorry, Miss Emily."

"This can't be right," Emily said. The room began to spin. She tried to stand up but her knees buckled. Captain Wyatt caught her before she hit the floor.

When Emily opened her eyes, she was lying on her bed and Mrs. Ortiz was leaning over her. Captain Wyatt was nowhere in sight, and Emily thought that she must have dreamed their conversation.

"Are you alright, dear? You gave us quite a scare! That nice Captain Wyatt carried you up here."

Emily groaned. It hadn't been a dream. Abel Brown—or whatever his name was—her husband, was a murderer.

"Sit up, Miss Emily, and drink this." Mrs. Ortiz gave her a glass of water. "You've had quite a morning. Captain Wyatt told me what happened. I never did like Mr. Brown, er, Parker. He was not a nice man!"

Emily gulped the water. She was having a hard time taking in the information that Captain Wyatt had told her. She couldn't think of what to do or who to turn to.

"Is there anyone I can fetch for you, Miss Emily?" Mrs. Ortiz asked gently.

"I don't know. I can't think." Then her eyes cleared. "Wait. Would you please tell Nellie—Mrs. Mueller—Reverend Mueller's wife at Mr. Weiss's store that I need her?"

"Of course, dear. You rest until I get back." And she left Emily alone.

Ten minutes later, Nellie was with Emily, who told her about Abel's arrest.

"That scoundrel! I've never trusted him! And to think he's a murderer!" Nellie said vehemently. "That doesn't surprise me, Emily. There was always something sinister about him. Where is he now?"

"He's in the cell in the government building. The marshal is going to take him to Kentucky to stand trial. They say he'll hang, Nellie." Emily shivered.

Nellie glanced at her sharply. "You don't have any feelings for him, do you Emily?"

Emily looked horrified. "No! I have never in my life been as miserable as I have been in this marriage, Nellie. You have no idea what I have had to endure. And now to find out that he's killed someone! I hope I never lay eyes on him again!"

Nellie watched Emily carefully. A year ago she would have dissolved into tears. Now she was matter-of-fact and resolute.

"Good. That's the spirit. What are your plans, Emily?"

"I don't know, Nellie. I can't think about that now. I know Abel paid our room and board here until the end of the year. Beyond that I don't know what I'll do."

"You always have a home with us, Emily."

The two women hugged each other, and Buster jumped up and down happily.

Discovery

Chapter Thirty-Nine

The next morning, Marshal Thompson visited Emily briefly. "Your husband has asked to see you. You can visit him if you'd like, but we'll be leaving shortly for California."

"I have nothing to say to him, Marshal. I'm glad that you found him. It's time he pays the consequences for his foul deeds."

"He'll get a fair trial in Kentucky, Ma'am."

The marshal left, and Emily felt like she could breathe again. In the afternoon, she had a surge of energy. She cleaned the room from top to bottom. She was determined to get rid of all traces of Abel Brown. After she finished, she went to the wardrobe, took out his clothes, and laid them on the bed. These she would give to Reverend Mueller to pass on to someone needy. As she was folding Abel's long black coat, she felt something stiff in the lining.

"What is this?" she wondered as she opened the coat to the inside. A little searching revealed a secret pocket. She reached inside and pulled out a handful of bills—hundreds of dollars and more inside!

"Just like Abel not to trust a bank!" she muttered. "This must be his gambling winnings." She had a momentary urge to throw it all out the window. She shook her head and pulled the rest of the cash from the coat. Then she carefully went through the rest of his clothing, but found nothing else. She counted up the bills.

"Seventeen hundred dollars!" She knew he had money, but he never told her how much he had or where it was. She fanned it out in her hands. This was more money than she had ever seen before. What would she do with it? That would take careful consideration.

Two days later, Emily received a letter from Michael Pound in Ohio. It had come on the last mail train in to Oregon City and had sat in the post office for two weeks. It was dated April 23, 1852.

"Mr. Pound, Daddy's lawyer," she mused as she opened the envelope. Inside she found a short note from Mr. Pound, and another letter. She read Mr. Pound's note first.

April 23, 1852

Dear Emily,

You most likely have received a letter from Mrs. Lawton informing you of your father's passing. I am deeply sorry. He was my friend and client for many years, and I will miss him. I read his will earlier this month, and it has taken me a few weeks to get his finances in order. Everything is detailed in the enclosed letter to you, which he wrote last year. He has entrusted me to make sure that his wishes are carried out, and I will do everything in my power to make this happen. Either I or a trusted colleague will deliver your estate to you next year when the trail is passable.

Until then I remain your trusted servant,

Michael Pound, Esq.

Emily was confused. What was Mr. Pound referring to? With shaking hands, she opened the larger letter from her father.

September 6, 1851

Dearest Emily,

If you are reading this, I am no longer of this world. Hopefully you are a mature woman and I died an old man.

There are some things I have to tell you and it is not easy. I had always hoped to keep you close to me, but I can see that Ernest is bound and determined to take you across this country to Oregon, and I have no power to stop him. This grieves my heart, and I can only hope that someday I will see you again.

Emily had to wipe the tears from her eyes before she was able to continue.

The woman you have always thought of as your mother is, in reality, your stepmother. Your real mother was a mulatto slave from my plantation in Virginia. Her name was Patricia. She was a beautiful and vibrant young woman, and I loved her. She died in childbirth. You survived, however, and when I first held you in my arms, I knew that you would always be my special little girl.

Emily's tears were flowing freely now.

Then, imagine my amazement when a second child was born. Your twin is a boy who resembles me more than Patricia except for his dark skin. He lives with his grandmother in Virginia. I wanted to keep him also, but your grandmother had serious misgivings. She had been my house slave and my father's before me for many years, and I respected her opinion. She knew I was planning on moving to Ohio, and that I would free the slaves I had in Virginia. She told me to take you and pass you as white. She said you would have the chance at a real life of privilege never known to anyone in all the generations of her family. She would take the boy and raise him. I regret to say that I did as she asked.

"A brother and a grandmother!" Emily marveled.

I set up a trust fund for him and for your grandmother after we parted. Mr. Pound is the executor. I have not seen this boy since his birth, and I have had no further communication with your grand-mother. I don't know what she has told him about his father and his twin. I thought to keep this to myself, but I think if I were in your position, I would want to know. I hope this is not too much of a shock, and that you will do with this information what you think best. The last address for your grandmother was: Mrs. Leticia Cross, Lynchburg, Virginia.

Finally, my estate has been divided in the following way: Your stepbrothers will inherit the farm with all the land, the house, and the property. You will inherit my investments and other assets. I have a small fortune in gold. Mr. Pound will apprise you of this when he gets everything in order. You have a good head on your shoulders, Emily, and I know you will invest this money carefully. I believe the sum will end up being around $500,000.

Emily almost dropped the letter. "Five hundred thousand dollars!"

I have recently told your stepmother about your real mother. I have not told her about your brother and grandmother. Mrs. Lawton was never a good mother to you like I hoped she would be, Emily. For this reason, I wanted to make sure that you would receive your fair share of the inheritance.

Please take care of yourself in the west. I do now and will always cherish you.

Your loving father

Emily read the letter a second and then a third time. Her head was spinning. How could her life take such a turn!

That afternoon she went to the bank and opened an account in her name. She deposited the $1700.00 from Abel's coat. The young teller who was helping her had heard what had happened to Abel.

"I'm very sorry about your husband, Mrs. Brown."

Emily murmured her thanks.

"Do you want to continue renting the safe deposit box?"

"Safe deposit box?"

258

He took her into the private room and left her with the box. Emily opened it and looked at all the deeds for land. Then she looked more carefully. All but one were in her name!

At the bottom of the box was a letter. She turned it over and saw that it was the letter her stepmother had written to her last April, safe and sound.

Epilogue

Two years later

Emily drove the buggy down Second Street to the Hanssons' barn. Ben and Hans were doing a thriving business as father and son blacksmiths. With the recent wagon trains and the influx of new immigrants, business was booming.

"Hello, Ben," she called when she saw him in the back of the barn working the bellows. He stopped his work to greet her.

"Emily, it's good to see you. Where have you been the last couple of weeks?"

She climbed down from the buggy. "I've been working hard trying to get everything organized. I can't believe the school will be opening next week. I'm so excited!" The school had been built a half mile from town in a quiet glen. It was two stories, and it had a bell to call the children to class. She had ordered books and slates from New York, and they had finally arrived. Everything was ready for the opening.

Ben wiped his brow with the back of his arm. "You've worked hard for this, Emily. I'm happy for you. Brenna's in the back if you want to see her."

"Thanks, Ben." Emily walked behind the barn to a round corral where Brenna was working with a young horse. The filly was trotting calmly around the circle and Brenna was encouraging her. When she saw Emily, she walked towards the filly's shoulder, and the horse stopped and faced Brenna.

"Good girl!' She rubbed the filly's nose affectionately. "Hi, Emily!" Brenna smiled, climbing out of the corral easily in her trousers. She had abandoned dresses for trousers and boots to work with her horses. Her dark hair was tied behind her neck in a ponytail that almost contained the wayward curls. She wore a man's cowboy style hat to keep the sun off her face.

"Hello, Brenna. Are you busy?"

Brenna looked at the filly, which had put her head over the top rail. "I was just finishing up with July, here."

"She's beautiful! Was she born in July?"

"Yes, a year ago last summer. I bought her after she was weaned. She's a sweetheart." She gave the filly a kiss on her nose. "Come inside where we can visit." They walked a short distance to a small house set back in the trees. Ben and Hans had purchased the house on ten acres off Second Street in town. Then they had built the barn for their blacksmithing, and another barn behind it for boarding and for Brenna's horses. The house was built from logs, and Brenna had made it very homey.

She took off her hat and hung it on a hook by the door. "Is the school finished?"

"Yes, and it's beautiful. You have to come and see it!" Emily's face was glowing. Her eyes danced with excitement.

"I want to definitely see it. Conor is excited about starting, and the Benson children can hardly wait. Sit down, Emily. Would you like coffee?" They were in Brenna's small cozy kitchen. A fireplace covered one wall, and a pot hung over it with hot water. A wooden table stood against another wall, covered with a cheerful table-cloth. Soft yellow chintz curtains covered the two sunny windows. The dry sink was under a window with a view to the barns, and a cook stove adjoined it.

"I'd love some coffee. How are your folks? I haven't seen them since the open house. Their house is wonderful. Your dad did a good job. The view is spectacular!"

"They are in seventh heaven! Conor and Da are planning to plant corn and wheat this spring now that the house is finished.

Ma had such a huge vegetable garden that she could barely keep up. Her pantry is full of all the fruits and vegetables she put up, and she sold a lot to Mr. Weiss.

Brenna went to the cupboard and grabbed two cups. She poured coffee into them from the pot on the stove.

"Ben likes to keep the coffee on all day. He comes in now and then and has a cup. Tell me about the school." She handed Emily her coffee and sat in a chair across from her. "I love how you used Abel's gambling money to build it."

Emily took a sip and put her cup down. "I knew I had to do something useful with the money—something to benefit everyone. The school will function as a town hall also, and since it's my building on my land, I am on the town council."

Brenna nodded approvingly. "How many children will start next week?"

"There are thirteen, and with the latest wagon trains the number will double I'm sure."

"Thirteen?" Brenna marveled.

"The older children will most likely miss school in the spring and fall. They'll be busy on the farms." Emily paused and took a breath. "I need you to help me, Brenna. Would you consider teaching? You can take the little ones and I'll teach the older children. What do you think?" Emily looked at Brenna expectantly.

Brenna was taken aback. She had never imagined herself as a teacher, not of children, anyway. She wondered how teaching children would differ from teaching horses.

Emily took Brenna's hands in hers. "You'd be wonderful, Brenna. You're so good with children. I'll pay you whatever you want, and we'll work together to make this a great school. Please say you'll think about it!" Emily's eyes were shining.

"I will. I'll think about it, and of course I have to talk it over with Ben." Her face flushed with excitement. "Oh Emily! I'm excited!" They spent an hour visiting and planning.

Emily left the Hanssons' home in high spirits. As she climbed into the buggy and waved to Ben, she knew he wouldn't object to Brenna's teaching when he saw how excited she was. He would do anything for her. They had been married in June, and theirs had been the first wedding in Reverend John's new church. She smiled when she remembered John showing her the plans for the church last fall. He had been so excited when she told him she wanted to fund his church. Nellie had hugged her and said she was an answer to their prayers.

She pulled up in front of Weiss's store. George had ordered many of the things she needed for the new school. When she went inside, Rebecca and James were there picking up supplies. Nellie still helped out in the store, and she was visiting with the Cardells.

"Emily! It's good to see you! We're so excited about the new school!" Rebecca said, hugging Emily warmly. She was holding a three-month-old baby in her arms.

"She's beautiful, Rebecca." Emily smiled at the baby and she smiled back.

"Have your parents finished their house?"

"Almost. Dad and James are doing the finishing touches inside. It's a big house, thanks to you and your donation of all the timber."

Emily smiled. She had provided timber to many of the people who had been on the wagon train with her. John and Nellie had built the church with some of it. Ben, Brenna, and Hans had built their barns. "And your house? When will you start on it?"

Rebecca looked at James, and they both smiled. "That's been put on the back burner for a little while," James said. "This past spring I planted all of the seedlings Mr. Luelling gave me from his orchards, and that's taken up all of our time." He paused to tickle little Ruth who cooed happily. "Well, not all our time. This one keeps us busy too."

"We plan on starting it in a couple of months," Rebecca said. "Dad should be finished with theirs, and he can help us with ours until spring planting. In the meantime, we're living with the family in the rented house."

"How is Mary? I miss all of her stories!"

Rebecca laughed. "She's started a little performance group. They've written a play and they rehearse in the barn behind the house. She's the director, of course. She has a troupe of six, and they're planning on putting on a show. You'll have to come."

"How wonderful! I'll talk to her about putting on her play at the school."

"Oh, she'd love that!"

After checking on her order with Nellie, Emily headed to the bank. When she walked in the front door, Mr. Moran, the bank president, hurried up to her. He was a small chubby man with round wire-rim glasses and a balding head.

"Miss Emily! So good to see you," he said, taking her hands. Emily smiled. He had been overjoyed when Michael Pound had showed up with Emily's inheritance and they had deposited it in the bank. Michael hadn't brought all of her money. She remembered their conversation.

"Miss Emily, I thought long and hard about this, and if you disagree, I will bring the rest of your inheritance next year. I've left half of it in interest bearing accounts in eastern banks. Perhaps in a few years, when these western banks are insured, your funds will be safer. For now, I'm uncomfortable with their risk."

She had agreed. Half of five hundred thousand dollars was still a fortune.

"There's talk of the railroad extending to California. That will make these cross country trips shorter and so much easier."

Mr. Moran said, "What can I help you with today, Miss Emily?"

"I'd like to carry on our discussion about what I'd like to do with some of my land," she said. She had returned the deed to Mr. and Mrs. Warren, and they had been elated. Abel's deed was forfeited, and she had quite a lot of land left in her name. Mr. Moran had helped her change her name back to Lawton, her maiden name.

"Of course, let's go to my office, Miss Emily."

Caliope, her mare, knew the way home, and Emily hardly had to touch the reins. Buster sat resolutely in the seat beside her. He had turned into a carriage dog, and she couldn't go anywhere without him. It had been a long day, and she knew Caliope was looking forward to her rubdown and her dinner. Dan Christopher, her groom, would be waiting for them, and he would make sure Caliope was taken care of.

He lived in the quarters alongside the barn. He had been on the wagon train and had lost his wagon in a river crossing. He also owed Abel money from poker games. Abel had taken it out on Dan in backbreaking work, but Dan had never complained. He had a way with animals, and Emily had hired him to work for her.

As horse and buggy made their way down the long lane to her home, Emily looked at it with pride. It was beautiful. She had met with the architect shortly after Abel's arrest and told him there would be some changes to the plans. There would be no colonial style. Instead, her home was a white wooden two story with a sun porch in the back and a wraparound porch in the front. Inside there was a dining room, a library with a study, and a parlor and sitting room. The kitchen was in the back, and Mrs. Ortiz baked special treats every day. She smiled, remembering Mrs. Ortiz's pleasure when Emily had asked her to be her housekeeper. Upstairs there were six bedrooms. The house was an exact replica of the one she had grown up in, and she loved it.

Soon she hoped to have her brother and grandmother from Virginia living with her. She had written to her grandmother, and she was hoping for a reply.

Her memories, the ones she chose to reflect on, were happy ones, but she didn't spend much time in the past. She didn't think much about the future, either. Her day-to-day life was too full and rich. Her overland journey had taken six months. She had met the people who were her new family. Her inward journey would take a lifetime, and she would meet it one day at a time.

Made in the USA
Monee, IL
10 October 2022

15606227R00153